"LOVING . . .
THE ANSWER . . .

His hands tightened as they slid into her hair, slipping slowly down her neck until his fingers rested lightly at her throat. Gently Richard massaged her velvety flesh before allowing his palms to roam over her shoulders, then down her back, his fingers spread wide as if probing the boundaries of her; farther to encircle her waist. . . .

Pulling her into him, Richard overwhelmed Bridget. He lowered his mouth to hers, devouring her lips, forcing them open with a power he had never felt before, tasting her in a way he had never done before. Bridget grasped him about the neck violently, pushing her body into his, as the long-dormant flame now blazed fiercely in them both.

They were falling, falling to the floor. Ever so gently they rolled over each other murmuring and biting and touching, each unable to get enough of the other. Richard's mouth was on Bridget's shoulders as his hands ripped her fine new clothes away. His lips slid over the swell of her breasts as she writhed beneath him, begging him not to stop.

Gone were the frantic demons that at once drew him away from her even as they threw him back, making him unable to live without her.

A Memorable Collection of Regency Romances

BY ANTHEA MALCOLM AND VALERIE KING

THE COUNTERFEIT HEART   (3425, $3.95/$4.95)
by Anthea Malcolm

Nicola Crawford was hardly surprised when her cousin's betrothed disappeared on some mysterious quest. Anyone engaged to such an unromantic, but handsome man was bound to run off sooner or later. Nicola could never entrust her heart to such a conventional, but so deucedly handsome man. . . .

THE COURTING OF PHILIPPA   (2714, $3.95/$4.95)
by Anthea Malcolm

Miss Philippa was a very successful author of romantic novels. Thus she was chagrined to be snubbed by the handsome writer Henry Ashton whose own books she admired. And when she learned he considered love stories completely beneath his notice, she vowed to teach him a thing or two about the subject of love. . . .

THE WIDOW'S GAMBIT   (2357, $3.50/$4.50)
by Anthea Malcolm

The eldest of the orphaned Neville sisters needed a chaperone for a London season. So the ever-resourceful Livia added several years to her age, invented a deceased husband, and became the respectable Widow Royce. She was certain she'd never regret abandoning her girlhood until she met dashing Nicholas Warwick. . . .

A DARING WAGER   (2558, $3.95/$4.95)
by Valerie King

Ellie Dearborne's penchant for gaming had finally led her to ruin. It seemed like such a lark, wagering her devious cousin George that she would obtain the snuffboxes of three of society's most dashing peers in one month's time. She could easily succeed, too, were it not for that exasperating Lord Ravenworth. . . .

THE WILLFUL WIDOW   (3323, $3.95/$4.95)
by Valerie King

The lovely young widow, Mrs. Henrietta Harte, was not all inclined to pursue the sort of romantic folly the persistent King Brandish had in mind. She had to concentrate on marrying off her penniless sisters and managing her spendthrift mama. Surely Mr. Brandish could fit in with her plans somehow . . .

Available wherever paperbacks are sold, or order direct from the Publisher. Send cover price plus 50¢ per copy for mailing and handling to Zebra Books, Dept. 3837, 475 Park Avenue South, New York, N.Y. 10016. Residents of New York and Tennessee must include sales tax. DO NOT SEND CASH. For a free Zebra/ Pinnacle catalog please write to the above address.

REBECCA FORSTER

Rainbow's End

ZEBRA BOOKS
KENSINGTON PUBLISHING CORP.

ZEBRA BOOKS

are published by

Kensington Publishing Corp.
475 Park Avenue South
New York, NY 10016

First printing: September, 1992

Printed in the United States of America

To my grandmother,
Martha Boehm,
thanks for the love and
apple cake

Chapter One

The first time Bridget Devlin saw Richard Hudson it was a cold day in January.

A fire had been laid in the cavernous marble hearth to cut the chill, though the stately home had long ago been fitted with central heating. The kitchen, far removed from the living area, was functioning like clockwork under the watchful eye of Mrs. Reilly. On the ground floor the rich smell of roast and potatoes wafted invitingly into every corner of every room. The aromas were so lovely they seemed to prolong the almost-gone holiday season.

Outside the grand, leaded window the San Francisco Bay lay under a blanket of thick fog that almost hid the Golden Gate Bridge. High above all this, the sun had actually risen and was doing its best to poke a few bright, warm rays through the obstinate clouds. But the fog would have none of it. Like a horrid child it simply lay there, refusing the cajoling of the sun or the prodding of the sea breeze.

Not that the fog bothered Bridget in the least. In

7

fact, she loved it. Staring wistfully through the window, she thought of home; she remembered Kilmartin. Here in California, or thousands of miles away in Ireland, the rolling fog served only to soften the world. Voices were hushed and people bundled tighter in their coats, smiling when they lifted their faces to walk through the cool white mist. The thick fog made people romantic and lazy and not necessarily in that order.

So it was, on that January day, that Bridget stopped to look out the window, frivolously tracing the path of a water droplet that coursed down the glass. She was humming, feeling, Lord help her, just a little bit perfect. Draped over her shoulders was a lovely pink sweater Mrs. Kilburn had surprised her with only that morning. Bridget's hair, unruly once she stepped outside, was a mass of beautifully-tended russet-colored curls inside the warm house. She had lost those extra pounds put on during the holidays.

And so, saying a bit of an apology to the Virgin for feeling as though she was exemplary in every way, Bridget was almost away from the window and ready to go about her chores, when she saw a small movement and turned back to look.

On the street below, coming out of the fog and straight up the drive, thank you very much, was a man so lovely the mere sight of him took her breath away.

She leaned forward, the water drop she had been contemplating now completely forgotten. Bridget lifted her hand and laid it flat on the cool pane, before pressing her cheek to her own warm flesh as she watched him.

Sure he seemed like a spirit, confusing heaven's pavement with this earthly fog, he came so slowly. He stopped for a moment to adjust his overcoat. Double-breasted, falling below the knee, Bridget could see it was the color of camel, a shade darker than his hair. His slacks were gray and, peeking from the upturned collar, she could just make out his starched white dress shirt brightened by the impeccable knot of a red silk tie.

The man turned his head, surveying the street as though wishing to recapture a moment from the past in a long-unvisited place. Bridget almost averted her eyes, feeling that she was intruding upon his thoughts. The small smile on his fine lips told her that he saw a world of memories here. His eyes were hidden from her, but Bridget could study his profile and admire the hollow below his high cheekbone, the broadness of his forehead and the shape of his nose. It was a bit long by American standards, she believed, but Bridget thought it noble and beautiful. She imagined the coolness of the man's skin and the dampness of his hair. The fog closed in on him once again, swirling about him like the fingers of a phantom lover.

Then—a miracle. Just as his well-shod foot took the first step toward the house, the mist parted and a ray of sunlight broke through, falling upon him. The man shone under the fleeting brightness. His blond hair was like a polished helmet, his skin was iridescent like the shimmer of standing wheat on a

9

summer day. And when he looked up toward the house, toward the very window at which Bridget Devlin stood, he smiled. Behind him the light reflected off the fog, framing him in the colors of the rainbow. Just like that, a fairy tale come true. Surely there was a treasure at the end of the rainbow; but it wasn't a pot of gold, and it had nothing to do with the little people. Then he. . . .

"Bridget, my girl, are you going to sit with your chin in your hand, staring out that window all afternoon, or are you going to manage to make a move before the day is out!"

Startled by Mrs. Kilburn's merry reprimand, Bridget jerked out of her daydream. Her chin slipped off her upturned palm as her hand fell onto the game table with a thud.

"Dear girl!" Maura Kilburn said with a laugh, watching the chess pieces scatter.

"Oh, Mrs. Kilburn. I'm so sorry. Look now what I've done," Bridget clucked, her brogue thickening the more agitated she became. "Ah, well, it's useless now. 'Tis afraid I am that the game is ruined." She sat back clutching a white pawn and the black king with her long fingers as she looked forlornly at the elegant, inlaid game table. Without really seeing it, she sighed. "Just as well. You were winning as usual. Sure I'm getting just a wee bit tired of you always beating the bloomers off me."

"Bridget Devlin, you don't know whether I was winning or not. Your mind was a million miles away," Mrs. Kilburn accused happily. "How dare you try to tell me different. I've always said you were full of the blarney. Beautiful, but full of the blarney nonetheless."

"I'll thank you to keep that information to yourself," Bridget teased and began to reset the pieces for a future game. "There aren't many in America who come by the blarney naturally, the way I do. It would pain me to have them jealous if they ever found out I've a talent for it."

"I'm sure it would, my dear. Now tell me, where was your mind? It must have been someplace wonderful. Those green eyes of yours were clear as a pond on an April morning. Were you thinking of home?"

"Not so far away, Mrs. Kilburn. I was just thinking that the weather hadn't changed much since Christmas." Bridget told her tale smoothly. Her remembrance of another holiday season so many years ago wasn't for sharing. At least not yet. "We've had such heavy fog this year. It always makes me sort of dreamy."

"That we have." Now it was Maura's turn to look wistfully toward the bay window. "I've been so lucky in my life, Bridget, to have seen so many fog-filled days. First in Ireland, then here in the United States." The old woman sighed, happy with her memories. "You know, I hadn't wanted to come to the United States, but Mr. Kilburn, he insisted. He told me 'Maura, we canna make it in style here in Ireland, and you're not one to sit under the pitch till the end of your days. We've got to go, my girl.'

11

"Well, I'll tell you, it wasn't like today, when you go someplace and it's easy as pie to get back to where you started. When I followed him, and my heart, and came here, I thought I would never see my home again. But the years sped by and we both worked so hard. Before I knew it we were a lady and a gentleman. The planes got faster. We became richer. The world got smaller.

"Sometimes I wish Ireland were just across that gorgeous Bay out there. I can hardly remember what my home village looked like. I can't remember the last time I went back. My memory is fading. But I still think I must be the luckiest woman in the world to have my wonderful family, my good fortune, and so many years on this earth."

Bridget stopped gathering up the chessmen as she listened, a chill coursing up her spine. Mentally she crossed herself. More often than not, her friend and employer talked as though the only way to look was backward. Of course Bridget was well aware the woman was eighty-eight. Yet Bridget couldn't bear to think of Maura as old or her time as limited. Despite her nurse's training, Bridget had committed the worst of sins—she had become attached to her charge. Maura Kilburn was the grandmother and mother Bridget never knew. She absolutely refused to take these nostalgic turns seriously. Instead the Irish bubbled up, and Bridget was all a-chatter.

"Well, of course you can't remember the last time you saw Cork," she scoffed, hurrying to complete her cleanup. "You've been far too busy over the years to worry about when it was that you set foot on the Emerald Isle."

"You're probably right, my dear. I suppose what's really *important* is that I don't forget the *important* things, isn't that so?" She watched her red-haired nurse with twinkling eyes and folded her hands in her lap.

Bridget laughed. "Now isn't that one way of putting it! And there is nothing more important than remembering who it is that loves you."

"That's so true," Mrs. Kilburn mused, her faded blue eyes thoughtfully placed on Bridget, who abandoned the game table and plumped the sofa pillows. "I think I have a very good idea of who loves me. A very good idea, indeed."

"Well, I should hope so," Bridget answered, unaware that she was the object of the old woman's scrutiny. Crossing her arms, Bridget surveyed the lovely living room. Everything was in its place, dinner was done, and the evening was coming on. She heaved a satisfied sigh and smiled at Maura. "Seems to me you must be the luckiest person in the world with the amount of love comes your way. Sure isn't your family one of the most special I've ever had the privilege to know."

"As are you, my dear," Mrs. Kilburn rejoined gently.

Bridget, hearing the unprecedented emotion in the usually-clipped and confident voice of her patient, went to Mrs. Kilburn and crouched beside her chair.

"Isn't that a lovely sentiment. It seems only yesterday I heard about some American lady from a friend of mine. An American lady who wanted an Irish lass to tend her is what my friend said. How funny that I should even have made that call, me just visiting, as it was, and not really having a clear idea of where I was to settle.

"But that was seven years ago, when I came here to be with you. I hadn't expected to stay so long, nor to feel so welcome. You've treated me as though I were one of the family. I shall never forget that, Mrs. Kilburn. Not as long as I live. And if you go on the way you are, you shall have to be caring for me in my old age."

Maura Kilburn patted Bridget's hand. "But you are part of the family. And I'm afraid you've given me much more than I have given you. Every time I hear the lilt in your voice, or you turn a phrase just so, I seem to be transported back to the years when I was a lovely young girl like you. Twenty-seven is hardly on your way to old age, you know."

"Aye, I know that."

"But then again," Mrs. Kilburn said wisely, "twenty-seven is an age when young women should think of more than their work, isn't that so, Bridget? I'm afraid I've been very selfish these last years, keeping you at my beck and call, when you should have been courted right to the altar by now."

"Oh, Mrs. Kilburn," Bridget scoffed. She pushed herself up so the woman wouldn't see how wonderful that idea sounded, especially the way things were happening now. "Isn't there plenty of time for me to worry about a husband and babies and all that nonsense?"

"There's that blarney again, my girl," Maura chided gently. She was not one to be fooled. She had eyes and was well aware of what had been going on under her own roof in the past three months. Lightening the mood, she slapped the arms of her chair. "Aren't we the two, sitting like a pair of spinsters gossiping about marriage and such. Well, I've had enough of that for today. Oh, and look," Mrs. Kilburn said suddenly, brightening as she caught sight of a visitor, "here's just the one to liven things up a bit before bed. That daughter of mine certainly does cut a fine figure, if I do say so myself."

Following Mrs. Kilburn's gaze, Bridget saw Kathy Hudson as she reached the front door. Looking stunning as usual, her short cap of dark hair was perfectly groomed. And her sunglasses, still atop her head added just the right touch of panache, covering her beautiful big brown eyes only when the sun shone brightly. Today Kathy was casually dressed in black trousers, Italian kid boots and a blouse of taupe silk. A huge black wool scarf was draped dramatically over her shoulders and rippled in the wake she created with her quick and accurate steps. She was just putting away her leather key case when Bridget opened the door.

"Mrs. Hudson!" Bridget greeted her happily. "We didn't expect you this evening."

"Will I ever cure you?" Kathy's gentle chide was substituted for a hello as she swept past. Bridget

15

stepped back, breathing in the fabulous scent of Kathy's perfume, Pheromone. "My name is Kathy, not Mrs. Hudson. Mrs. Hudson is my husband's mother. I'm hurt that you think I'm so ancient as to feel it necessary to call me by that title. I want you to call me by my given name, like a friend should."

" 'Tis a habit you'll very likely never break me of," Bridget said with a laugh, closing the door behind the lady.

"I'll just keep trying to pound it into you, then. Where's Mother?"

But Kathy had no need of Bridget's assistance. By the time she joined them in the living room, Kathy was well settled and deep in conversation with her mother.

"Don't you think so, too, Bridget?" Kathy and Mrs. Kilburn were both looking at her expectantly.

"I didn't hear the question," Bridget reminded them, her eyes dancing with delight. She could not have loved these two women more if they were blood relatives. Never once, from the moment she set foot in this house, had she been treated with anything but kindness, respect and acceptance; as a friend, not simply an employee.

"Of course you didn't, my dear," Mrs. Kilburn said patiently. "Kathy, we don't all run a mile a minute the way you do. You must remember that poor Bridget and I are mere mortals. Do try to give us time to acclimate ourselves to your rush of enthusiasm. After all, when it's just Bridget and me, I'm afraid this is a very quiet household. We're not used to planning one thing, talking about another

16

and agreeing to yet one more all at the same time."

"Oh, Mother, you are such a kidder," Kathy admonished playfully.

In that instant Bridget glimpsed the little girl who still lived inside Kathy Hudson's fifty-five-year-old body. And why shouldn't that child still be there? Her life had been full of the best things money could buy and none of the tragedy simple living could bring. She had never been poor, never had to work to exhaustion. Kathy had married a man who was not only handsome and kind, but who had worked hard enough to build a fortune that rivaled, if not exceeded, that of the Kilburns'. Yes, Kathy lived a charmed life. Even her son was nearly perfect, so why not let a bit of the wonderment of youth live on? No one had ever told Kathy there should come a time when childhood was put aside. She was a lucky, lucky lady.

Kathy held her mother's hand while she spoke to Bridget. "I was just saying that I think it would be wonderful if Mother went away with us for a bit. Ted and I were thinking of taking a long weekend in Mendocino. It's so lovely up there — quiet, not really much to do. We can take walks and eat at that marvelous little restaurant just off the main street —" Kathy knit her brow and snapped her well-manicured fingers, but gave up thinking when the name didn't dawn on her immediately. She waved her hand. "Well, it's marvelous and I'll know it when I see it. After all, there really isn't any possibility you can miss it up there. Not like Carmel. Mendocino hasn't given in to all that temptation to

17

cater to touristy-type things. So, what do you think?"

"Sure doesn't that sound lovely! I was there once and thought 'twas the most beautiful place—other than my island, you understand—that I'd ever seen. What do you think, Mrs. Kilburn? Are you up for a trip?"

"I'd love to go." Maura squeezed her daughter's hand in gratitude.

"Wonderful! The day after tomorrow, then. Thursday. Now, Bridget, you won't forget to check with the doctor about any medication Mother will need, will you?"

"Not to worry. I'll take care of everything."

"Good. Then jot down all the instructions and everything I have to remember. I'd hate to do anything wrong." Kathy was up and leaning toward the gilt-framed mirror over the fireplace to check her lipstick. Satisfied with what she saw, Kathy smiled at Bridget's reflection.

"But surely, Kathy, I'll be there to take care of all that. You and Mr. Hudson won't need to worry your heads," Bridget objected.

"Oh, don't be silly. We're leaving you home. This is suppose to be as much a vacation for you as it is for Mother. Don't you think we know how horrible she can be to work for?" Kathy turned and winked broadly at Bridget.

"Of course I am," Maura interjected. "That's why the poor girl has remained here all these years. She absolutely adores abuse, don't you, Bridget?"

"I'd be hard-pressed to live without it," she

18

quipped, then added seriously, "but this is too kind. I'm not due for my vacation for a good long while."

"Well, you'll just have to suffer through two this year. I have a feeling you'll find something to keep you occupied."

This time she winked at her mother, who winked right back. Both hoped Bridget would fill her time in the company of someone they knew quite well.

"All right, Mother, that's settled. I'll make all the arrangements. You simply be ready Thursday and off we'll go on a holiday. And, Bridget, I have a ton of magazines for you. You must pop round sometime to get them, or I'll try to remember to give them to you next time you bring mother to Marin."

"Thanks so much," Bridget said as Kathy brushed by, pulling her keys out of her handbag.

"I'll be sure to be ready," Maura called after her daughter, who was already halfway to the front door. "You're a dear to think of it. I love you."

But Kathy was already gone, out of range. The endearment was lost in the sound of the heavy front door closing. Maura shrugged and Bridget giggled.

"Go on, now. Upstairs with you. It's getting late," Bridget ordered. "If you start getting too excited before you leave and your blood pressure gets out of hand, Doctor Perry won't let you go at all."

"Oh, pooh, all of you so concerned with this heart of mine. It is a nuisance," Maura pouted.

"I agree, but better a nuisance that's beating hale and hearty, so you can keep complaining, than one that's stopped beating at all."

"You have a point there," Maura said with a chuckle.

"Sure and aren't I glad you see it my way," Bridget answered. "Now up with you. Would you like some help with your nightgown?"

Maura laughed, declining Bridget's offer, and went slowly out of the room, the tip of her cane making a ladylike thump against the hardwood floors. Bridget cocked her head, listening, waiting. When she finally heard the whir of the lift that took her charge up to the third floor of the mansion and the bedroom suite, Bridget was satisfied. She would check in on Mrs. Kilburn after giving her a bit of time to herself.

Efficiently Bridget straightened the living room. Though Mrs. Reilly did the cleaning and cooking, Bridget took pride in doing her share. She had always kept her da's cottage neat as a pin. No sense in doing less, now that she lived in a mansion surrounded by objects both priceless and exotic.

Everything was in its place. Bridget paused once more at the picture window to watch the fog roll in off the Bay. It came slowly, the sunset fading to a pin dot of color behind it.

Crossing her arms, she leaned against the carved wooden sash, unable to keep the memory of that first moment she'd seen Richard from drifting slowly, sensually back into her mind. That cozy day when he'd walked out of the fog, the sun breaking through, shining on him. Bridget had thought he must be the pot of gold at the end of the rainbow. And then. . . .

Then he glanced up and Bridget could see he had noticed her in the window. He was looking at her like a man not used to being surprised. Sure hadn't they stood that way for a century or more? Mother in heaven, Bridget had been lost in his gaze, though she couldn't see the color of his eyes. She had drowned in an ocean of longing as that golden man parted his lips first in astonishment, then recognition and finally pleasure. And hadn't her heart skipped a beat, hadn't her lips met the cold glass as though they might kiss him, warming him and setting herself on fire?

Never in her entire life had she abandoned her will. But without it there was no need to wonder if what she was about was proper and right. Then the moment was gone, the century of desire between strangers had passed, and he was moving up the drive. Now he climbed the short flight of steps to the front door, still scrutinizing her as he came.

The closer he came the more his face changed. His expression became open and happy. His lips, so hard and handsome when he had first seen her, parted in a smile of such sunny proportions Bridget almost forgot the dampness of the day. And as he came very close, she could see that his eyes were golden brown, the color of autumn's first morning light. Finally he stood on the wide porch, raising his hand as though to knock on the heavy door before changing his mind. Instead he leaned over the wrought iron railing and put a finger to his lips, all the while gazing into Bridget's eyes. He took that finger and placed it on the glass playfully. Bridget shivered as though he had put it to her mouth.

When he smiled, Bridget looked to see if he was laughing at her and thanked her lucky stars he wasn't. He was simply smiling, enjoying a harmless little game. He was liking her, wondering about her. Then he pointed to the door, raised an eyebrow and asked to walk into her life. Without hesitation, she rushed to let him in. Enthralled by the mere sight of him, now she was going to learn exactly who he was and what he would mean to her.

Head held high, Bridget opened the door slowly so she could prepare herself to hear his first words. But his wasn't the voice she heard.

"Richard," Maura Kilburn called.

Bridget looked on as the golden man took the old lady tenderly in his arms, gently twirling her about. Bridget felt a bit disappointed but was impressed that he could lavish such sentiment on an old woman. Bridget could not be more attracted to him if she tried. She found her longing for him growing as she watched this display of love and affection.

"How is my best girl?" he asked in a voice as gentle as the night breeze and as deep as an echo in a cavern.

"Fine, fine. I thought you'd never come to see me. You've been in town three days already."

Maura Kilburn, much to Bridget's surprise, had become coquettish, and her handsome visitor obliged her mood.

"I came as soon as I was presentable," Richard said, laughing. "Do you think I would dare show up here, tired from my flight and wearing jeans and dirty tennis shoes? Weren't you always the one who told me that dressing well was a sign of respect to myself and to the people around me? You're such a hideously demanding woman."

He twirled Maura once more, pulled her even closer to him before setting her down gently on the white marble of the entry. Neither one of them released the other. Maura's frail, age-spotted hand lay in Richard's strong one with easy familiarity. Bridget looked away fearing that one of them might see how she, too, longed to touch his hand.

Bridget fell back a bit so that she could watch the sweet drama unfold without intruding. This man's mere presence was enough to bring back a girlish delight that Mrs. Kilburn had left behind long ago. Her years disappeared once she was in his arms and she was once more irresistible. Laughing, still, attempting to retain her dignity, she ordered him to "pay attention to your manners."

Mrs. Kilburn squeezed his hand and turned him about until he faced Bridget. Without thinking, she stepped forward. His eyes met hers without apology for his interest, and she thought she had never seen eyes like his before; eyes that one could get lost in happily.

"This is Bridget," Mrs. Kilburn said with pride.

"This is my new friend and companion, Bridget Devlin from Kilmartin, Ireland. Bridget, this is . . ."

"Bridget? Bridget Devlin! I'm going to my room now unless there's something else the missus needs."

Thankfully Bridget heard Mrs. Reilly before the cook and housekeeper found her staring out the window. Though Mrs. Reilly appeared moments after her call, Bridget had just enough time to pretend she was actually busy. Quickly she grabbed up a pillow and fluffed it.

"Just fine, Mrs. Reilly, there won't be anything else tonight," she said as the woman looked in.

Mrs. Reilly saw that the room was almost as put together as if she'd done it herself, then gave Bridget a curt good-night before she went to her room.

Embarrassed to have almost been caught daydreaming again, Bridget put the pillow back on the sofa and climbed the long flights of stairs to Mrs. Kilburn's room. It was time to get back to work. Knocking gently, she opened the door.

"Time for your check," Bridget said softly, smiling broadly at the old lady who had settled herself quite nicely in the high antique bed.

"If you must," Maura sighed, putting her book aside.

"I must and you know it," Bridget insisted. In moments she had the stethoscope in her ears and was leaning over her patient.

Closing her eyes, she listened carefully as she held the instrument against the pulse point in the crook of Mrs. Kilburn's arm. A moment later Bridget smiled, snapped it out of her ears and hung it about her neck.

"That's it for this evening, Mrs. Kilburn. All's well, though I must tell you that skip is a bit more pronounced. I am going to call Dr. Perry first thing in the morning. Blood pressure is perfect."

"Oh, please. Just do what you have to do. I don't want to hear a report. I'm an old woman. I'm not planning on joining an aerobics program. Of course my heart's going to skip a beat now and again. It's tired. It deserves to be, after the life I've had."

Bridget hid her smile, "Well, then, if you're sure that's how you feel, I won't even give you a bit of an idea of what I'm going to recommend to the doctor about your going away with Mr. and Mrs. Hudson."

"Don't be silly, girl, you think I don't know you well enough by now? You're going to tell him it would be the best medicine in the world for me."

Bridget shrugged. "Aye, right you are. I just wanted to see if I could threaten you into turning out the light and going to sleep."

"I've given an inch, Bridget Devlin, and you must be satisfied with that. In the old days I wouldn't even be in my bedroom until three in the morning. Now I'm imprisoned here at nine o'clock."

"Only when you're tired. And I can see you are."

Bridget stood by the bed, carefully replacing the tools of her trade.

"All right. I am a bit. But leave me alone now. I'm going to read for a while, then I can turn off my own light. I'm a big girl. I've had all my pills, and you've listened enough to my insides. A bit of privacy is the only thing I need at the moment. Why don't you go downstairs and watch television." Maura made a shooing gesture with one hand.

"If you're sure." Bridget handed her the Tennyson anthology she'd been reading.

"I'm sure. Go," she ordered, opening her book and sticking her nose in.

"I'll have the monitor with me, so call if you need anything. Otherwise, I'll come up in an hour or so and make sure you're asleep."

"I won't be. Out, Bridget, before I make believe I am an invalid and insist you read to me."

Bridget laughed. "A fate worse than death to be sure. I'll leave, but only because I have some mending to do and there is a movie I want to see on television. I'll be back, mind you, so no carousing in your boudoir."

"I'll keep the men quiet," Mrs. Kilburn joked.

"Good night, then."

"Good night, Bridget."

Downstairs, house locked up for the night, Mrs. Reilly in her room, Bridget's face scrubbed clean, she put on her nightgown and settled into the soft plaid sofa in the den and turned on the television. In her hands was a threaded needle, her torn jeans

26

pinned and ready for stitching. Her eyes were trained on the flickering screen, but her mind drifted back to where it had been all day . . . to the moment seven years ago when he had turned his full attention to her for the first time and Mrs. Kilburn had said. . . .

"Bridget Devlin, this is my grandson, Richard Hudson."

"Pleased to meet you, Mr. Hudson."

Bridget managed to say his name despite her dry throat. She could feel her lips moving to form the words, then trembling the next moment as though they couldn't let go of his name.

He moved toward her, easily relinquishing his hold on his grandmother. Maura Kilburn would not leave the place in which he had put her, but Bridget was another matter. She could feel his energy, the urgency in him as he came close to her. He put out his hand to touch her, and she was powerless to reach out to him. If she did, she was afraid she might find out he wasn't real, only part of a dream.

In the next instant he was shaking her hand. She was doing a fine job, pretending she was simply pleased to meet him, until his other hand covered hers. When he cradled her slender palm in the warmth of his strong grasp, Bridget's composure faltered. The gesture was infused with an energy and promise beyond a mere introduction.

As sure as St. Patrick drove the vipers into the sea, Bridget felt his touch drive the breath from her. Riveted by the depth of her reaction, Bridget looked up into his eyes. His gaze, so frankly appraising, seemed to release her. She breathed again as he spoke.

"I've heard a lot about you, Bridget Devlin. And I must confess, both my grandmother and my mother have not done you justice."

He smiled. Bridget was sure in the next moment he was going to slide his hands, not from hers, but around her waist, pulling her close to him so that their lips and arms would close around each other and they would loose themselves in. . . .

Bridget felt the resonance of the door chimes before the actual sound intruded on her memories. She almost laughed, thinking how Richard had made her weak with desire that first time she had seen him and during his infrequent visits since then. But she'd been seven years younger. A mere girl. Now things were so marvelously different. Richard was no longer living on the other side of the United States. He had moved back to San Francisco, and it was with Bridget he was choosing to spend a good deal of his time.

The chimes sounded again. Resignedly she got up from the sofa, knowing her memories had to be put away for now.

Glancing at the hall clock, she saw it was almost ten. Late for a caller. Her lips were set against her rising irritation as the chime sounded insistently once again.

"I'm coming as fast as I can," Bridget muttered,

hurrying down the hall. Anyone familiar with the house would know it took a good while to go from the back rooms and through the halls before eventually reaching the front door.

Approaching cautiously, Bridget put her fingertips to the curtains that had been drawn over the glass beside the carved door. But before she could glimpse the visitor, the chimes rang yet again. Furious, she was just about to give the caller a piece of her mind when a knock sounded and a familiar voice called out.

"Grandmother! Bridget! Let me in. It's Richard!"

In an instant Bridget was fumbling with the chain, forgetting her nightgown, forgetting her wrath, forgetting her lovely memories. Reality was much more enticing than her dream.

"Richard? What on earth are you doing here so late?"

He stood at attention on the porch, his hands clasped behind his back as if trying to restrain himself. His face was aglow, his fine features lit with good humor. But when his dancing eyes met hers, when he opened his lips to greet her, Bridget saw his face change and soften with appreciation.

It was then she realized her linen and lace nightgown was cut perhaps a bit too low, and the light from behind her shone through the voluminous gown silhouetting the length of her legs, the nip of her waist, and the rise of her breasts.

"Incredible," Richard murmured.

Chapter Two

"Richard!" Bridget chided, stepping back as she opened the door wider, keeping herself out of the direct light. Knowing he could no longer see through her gown did nothing to ease the sensation of intimacy. "I should have put a robe on before I opened the door," Bridget apologized teasingly.

"Not on my account, I hope," Richard murmured, leaning into her for a kiss.

She obliged him, raising her lips willingly, feeling the now familiar wave of desire run through her as his lips lingered against hers. It was as though Richard preferred to drink in the essence of her slowly and surely. He could be a most baffling man.

"Especially on your account," she reminded him when they finally parted.

Her green eyes flashed with what she hoped he interpreted as confidence, though that was the last thing she felt. Weak with the closeness of the moment, Bridget felt almost naked standing alone with him in the soft night light. Never had a man gazed at her the way Richard did, and there could never be a more private look than the one they had just shared. They'd come so far. Yet Bridget still wasn't sure if Richard held the same burning love for her that she did for him. Forcing an expression of nonchalance, Bridget changed the subject, holding her sewing in front of her in a charming gesture of modesty.

"You've interrupted a most exciting night of mending. I didn't expect you tonight at all. Sure I didn't forget we were suppose to be seeing each other, did I?"

"No, of course not. Not only is your memory impeccable, I know it would be impossible for you to forget about an evening with me." Richard joked but both knew how true the statement was. "Actually, I didn't exactly expect to be here, either. But since grandmother is leaving day after tomorrow, I thought I'd better come see you tonight. I've had a particularly busy and fruitful day. I knew you two would like to hear about it."

"Really? And would that mean that you're now an employed attorney?" Bridget queried.

"Hardly," Richard laughed.

The look of preoccupied exhaustion in his eyes when he'd returned to San Francisco three months ago had almost vanished. Now Bridget saw a ghost of it and was sorry she had brought up the subject of work.

"I'm afraid I'm still not ready to welcome a full-time position as good news. Seven years at the Attorney General's Office in Washington were enough to make me want to sail off to Tahiti and never come back. I'm afraid I took it as a personal affront that, even if I worked forty hours a day instead of a week, I couldn't win the war against drugs on my own." The sparkle of self-possession came back into his eyes. "But I suppose if I stick to my plan to use this hiatus to recoup my energies, I might find I am suited for a lifetime of public service. In fact, I have the sneaking suspicion that I'm beginning to believe I can conquer the world again, and I've only been unemployed for three months."

"I know you will, Richard. I've never seen anyone in my life with as much self-confidence as you. If the world needs conquering, I imagine you'll be the one to do it," Bridget assured him emphatically, knowing it to be true. Look how easily he had conquered her heart once they were in the same town together. As far as she was concerned there was nothing Richard Hudson could not do or have, if he wished it so.

"Why thank you, my lady. I appreciate that vote of support."

Bridget rolled her eyes. "As if you needed it. Sure isn't it everyone who tells you how perfect you are, Richard Hudson."

"But it isn't everyone who matters, is it, Bridget Devlin?" Before she could even think of a fitting response, Richard was off again, his mind snapping back to the news that had brought him to the Kilburn household. "Anyway my news is much more exciting than a mere job. Is Grandmother still up? I want you both to hear about it. In fact, I felt so festive I stopped and picked these up just for you."

Both hands, hidden before, now appeared holding a most beautiful bouquet toward her. The fabulous arrangement of daisies, carnations, stalks, a water lily, a bit of heather and riotous greenery all around, was the kind of spray a man picked when left to his own devices in a roomful of cut flowers. Richard selected them, not because they complemented one another as a whole, but because each flower attracted him with its unique beauty or scent. It wouldn't have occurred to him to make any other choice.

"How lovely." Bridget buried her nose in the petals' velvety softness, loving the fact that he'd picked a bit of everything. Her da used to say that was how a man went courting. So many lovely lasses to choose from, each one like a sweet-smelling flower that he gathered to him in a great beautiful bouquet until he decided which one he liked the best.

Bridget laughed delightedly, unaware of Richard's eyes on her, drinking in the sight of her loose coppery hair, her pale skin and the frame of flowers around her heart-shaped face. When he turned away, she had no idea it was because he feared the next moment would find him reaching out for her, crushing her to him, flowers and all.

That might have been fine behavior with the worldly women in Washington, but with Bridget he wanted no frivolous gestures. Richard wanted to be quite sure he meant every word he spoke to her as they explored what they meant to each other.

"I can't thank you enough, Richard. It's surely a lovely surprise," Bridget exclaimed, following him as he ambled toward the staircase where he looked up expectantly.

"I hope not too much of a surprise," he said, laughing, unable to keep himself from peering back into her upturned face. Instinctively he reached out and touched a tendril of long, red-brown hair that had fallen into the bouquet. Deftly he brushed it back over her shoulder, thinking it felt as soft as rose petals.

Before he could say another word, just as he was about to pull her toward him, Bridget's monitor beeped obstinately. Laughing together, both acknowledged that there could be no ignoring the summons. Maura Kilburn wanted to know who was at the door—and she wanted to know immediately.

Shrugging prettily, Bridget said, "You might as well go on up, then. She'd be furious to know that you were here, and me keeping you all to myself."

"I can't think of anyone I would rather have keep me," he said, leaning forward to whisper in her ear.

Bridget lowered her lashes, throwing off Richard's compliment. Sometimes the surety of his words made her feel powerless, without a will of her own. But what sweet helplessness.

"What a charming way you barristers have with words," she bantered even as her heart soared. "It must take many a year to learn how to lie so smoothly."

"And even longer to learn how to tell the truth properly," Richard responded quietly as he grasped the banister. Bridget's carefree smile faded from her lips, her eyes softening appreciatively. Reaching out once more, Richard pulled a perfect white carnation from the bunch of flowers in her arms. "For Grandmother, if you don't mind." Bridget shook her head. "Perhaps we can discuss my ethical education in greater depth as soon as I've seen her."

"Perhaps there might be time," she agreed.

Without another word Richard bounded up the stairs. Unthinking, Bridget moved to the foot of the steps, watching his long denim-encased legs, his broad, strong back and shoulders move gracefully upward. His blond hair, a bit long in the back, was styled so beautifully it seemed to have the depth of well-cut velvet. At the top of the first landing he stopped. Casually he leaned over the banister.

"Do you think a cup of tea would keep Grandmother awake all night?"

Bridget, her alabaster face tilted up to him expectantly, shook her head. "Of course not."

"Would you mind?"

"I'll be up in ten minutes with a steaming pot," Bridget answered with a smile, reluctant to let him go, yet feeling content just to have him in the huge house. He watched her a moment longer before disappearing, winding up the amazing sweep of staircase to his grandmother's room.

In the kitchen Bridget hummed as she primped the flowers in Mrs. Kilburn's finest Waterford vase while waiting for the water to boil. The flowers were placed in the center of the satinwood drum table in the middle of the foyer. Standing back, Bridget admired the inlaid antique furniture, the simplicity of the crystal vase and her floral handiwork.

"Ah, Bridget, you clever girl. Imagine what you could do if only you had the money," she muttered, then laughed at the silliness of it all.

Proud as she was of her profession, it would never lead to wealth, yet there were moments when that was what she dreamed of. Not the amazing wealth of Mrs. Kilburn or the Hudsons, but just enough to allow her to fly home to visit her da every now and again without having to worry. Or enough to put up proper street lights in Kilmartin. No, no. Enough money to pave the main street and build a new school. No . . .

At this final, extravagant thought Bridget laughed out loud. She might be silly, but at least she had dreams, and that was more than she could say for many people walking around this world. Shaking her head, Bridget went back to the kitchen, thinking not of Kilmartin or what a fine lady she would be if she were wealthy, but of the man upstairs. If he ever loved her true enough to marry, she wouldn't care if he were rich or poor.

And there was the rub. Though exciting, though promising, their quickly-blossoming relationship was just that for him — new and wonderful. But Bridget had loved him through the years, cherishing Richard's infrequent visits. She dreamed of him when Mrs. Kilburn read aloud his more regular letters. And now that he was home to stay, now that he sought Bridget out, she loved Richard Hudson deeper and dearer than she had thought humanly possible. But since he hadn't declared himself, Bridget Devlin would not act the fool and be the first to speak of love.

Dashing up to her room for a robe, she was back to the teakettle by the time it whistled its tune. All she really wanted was to be near Richard Hudson.

"I hope you're going to pack for cool weather. Nothing fancy. And watch out at night up there because there aren't any street lamps," Richard warned. He knew his grandmother was only heading up the coast for a long weekend, but he was also sure that she would try to act like she was sixty instead of eighty-eight if given the chance.

"Oh, stop it," Maura commanded playfully. "You sound just like your mother. She always gets that horrible, clipped, boarding-school-mistress tone when she gives directions. Sometimes I wish she had married a little less successfully. Your father's marvelous head for business only lets her have enough money to reinforce all the uppity habits she learned when we sent her to those fancy schools."

"And you wouldn't have her or me any other way," Richard reminded his grandmother.

"True. Somehow the two of you can pull it off and still remain totally lovable," Maura admitted. "But enough of this trip nonsense. I don't want to hear about Mendocino. What I want to hear is what has brought you here at ten o'clock in the evening."

Richard pushed himself off the side of his grandmother's bed, where he had initially perched, then settled himself in the little satin chair to the right of her.

With an expectant glance toward the door he answered, "I'd like to wait for Bridget if you don't mind. Good news is better told just once. Otherwise it loses that edge of excitement, if you know what I mean."

"Of course we can wait, dear." Maura nodded, letting a comfortable silence settle between them. It didn't last long. Maura Kilburn couldn't contain her curiosity despite her promise. Rationalizing her next question, she decided it was a universal assumption that an old woman would poke her nose into everyone's business. She put it to him bluntly.

"You like her, don't you, Richard? Bridget, I mean."

Richard slid down in the chair and let his head rest on the tufted back. His hands were crossed over his flat stomach, his strong fingers intertwined. He stretched his long legs before him, crossing them at the ankle. Richard looked as relaxed as could be until Maura began to study his face. It was then she saw what made him such a formidable attorney.

His eyes were hooded, his face the picture of composure. Not a muscle twitched nor did his lashes close as though to hide his thoughts. The only evidence that Richard was thinking deeply was a slight crease of his brow. Or perhaps it was the exceptional stillness of his body, the almost total lack of animation, as though he had drawn into himself to find the proper answer to Maura's question. That pleased her.

Richard had grown into a fine man, not just a young man seeking the next pleasure in life. He would go far with or without anyone's help. Of that Maura Kilburn had no doubt. She knew, though, that for success to mean anything to Richard, it had to be earned rather than given. His eyes flickered to hers, and Maura Kilburn realized her grandson was about to speak more seriously than she had imagined.

"Yes, I like her very much."

"I thought so." Maura nodded, knowing the tone of his answer left room for discussion. "I gather you aren't going to sweep her off her feet and marry her before I decide to die, though."

"I don't exactly intend to run away with her tomorrow, if that's what you mean, but I wouldn't give up hope. I have a feeling you'll be around when I take the big step. Hell, you'll probably dance the longest at my wedding. I'm just not sure that gorgeous Irish lass you've had tending you is destined to be the bride." He hesitated for only a moment before continuing, then he spoke as though to himself.

"She is so different, Grandmother. She's guileless. She says what she means. I mean really says it. Bridget doesn't couch her words in terms she thinks I want to hear, and she doesn't talk simply to be heard. Do you know how long it's been since I've been with a woman who actually feels comfortable with silence?"

Richard sighed, stretching his arms around the back of his head, lacing his fingers to create a cradle.

"We're good together. She doesn't push me or

pull me or demand anything. Sometimes I think I'll go out of my mind if I don't have her, and other times I simply like to be with her. If that's love, then it's the strangest feeling I've ever had. I thought you were suppose to walk around with your feet barely touching the ground. Bridget makes me feel as if I'm all here. She makes me feel solid and comfortable in all sorts of ways I don't think I ever felt before. This is a tough call. Maybe I'm not ready to settle down completely yet."

"You'll know when the time is right, Richard. And when you do, I hope you choose your young lady for who she is, not what she appears to be or what she has."

"I hope I'm wise enough to do that," Richard admitted. "And I think I will. After all, I had two marvelous examples of what to look for in a woman—you and Mom. The more I get to know about Bridget the more I think she's what I'm looking for. And I might be what Bridget is looking for, too."

"What might Bridget be looking for?" Bridget asked, hearing the last part of Richard's statement. She had pushed open the door to Mrs. Kilburn's bedroom with her derrière, turning gracefully so the huge tray she carried skimmed past the jamb without a cup rattling.

Realizing their conversation should remain private until Richard decided differently, Maura Kilburn quickly covered the real topic of their conversation by blurting out the first thing that came to mind.

"He was just saying that Bridget might want to look into a new law regarding the Irish quotas."

Maura glanced helplessly at Richard, knowing he had been researching Bridget's legal status. Her temporary working papers had lapsed, and frustrated by quota restrictions and red tape, her green card had never materialized.

"Right." Richard caught on immediately, grateful for his grandmother's tactful segue. "I just read about the Morrison Act the other day. It provides 48,000 more visas for the Irish. If you have the written promise of work you're almost guaranteed a card."

"Sure and I've heard of it," Bridget said, putting down the tray and fussing about with the pot. "My friend Tess applied and was rejected, though she worked three years in this country. She's being sent back soon, because they say she didn't qualify. No, thank you. I think I'll take my chances and leave things as they are."

"Bridget!" Maura cried but Richard silenced her with a raised hand.

"It's all right, Grandmother. When I finally settle myself in a new firm I'll make sure this gets straightened out. As long as she is permanently employed, I don't think there will be much trouble."

"Thank you for understanding and promising to help," Bridget said, offering him a delicate Limoge cup filled with Earl Grey tea. "Now, can we please forget about me and find out what Richard's news is? Unless, of course, he's already told you."

Maura took her cup and shook her head. "Of course not. He wouldn't breathe a word without you in the room."

Bridget slid her eyes Richard's way and smiled before settling back on the sofa at the end of the bed. "Sure and if I'm not flattered," she said quietly. "Well, now I'm here and Mrs. Kilburn looks as though she's ready to burst with curiosity so tell us. What have you done with yourself today, Richard?"

Happy to have center stage, he cleared his throat and polished his nails on his shirt as he grinned.

"I want you to be the first to know that you are looking at a home owner. I signed the papers this evening. I haven't even told Mom and Dad yet."

"Richard, I'm so pleased," Maura cried. "This is the first time I've felt your move to the West Coast is real. How marvelous that we'll be a family again. No more of you popping in and out on the odd holiday. I always hated the fact you weren't close enough to even show your face on Christmas most years," Maura exclaimed.

"And you, Bridget?" Richard asked. "Are you happy, too?" Bridget's cup hovered between saucer and lips. She looked hard at him, wondering if his decision to buy a house had anything to do with her. Before she could respond, he said gently, "Say something nice now. I've never committed to anything quite so permanent in my life, and it scares me to death." Laughing, he added, "That piece of information, however, is not to get out of this room. It would ruin my reputation as a formidable attorney and all-around macho guy."

"You have my promise," Bridget swore playfully, never taking her eyes from his. "And aye, 'tis wonderful. Congratulations, Richard."

They were so lost in each other that neither noticed Maura contentedly watching them. Perhaps, she thought, she might even be around for her first great-grandchild, the way things appeared to be going.

"It's unanimous, Richard. We're both delighted," Maura said affectionately, feeling the silence was becoming a bit too heavy with longing. "You must show it to Bridget while I'm gone. After all, she'll be rambling about this place all by herself for four days. Even Mrs. Reilly has decided to venture out.

"But now, I'm afraid, we'll have to call an end to the celebration. I'm awfully tired. I'm afraid if I don't close these old eyes this minute, I'll never get them open in time to go day after tomorrow."

Bridget was up before Richard could move. She had been enjoying this intimate moment so much she hadn't noticed her patient's face pale.

Deftly her long fingers found the pulse point on the old woman's fragile wrist.

"You take good care of me, Bridget, dear," Maura whispered, her eyes already closing.

"No more late-night parties for you, Mrs. Kilburn," Bridget whispered as she helped Maura settle herself. Turning away, once the covers were properly tucked, Bridget took a few steps toward Richard. "Not too long. I'm afraid we've worn the dear woman to a frazzle.

Richard nodded. "I'll just be a minute."

Just as she walked out of the room, Bridget turned back to remind Mrs. Kilburn of her doctor's appointment the next day, but closed her mouth instantly.

Richard Hudson was half sitting on his grandmother's bed. Gently he bent down and kissed her forehead. She smiled as he turned off the light in the bedroom. But the hall light illuminated the pair enough for Bridget to see Richard pick up his grandmother's hand and raise it to his lips. Quietly she left them to their private time.

True to his word, he stayed only a few minutes and sought Bridget the moment he'd closed the door to the room. It had taken him years to pay attention to the fact that Bridget existed. Now, at times, he wondered how he could exist without her.

"There you are," he said a short while later as he stood in the kitchen door watching her. "I thought I was going to have to burst into your bedroom like one of those literary rogues just so I could say good-night and thank you.

Pleased he had come to find her, Bridget smiled, looking over her shoulder as she dried the last cup.

"I think a knock would have gained you entrance. No sense ruining one of these lovely oak doors," Bridget murmured. Still she indulged herself with the image of Richard flinging open her bedroom door dressed in a doublet, a sword dangling against his muscular thigh.

"I would have helped if you weren't so efficient. I had a cleaning lady in Washington but I managed to learn to dry dishes quite nicely." His offer banished the dashing image. Richard Hudson was an all-American, all-modern man.

Bridget's curls danced about her shoulders and down her back as she shook her head in amused disbelief. She hadn't bothered with the overhead kitchen lights, opting to turn on the little spotlight above the sink. Her hair caught the subdued rays, twisting them into a red-gold halo. Richard moved toward her, reaching out to touch the bright tumble.

"I'm afraid it's all done now. Just a wipe here and there."

"Well, then, since I can't be of help, I suppose I'd better be going." His voice was deep and velvety like the night around them.

"Then I'll be saying good-night, too," she answered softly.

Contentedly she followed his languorous lead, enjoying the anticipation of the moment they took their leave. It was becoming more difficult each time they saw each other to say goodbye. Soon, Bridget knew, they would no longer pretend a kiss was enough, an embrace satisfying.

Watching Richard through lowered lashes she saw him lean back against the sink, leaving only a hairbreadth between them. His arms were crossed, his muscular shoulder inclined toward her more delicate one. Bridget could smell the starch in his shirt, and the scent he wore reminded her of the beach on a hot summer day.

Beneath the belt of her robe, Bridget felt a hole of raw desire that swallowed everything about her, including the ability to speak. Suddenly her body began to tremble with expectation. The kitchen was dark, the house silent. It had been coming to this for weeks, months. Perhaps they had been moving unconsciously toward this moment since the first time they met. But when it was that the passion had been kindled was irrelevant. Right here and now was the time of reckoning. And Bridget wanted it more than anything else in the world.

"I know I should leave," Richard whispered with an urgency that demanded she look at him, tell him there was no need.

"Sure you should," she murmured, aching with unspoken desire, keeping her body still while her mind whirled.

"Then why do I find it so hard?"

Richard reached out and took her hand just as she laid the dish towel down. Bridget closed her eyes for a moment, suddenly aware of how small and delicate her hands were, after years of thinking of them only as competent working tools. Richard was changing the way she imagined herself. He was a magician and she a subject willing to be transformed.

Richard touched her chin bringing her face up, turning her head so he could gaze into her eyes, study them intently. He seemed to be memorizing the position of each fleck of gold swimming in her emerald-green eyes, the shading of each long lash as they fluttered closed against her cheek.

"If it was easy, then I'd say there'd be no reason for you to ever come back," she breathed. He laughed a little, a sweet and gentle sound that surrounded her and lifted her heart. His smile dispelled the trepidation that had lain between them momentarily.

"A bit convoluted, but logical reasoning, I must say," he whispered back, his head bowing until their foreheads met and they spoke to each other in the softest way. "You know, there was a time I wasn't sure if I should think of you as a sister or a friend. You've become such a part of our family. All those years I heard about you from my mother and grandmother—their letters and phone calls were full of news about Bridget. Now, since I moved back here, since we started seeing each other, I can't imagine you as anything but . . ."

Richard hesitated. Bridget moved into his touch, forcing his hand to slide around her head, his fingers to bury themselves in her mass of hair.

"But what?" she asked boldly, raising only her eyes to him not her voice, anxious to follow the path he had put them on.

"Anything but a lover," he said, moving his head away from her, drawing her face closer to his.

His lips hovered just above Bridget's as he searched her face. Maybe there he could find a clue to the words that would make her understand how much he cared, how unusual and new these emotions were raging inside him.

"A lover, Bridget," he insisted, needing to hear the word to make sure it was real. "Perhaps I should have been thinking of you as a lover all this time. We've been so polite, so careful. We've been friends until now. I'm not sure I want the caution to end. This could be so important — to both of us. We have to be sure of one another."

Tentatively, so gently she wasn't sure she had felt the touch, Richard kissed her, and in that caress was a promise of something wonderful. Bridget felt her body instinctively curve into his, yet still they didn't embrace. Rather they swayed together, drawing out the pleasure of expectation, holding each other with only the force of their longing.

"I want that, too, Richard. Sure hasn't it been in my eyes these months you've been home? I don't just want one thing or the other. I've known it such a long time. Do you think I like walking out with you, and you not knowing how I feel? I promise to be careful. I'm not a child. I can wait while we see where this leads."

"I don't want you to be like the others."

"What others?" Bridget demanded gently, her hand now framing his face tenderly as she forced him to pay close attention to her words. "I'm only myself, Richard Hudson, no other. Sure I can't be compared and neither can you. If we do that, then we've lost before we've begun. Now tell me true. Do you want to begin? Because if you do, I'm ready. I don't ask much from you. Only that if you love me, love me true. And if you don't, don't pretend. Can you do that, man?"

"Aye, that I can do," Richard laughed, gently teasing her with his poor imitation of a brogue. Grinning, he abandoned the luxury of caressing her hair and encircled her waist, pulling her toward him. "And I'll start my honest relationship with you right now. I honestly like you much better in that nightgown of yours. Robes are definitely not my favorite piece of clothing."

"Well, now, I suppose we are going to have to talk about that aren't we?" Bridget sighed, completely and happily helpless in his arms.

"Talking wasn't exactly what I had in mind."

"Then take your mind elsewhere for tonight. Remember, this is your grandmother's house and, though a man you may be, under her roof you are still her grandchild. Much as it pains me, I'm going to show you to the door."

"I thought you might. And this time I'll let you. But not before we share a proper goodnight."

Before she could say another word Richard's lips were on hers, his mouth parting slightly so that his breath mingled with hers, and the warmth of it made her shiver with delight. Richard's broad hands spread over her back, and Bridget's arms went about his neck, feeling for the first time the tautness of his skin, the silkiness of his golden hair. Her eyes closed, and behind them she saw every beautiful feature of his face dancing before her. This was heaven. This was what she had waited so long for and traveled so far to find. Wrapped in his arms, Bridget reveled in feeling him wanting her.

Chapter Three

"Do you think they're in Mendocino by now?" Bridget asked. She rested her head on the leather seat of Richard's Porsche, keeping her eyes shut as he had instructed. Talking kept her from thinking about the never-ending curves that made the car sway as they headed toward Richard's new home.

"Of course they are. Even if they left a bit late it's only a four-hour drive or so. Let's see, it's almost eight —"

"Eight!" Bridget's eyes popped open in surprise. Where had the day gone?

"Close those eyes," Richard commanded, a chuckle in his voice. He reached out, gently caressing her forehead, forcing her lids down. "You promised not to peek until I told you to look."

"But I'll get seasick if this goes on much longer," she protested.

"Then thank your lucky stars we're almost there," he said, laughing. "And I don't know how you can be surprised by the time. I think that was the longest brunch I've ever had. Let's see. We started at noon at the Cliff House, two omelettes, two Bloody Mary's and two pieces of cheesecake, not to mention a couple of hours of conversation. It was three by the time we left there. Then there were two or three design studios we stopped at, that little antique place, lingered over a cup of cappuccino, watched a street mime for half an hour down by the wharf and stopped for a few hugs now and again. And you wonder where the day went! Hah."

"I suppose you're right. It just isn't fair that we have four days to ourselves and one is gone already," Bridget said as Richard slowed the car and made a final turn. Even with her eyes shut she could tell the difference between the dark of night and the dark of a garage. Breathing a sigh of relief, she rested, thankful the car had stopped moving.

Richard's door opened, then closed again. The next instant hers was open. Richard leaned over, kissed her gently and let his lips linger on hers while he whispered against them.

"It's time to see my home, Bridget Devlin. Wait to open your eyes, and I'll show you my new world. Maybe you'll like it enough to stay awhile."

"Perhaps I will," she answered softly, her fingertips floating toward his face, touching it.

In her self-imposed blindness Bridget found him even dearer. She never realized how exhilarating a mere touch could be. Through her finger-tips she could feel not only flesh but character and emotion. She could feel his small and affectionate smile. For a long while they remained that way, reveling in the exchanged tenderness until Bridget reminded him, "Lead me where you will."

And the moment was gone—their desire once more put aside.

When Bridget grinned, Richard could see the pearly whiteness of her teeth. Taking up her hands he warned, "Okay. Your eyes are shut tight. Here we go."

Excited as a small boy, Richard helped her from the car, through the garage and into the empty house.

"By the saints this sounds spooky indeed," Bridget whispered, her low-heeled shoes sounding like an orchestra of drums on the hardwood floors.

"I know. It's great, isn't it? This is probably the last time this house will be so empty. Absolutely nothing here. Just you and me and—"

Richard stopped, drawing Bridget in front of him. He wrapped one arm about her shoulders so her chin rested on his forearm. With the other he held her waist. His fingers dug into the thick cables of the fisherman-knit sweater she wore against the chill of the day.

"Open your eyes, Bridget, and you'll see why I had to have this house."

She didn't need a second invitation. Her eyes flew open, her exclamation of wonderment echoing eerily through the house. Her gaze flitted over the scene in front of her.

"Ah, Richard," Bridget breathed, easily slipping out of his arms and moving tentatively toward the floor-to-ceiling leaded windows.

One hand reached out, then the other, until she was pressing against the glass like a child silently begging to go out and play. In front of her lay San Francisco, spread out in all its glittering night glory, a mosaic of brilliant lights. And behind every light, a story: a family sitting down to dinner; lovers standing naked and unashamed before each other; an old woman looking at pictures, her memories as bright as the light in her sitting room. Cars were speeding over the Bay Bridge, their headlights melting into a liquid stream of brilliance.

"What do you think?" Richard was behind her now, resting his hands lightly on her shoulders.

"Sure I think I must have died and gone to heaven. By God, the streets are paved with gold from this perch," Bridget breathed, finally finding her voice. "I've never seen anything so lovely. You *are* lucky to have a place like this. You have no idea how fortunate you are."

"That's where you're wrong. I know exactly how blessed I am. I hope I never forget it."

Bridget tilted her head to look back at him. Turning reluctantly from the view, she watched

55

Richard closely, seeing he did indeed appreciate his status as a favored child. That was good. But he was so sure his fortune was for eternity that Bridget wondered what would happen if his marvelous world was ever threatened. What kind of man would he be then? Yet through her love Bridget knew the answer. He would still be Richard; confident, happy Richard. Of that she was sure.

"You won't forget," she assured him. "I have a feeling you'll always be true to your heart. That's a fine thing. An unusual thing. At least in an American man."

It took a moment for Richard to realize Bridget was baiting him. When he did, he laughed, "I'm so glad you approve. You ladies from overseas can be so difficult to please."

"That is the truth, Lord help me," Bridget said giggling. "Now, before I'm totally taken with the view and haven't an ounce of desire to see anything else, you'd better show me the rest of this cottage of yours."

"Your wish is my command," Richard answered gallantly. "This, as you've guessed, is the living room. Fabulous view here." He pointed to the window. "Exceptional marble fireplace there." Now he pointed to the opposite side of the huge room. "We have ceiling moldings and lath-and-plaster walls. I have a feeling we're not going to be putting black leather and plastic in this room."

"I should say not," Bridget agreed, her heart fluttering each time he spoke the word *we*. "But, Richard, I've no idea what you would put in here to make it perfect. This one room is bigger than my da's entire house."

"Methinks you exaggerate." Richard took her hand and led her into a lovely dining room complete with wainscotting and a carved breakfront built into the wall. "It doesn't matter, anyway. After everything we've seen today I realize I'm going to be decorating very, very slowly. If perfection is the goal then the strategy is precise buying."

"I suppose that makes sense," she agreed, thinking all the while that it took her mother and father two years to save for their bedroom set. That was about as precise as one could get, but she doubted cost was Richard's concern.

Not wishing to bother him now with tales of how the other half lived, Bridget followed him from room to room, one grander than the next. The kitchen was huge with hand-painted tiles. The den was a man's place, paneled with beautiful, dark wood. And there was an imposing room that seemed to Bridget to have no purpose whatsoever.

Upstairs the landing was pitch black. Richard held tight to her hand, but each bedroom was awash in the dim, pearly light from the street below. When they came to the largest room, Richard stopped.

"This will be the master suite. There's an attached bath and a small room just to the right that the broker told me was put there for the new babies. Sort of a little nursery before they were sent to the big nursery."

"Sure isn't that a lovely idea. So the mum could hear the wee one easily. 'Tis a charming idea."

"I think I'll use it for my exercise equipment," Richard said casually.

"You'll do no such thing," Bridget objected. "It's such a beautiful little room. You leave it for the baby."

"But I haven't got one."

"But you will someday," Bridget insisted.

"You sure about that?" he asked, leaning back against the wall.

"I just hope you do, that's all. You'd make a grand father I think. Now stop teasing me. It's getting late and I'm starving. Since I probably couldn't count on you to cook me a meal even if the lights were on and the place was stuffed with furniture, we'll be going out I imagine."

"Bridget Devlin, you are getting so pushy."

"I am not, but it's no less than you promised me. Now, let's be on our way," she prodded, taking him by the shoulders and pointing him toward the door.

But he stopped suddenly and turned back to take her in his arms. "You know, you're lucky tonight. Sometime I'm not going to let you out of here so easily. You do understand that, don't you?" He spoke with the assurance of a man used to getting what he wanted.

Bridget nodded, accepting the inevitability of it with pleasure. "That I do," she answered with an unwavering gaze.

Richard grinned. There was no doubt Bridget wanted that as much as he did. "Just wanted to make that perfectly clear in case you need a reason to run for the hills," he warned.

" 'Tisn't the hills that are interesting me, Richard Hudson," Bridget murmured.

"I was hoping you'd say something like that," he admitted frankly. "You know, I'm starving, too. Let's get something to eat."

"Sure don't I have a marvelous idea. Drive me back to your grandmother's. I'll be fixing you a roast chicken unlike any you've ever had. But first, stop at the pharmacy. If I don't drop this off to be filled, Dr. Perry will have my head come Monday."

"Are they open this late," Richard asked, guiding her back down the stairs.

"Till nine. So we must hurry. Then look out, bucko, because Bridget Devlin cooks tonight!"

"Here, stop here."

Bridget pointed to an old brick building sporting a row of renovated, glass-enclosed storefronts. Deftly he guided the Porsche to the curb, pulling to a stop. Bridget hopped out, leaning in for just a minute.

"I'll be back in a twinkle," she said lightly.

"Hurry. I'm not sure, but I think we have some frozen things in these bags," Richard grumbled, worried about the pristine interior of his car.

"As you say," Bridget assured him, then ran into the brightly-lit drugstore.

Inside, a shopper or two poked about the merchandise. A young sales clerk seemed bored at the register. And in the back, behind the high counter, the pharmacist was still at work.

"Late tonight, Mr. Payne," Bridget greeted him brightly.

"Miss Devlin. What brings you in at this hour?"

The man's eyes lit up, obviously delighted to see her. But she was oblivious to his marvelous smile, his quiet good looks. In his white jacket and his wire-rim glasses on his short straight nose, his hair combed back from his wide forehead, he looked like a very fashionable scientist. Fashionable or not, Bridget could think of nothing but getting back to Richard and the rest of their evening. She talked quickly, her brogue thickening as she looked forward to their heady evening to come.

"Just wanted to drop this off, if you please. No need to pick it up until Monday morning."

On tiptoe she handed the small piece of paper to him. He adjusted his glasses.

"I can get it for you now, if you care to wait. I wouldn't mind a little company before I close, then maybe—"

But Bridget had been distracted by the display of perfume and was allowing herself a spray of Opium, hardly hearing what he had to say.

"Thanks so much, Mr. Payne. Monday I'll be back then."

With a wave she was off, leaving Michael Payne to shrug and smile. Miss Devlin certainly looked good in her short, plaid skirt and that big, big sweater. He always did admire someone who wore clothes well, even if the style was a bit conservative.

"You know, Bridget, this is ridiculous. We could have bought an entire restaurant for what we paid for these groceries. Why don't we stash them at grandmother's and head out for a bite in the city," Richard complained.

"Now stop that. When was the last time you had a meal made from love, instead of Mrs. Reilly's perfect concoctions made with great skill but no heart?"

"I don't know. Let me think. Oh, yes, it was that beautiful Greek girl from the embassy in Washington. She made me—"

Bridget cut him short with a whack on the arm. He turned the car and they headed down the long road that led to his grandmother's street.

Bridget was on the verge of reprimanding Richard for bringing up a lost love, but fell silent as she caught sight of the house. It was a moment before her mind registered what she saw. When she did, she lay her hand gently on Richard's shoulder.

"There are lights on," she said quietly, the joy of the day draining from her.

"There are?" Richard frowned and made the last turn before coming abreast of the drive. For a moment the house was hidden by trees. Then it was in front of them, all three stories ablaze with light.

Richard stopped the car in the middle of the street. For a moment he and Bridget sat staring at the place as though they had never seen it before.

"Should we call the police?" Bridget whispered.

Richard shook his head. "No, I don't think so. No burglar in their right mind would go into an empty house and turn on all the lights."

"You're right, of course," Bridget agreed quietly, her eyes continuing to scan the facade, looking for any sign of life. But all was still.

"Perhaps it's Mrs. Reilly. Maybe she came back and was afraid to stay in the house alone."

Bridget shrugged. "Who else could it be?"

"I don't know," Richard answered thoughtfully. Releasing the brake, he stepped gently on the gas, letting the Porsche all but glide down the drive and roll to a stop in front of the door. This time Bridget didn't wait for him. She was out of the car by the time he rounded the back. Exchanging a glance, Richard took her elbow and guided her forward. Bridget had her key in hand. Inserting it into the door, she heard the lock click smoothly. It hadn't been tampered with. Opening the door slowly they stepped into the foyer. The brilliantly illuminated interior of the house was more frightening than welcoming. Bridget and Richard strained to hear any sign of life. It wasn't a sound, though, that caught their attention. It was a presence standing quietly on the first landing. Instinctively Richard pulled Bridget close as they whirled toward the staircase.

"Mom? What are you doing here?" Richard's shoulders fell with relief at the familiar figure. He took a step forward, his hand held out toward her.

Kathy's first step toward him was slow. Then, in a blink, she was down the stairs and in his arms. "Your grandmother wasn't feeling well. We came back an hour ago. I put her to bed . . ."

Bridget moved first, mumbling as she hurriedly unbuttoned her sweater and started past Kathy and Richard. "I'd better go to her. Has Dr. Perry been called? I knew I should have gone with you. It's probably nothing, just exhaustion. But I'm glad — "

Richard felt his mother tense, his eyes filling with sudden tears as he understood everything, seeing the situation in exquisite detail. They were all there in his grandmother's house: her devoted friend and nurse, her daughter and son-in-law, her grandson. All there and. . . .

Kathy pulled away from her son, straightening as she put a hand out and took Bridget's arm as she passed. Bridget swiveled toward the other woman, and Kathy saw her peevishness just before she hid it. Kathy Hudson's chin fell to her chest for an instant then her head came up and she held it high.

"Dr. Perry has already left, Bridget. There was nothing he could have done. Nothing you could have done. It was very peaceful, my dear."

Aghast, her lungs constricting with such force that her chest hurt, Bridget stared at Kathy Hudson for what seemed an eternity. Then Bridget was running up the stairs two at a time. In the hall below, Kathy and Richard were in each other's arms. Above was Mrs. Kilburn.

"Please, sweet Jesus," Bridget sobbed, knowing that a prayer was useless, for certainly it was Mrs. Kilburn who had the good Lord's ear now. But hope would not die and Bridget sprinted faster up the stairs, faltering for only the blink of an eye when she reached Maura's bedroom. Crossing herself, Bridget pushed open the door and stepped into the almost-dark room.

Slowly she moved forward, first one step then two, until she had managed to walk across the room and slide reverently into the little satin chair before her knees gave out.

At rest on the bed she had shared with her husband, the bed she had retired to alone so many years after he passed on, lay Mrs. Maura Kilburn. Kathy Hudson had been right. The passing had been brief and peaceful, for Mrs. Kilburn looked as lovely as if she were asleep. Knowing the lady was in heaven, though, did nothing to ease the pain and sorrow Bridget felt so deep in her heart.

Grief stricken, she folded her arms on the cover of the bed and lay her head upon them, the tears flowing down her cheeks as though from a perpetual font. And buried deep in her heart was the knowledge that she cried not only for her friend, but for herself, as well. Without Maura Kilburn, who was Bridget Devlin, except a young woman who didn't belong in this great big country? Without Maura Kilburn, Bridget had no center, no reason for being. She was adrift.

Chapter Four

Bridget smoothed the medallion on the chenille spread so that it was perfectly centered with the four king-sized pillows. The bed was the last chore after a morning spent putting Mrs. Kilburn's room in order, disturbing as little as possible. A final tug on the quilt, which lay folded at the foot of the high bed, finished the work. At the doorway Bridget turned as though she had forgotten something. But there was nothing. Everything was perfect. Now Kathy Hudson would be able to sit in this most intimate room and remember her mother properly when the time was right.

Without warning Bridget's throat constricted. Her shoulders trembled as a great sob expanded her lungs and crawled toward her throat. Hand to mouth, she fought it back. Her crying was done. By God, she was a nurse, not a wee girl to whom death was a mystery. She knew better than to grieve too greatly for an old woman like Mrs. Kilburn.

Her passing had been peaceful. She had seen and spoken with everyone she loved before she died, and her affairs were in order. Sure wasn't this the way every human being wished to pass on? But Bridget's heart got the better of her logical mind, and emotion broke through the dam she had tried to erect.

Squeezing her eyes tightly, Bridget tried to halt the tears. Clamping her lips shut she tried not to give vent to heart-wrenching sobs. The house was quiet now. Turning to the wall, Bridget let her head rest on her crossed arms until her sobs became sniffles and the tears on her cheeks were dry. How hard all this was! Mrs. Kilburn had been more than a patient and companion, she had been a dear friend, whom Bridget would forever miss.

Taking a deep, tremulous breath, Bridget composed herself once again as she had been forced to do off and on for the last two days. It was more difficult now, though, since everyone was gone. There wasn't a soul in the house who Bridget felt the need to be brave for.

The first day, Kathy and Richard had been here, going through Mrs. Kilburn's papers and doing all those things relatives must do. Bridget wasn't sure how much they had accomplished between Richard seeking her out just to hold her and Kathy launching into detailed memories of Maura each time Bridget brought her a cup of tea or offered to help. So they had finally given up and gone to the Hudsons' home to make funeral arrangements, leaving Bridget with no one to bring tea to, no one to hold her, no one to talk to.

"There now, lass," she said quietly to herself, "enough of that. Time to get yourself dressed."

Turning sharply on her heel, Bridget reverently drew the door to Mrs. Kilburn's room closed. She surveyed every detail of the house as she went through the upper wing toward her own room. There, fully intending to fix herself for the day ahead, she couldn't help reaching for the envelope on her dresser. Sitting down she read once again the letter Maura Kilburn had left for her.

My Dearest Bridget,

I shall be gone from you for four days. Time enough for you to get over any embarrassment this letter may cause.

Bridget dear, I'm delighted you and Richard have found each other. From Richard you can learn how to live with confidence in a sophisticated world that often will not understand your kind heart, or appreciate it the way he does. From you Richard will learn to value the privilege he has always enjoyed.

I want for you all the riches life can provide, so that your dreams may come true here or in Ireland as the fates allow. Love

Richard if that's what is meant to be. If it isn't, know that you will always be a part of my heart and my heritage and my family. With love and affection,
  Maura Kilburn

Carefully Bridget folded the letter, put it in the envelope and held it to her breast. How easily she had written about the future, but without Mrs. Kilburn, Bridget wasn't sure there was a future.

Her options were limited and tenuous. She could try to find another position and hope she was not asked for the proper papers. Or if she was asked, she could hope her prospective employers wouldn't become suspicious of the story she would have to tell and turn her into Immigration. Of course the third, final and thrilling option was always there. With Richard by her side there would be no problems with Immigration, and she would be making a commitment to the man she loved. A man who, she felt sure, loved her. Perhaps he hadn't been ready to commit to her while his grandmother lived, but now things were so different. Bridget was positive he wouldn't let anything happen to her.

So, in her heart, sorrow warred with happiness. Knowing it was Mrs. Kilburn's death that brought her and Richard to this bittersweet point in their relationship was so hard to accept yet accepted it was. Bridget put her letter down and tried not to think of tomorrow. Today was what mattered. Today she would say goodbye to a lady who loved her. Then she would worry about the rest.

The sudden ringing of the phone startled Bridget out of her reverie. The normally comforting jangling, the noise that let her know she was not forgotten by the outside world, seemed strangely frightening as it echoed through the sad house. Bridget answered it immediately.

"Mrs. Kilburn's residence," Bridget said softly.

There was a silence on the other end before Richard's lovely deep voice came over the line. "I'm sorry, Bridget, I had to stop and think for a moment. I half expected Mrs. Reilly, who would tell me Grandmother would be a moment longer."

Richard apologized so sweetly Bridget felt warmed to share the memory with him. "It feels strange to answer the phone this way now that she's gone," Bridget told him, understanding exactly how he felt. "I'm sure it feels even odd to hear it. Force of habit would make you ask for her."

"You're right. It will be a hard habit to break, thinking she's there for me."

Bridget pictured Richard putting his head to the side the way he did when he thought deeply about something. Respectfully she waited for him to speak. If he was remembering his grandmother, she had no desire to interrupt those memories. Sure and wouldn't they fade soon enough, as memories always did, if he didn't work at holding on to them?

"Well, this is silly," Richard breathed. Bridget heard a tremor deep in his throat. "I actually called for a reason, and the moment I got you on the phone my mind went blank."

"Ah, that's to be expected. How is your dear mother holding up?" Bridget hoped to draw him out with a bit of conversation about someone else.

"As well as can be expected," he answered with a melancholy sigh. "It's not going to be easy. Grandmother was so vital. It made her death that much harder to accept. If she'd truly been an invalid we might have considered her death a blessing. But this way, well, Mom's blaming herself."

"Sure that's the last thing she should do."

"She can't help it. It was her idea for the trip. She thinks if she had left Grandmother where she was, everything would have been fine."

"And if Mrs. Kilburn had passed on when your mother was away, would they have had those last few hours alone together? Sure they wouldn't," Bridget prodded gently. "Richard, you must remind your mother that Dr. Perry has been expecting this to happen for years. We are all lucky to have had your grandmother so long. No one, least of all your mother, did anything to hasten her passing."

"I know you're right. But I suppose we all assumed Grandmother was indestructible, since she held on the way she did and lived with such gusto despite her bad heart. Even I was guilty. I lived far away, writing the occasional letter and believing she would always be here when I decided to come home. Now I see how much time I've wasted."

"Hush, love, that's not what she would want to hear. Your grandmother was as proud as punch with what you were doing in the Attorney General's Office. Bragging about you all the time, she was. Mrs. Kilburn wouldn't have wanted you home just to wait for her to die. No, man, she was so happy you came back of your own accord, rather than returning like you were here for a death watch. Richard, she loved life too much for you not to live yours the way you saw fit."

Richard laughed softly and dearly, "Bridget, I am so glad that it was you Grandmother had with her all these years. You made the difference, keeping her from getting depressed over not being as active as she would have liked. You are a remarkable woman."

"It was all of us that made her life rich. Mrs. Kilburn surrounded herself with people who cared for her and loved her. She was extraordinarily lucky to have so many people like that," Bridget insisted.

"We should all be so lucky, to be loved and respected the way she was."

"I think we are that lucky, Richard," Bridget told him and there was no mistaking what she meant.

Bridget almost bit her tongue. She hadn't been able to help herself; the prodding just slipped out. She wanted to hear him say those all-important words. She needed to know that Richard loved her and would not let her go into the world on her own again. Her heart was too much his for her to think of moving on without him by her side.

But he missed the implication in her words and simply answered, "I suppose we are, Bridget. Listen, I really called to find out if you needed a ride to the church. I could be there in about forty minutes, then we'd have to be back here for the limousine pretty quick."

Bridget thought for a moment before deciding. "Thank you, but I have an errand to run before the service, and it's silly for you to come all the way from Marin just to go back again. I think it best if you and your family ride alone."

"Bridget, I know what you're doing. You think you'd be intruding. You know you're wrong."

"I'm thinking no such thing," she said indignantly, even though she, herself, could hear the false ring in her words. "Ah, Richard, no sense lying. I would feel better if you and your mom and dad had a bit more time together, just the three of you. I'll see you at the church."

"You are a special woman, Bridget Devlin. Is it any wonder I love you? I'll see you there."

Bridget's breath caught. He told her he loved her. Yet it was all wrong. He had rung off before she could savor the words. She hadn't heard exactly how they had been said or enjoyed the saying of them before the line went dead. Bridget clutched the receiver to her, unable to will him back to repeat those words. He was gone, turning his attention to others who needed him that day. Carefully Bridget replaced the receiver, her hand resting on it as if holding on to the memory of Richard's words.

As though burned, angry at her selfishness, Bridget stood up abruptly and went to the bathroom. Now was not the time to think of love. Showering quickly, she slipped into her good dress of dark blue faille. The white standing collar framed her face beautifully when she had her hair pinned up in free-falling curls. Stepping into the unaccustomed high heels, Bridget took her purse and, with one last glance in the mirror, left her room.

Still an hour before the service, Bridget felt a sudden odd need to hurry, as though if she didn't she would be shut out of the church, the doors closed against her and no way to get in. It was a premonition so compelling Bridget found her hand raised, heard herself whisper

"Richard." Startled by the intensity of her feelings, she swallowed hard and walked out of the house. Carefully locking the door, she headed down the steps without looking back.

Feeling at odds with herself, anxious to be away from the house, yet not sure where she should be going since the service didn't start until two, Bridget got off the bus to walk away the odd anxiety that gripped her. She hadn't planned well, though, since the church was only six blocks north. Slowly she moved ahead, looking in the windows of the businesses that peppered this almost exclusively-residential neighborhood. She stopped to smell the fresh-cut flowers haphazardly displayed outside a small grocery. Bridget sidestepped a stroller being pushed by a singled-minded young mother. She watched as the woman crossed the street and disappeared into the building on the corner. Bridget smiled, realizing it was Wilson's pharmacy she was staring at.

"If you look hard enough, the way is always pointed out," Bridget muttered.

Glancing both ways, she crossed the street quickly, thinking how sad it was that nothing really changed when someone died. The cable car still rang its lovely little bell, people still headed to work, cars still broke down in the middle of the street, and the sun still rose and set. Somewhere, too, women were giving birth, new little souls were coming into this world to replace the one that had left. But it seemed all wrong, all this normalcy. Bridget wanted a huge bell to toll somewhere. She wanted the world to stop and everyone in it to say, "We're sorry Mrs. Kilburn isn't with us any longer."

Thinking this, running across the street, cars honking, people walking, Bridget found herself near tears by the time she strode through the doorway of the drugstore. She knew she should have composed herself before seeking out the pharmacist. There was that warning little prick of tears behind her eyes, but she ignored it. Instead, thinking herself terribly professional and able to deal with death as any nurse should, Bridget walked straight up to the high counter behind which Mr. Payne stood, opened her mouth to speak, only to burst into tears without saying a word.

"Miss Devlin!"

The pharmacist was out of his glass cage in an instant, his arms surprisingly strong around her shoulders. As he led her back through the little swinging door to a chair behind the counter where no one would see her, Bridget covered her face with her hands, sobbing as great big tears slid down her face.

"Here, hold on now. Let me get you some water."

Bridget cried, sniffling as her shoulders quaked, while the pharmacist rummaged around in a small office. Then he was back, putting a tissue in her hand and guiding it to her eyes. Bridget hiccuped another sob, shook her head, whispering, "It's all right." At last she took a sip of the water he had brought her. Michael Payne, realizing the worst was over, sat on the floor at her feet, his back to the wall, oblivious to the state of his lab coat as it trailed on the floor.

"Feeling better?"

Bridget nodded and stammered, "Yes, thank you."

"Good. I don't get a whole lot of weeping women in here. Usually they're damn mad about the cost of their prescription. That I know how to handle. This, well, I wasn't quite sure what to do. Hope I covered all the bases," he said kindly.

"Yes, you did. Very nicely, thank you." Bridget's voice still wavered. Embarrassed, unable to look at him directly, she continued to dab at the side of her eyes, wishing there was a mirror handy. There was nothing she hated more than a lass with black streaks down her face from running mascara. A quick glance about told her mirrors were in short supply in Mr. Payne's place of business, so she sat where she was, her head bent so Michael Payne hopefully wouldn't see her face in disrepair.

"Who died?" he asked, his soft voice lighthearted.

"Mrs. Kilburn," Bridget answered, raising her

head to see him now, not caring whether or not she looked horrible. If she did, it would teach him not to be so flippant. But he wasn't laughing, nor was he staring in horror at her messed makeup. Rather Bridget saw his great regret for his offhand remark, and she was immediately sorry to have thought badly of him.

"I'm so sorry, Miss Devlin," he said, getting to his feet immediately and adjusting his glasses in embarrassment. "It was only an expression. I truly apologize."

"It's all right, Mr. Payne. There was no way you could have known."

"Of course there was. If I'd been a bit more observant, I would have noticed you're dressed rather soberly and not in your uniform. I also know that Mrs. Kilburn has been on rather powerful medication for the last few years. I suppose I just assumed, since she had done so well with it, that I would always be filling that particular prescription."

"Just as I thought I would be tending that particular patient," Bridget sighed. "It's funny how used to things we get."

"Yes, it is. I'm awfully used to having you come in. I suppose I won't be seeing much of you any longer. I'm as sorry about that as I am about Mrs. Kilburn."

"Thank you." Bridget raised the tissue to her eyes again, then reached into her purse for her pocket mirror and powdered her nose before smiling weakly at Michael Payne. "I appreciate that," she said, referring to his sentiment about Mrs. Kilburn.

She hadn't acknowledged his unhappiness at the prospect of not seeing her on a regular basis. How could she? Her mind was scrambled with so many thoughts, her heart with a million emotions. All Bridget Devlin could think about was making it through the rest of this awful day.

"You're welcome," Michael answered gravely. He took the glass of water Bridget held out and put it near a typewriter. "Are you sure you're feeling better?"

"Much, thank you. I don't know what came over me. Mrs. Kilburn passed away two days ago. I thought I was beyond a display like this. You must forgive me."

"Nothing to forgive. It's a delayed reaction. The professional you was on such a roll it just took a few days for the personal you to kick in." He grinned at Bridget as if to reinforce his prognosis that her reaction was anything but abnormal.

"You think so?" Bridget asked, amazed that he would have that kind of insight. He just didn't look like the type of man who would think about anything except precise prescriptions. Now she realized there was probably a lot more to him. He looked positively handsome towering above her the way he was.

"I know so," he said softly, his eyes filled with understanding behind his round, wire-rim glasses.

For the first time she noticed how incongruous those frames were with the rest of him. His face was squared off at the cheekbones and jaw, giving him the look of one of those models she saw on the cover of *GQ*. His baby-fine hair was cut shingle-straight across the back and combed straight back from his high forehead. Now, seeing him full-length rather than peering out at her from behind his high desk, Bridget realized he was a tall, well-proportioned man. For an instant she wondered what he looked like without his white coat, but that instant was barely a fleeting moment. She was on her feet and smoothing her dress before she even acknowledged it had entered her mind.

"Well, the thought makes me feel a wee bit better," Bridget acknowledged. "I thought I was turning into a hysterical female. I really only came by to tell you that you may close out Mrs. Kilburn's account."

Michael waved away the information as if there was plenty of time for the specifics.

"If I were you," he said, leaning toward her conspiratorially, "I wouldn't even try to feel a wee bit better. Just go with your emotions. There's nothing better than allowing yourself the pleasure of truly feeling your joy or your sorrow. Believe me. That's how life was meant to be lived."

"Mr. Payne, I'm sure you must be just a little Irish with an attitude like that." Bridget laughed through the remnants of her tears and held out her hand. "Sure and I appreciate the advice."

Michael took it and shook it solidly. "You'll feel a whole lot better when it's finally time to move on, if you gave it your all saying goodbye to Mrs. Kilburn."

"Yes, I can see that. But it still doesn't excuse this outburst. I should have had the decency to be in the privacy of my own room," Bridget said, still embarrassed. She let her palm slide from his and grasped her handbag tightly.

"Then I wouldn't have had the pleasure of coming to your rescue. Think of it as your good deed for the day. You've made my dull day quite exciting."

"Well, I'm glad some good came out of it."

"A lot of good came out of it." Michael Payne brushed back his hair then pointed up. "Though I never met her, I imagine Mrs. Kilburn is sitting on a cloud up there somewhere, cheering you on."

"How do you know she'd be doing that?" Bridget laughed, in spite of herself.

"Because she must have been a wonderful person if you stayed with her as long as you did. I don't think you would have stuck it out with someone you didn't love, or at least like a whole lot."

"Isn't that the truth. Pharmacology school must be an amazing place. You've learned quite a bit more than just how to count out capsules."

"It's life that's the amazing school," Michael told her.

"I'll remember that. Now I'd better be going. I only wanted to stop in and let you know that Mrs. Kilburn had passed away. I knew you would be needing the information for your records. I also wanted to be thanking you for all your help over the years. You've no idea how pleasant it was to have you remember my name and the name of my patient. I felt somehow that I was back home in my village where everyone knew everyone. That meant so much to me, Mr. Payne."

"My pleasure." Michael took her arm and steered her toward the door. "I'm glad to hear my bedside manner met with your approval."

"It did, indeed. Now I'm off. The service is due to start in ten minutes. Thank you again, Mr. Payne."

"Michael. My name is Michael. And you're welcome, Miss Devlin."

"Bridget," she said softly, returning the courtesy.

With that she left the pharmacy. Head held high, Bridget walked to the church, confident that Maura Kilburn was indeed sitting on a cloud surrounded by angels, entertaining them with stories about each and every person who was walking into the church to pay their respects. Realizing she was now late, Bridget hurried as best she could in her high heels, down the last two blocks.

In front of the church, the black hearse stood ready to receive the casket after the service. The steps leading to the door were empty. As in Bridget's premonition, the great metal doors of the structure were closed. She was late and she was the last. They hadn't waited for her.

Then, from behind one of the imposing pillars, a man stepped. Hands in his pockets, he looked first left then right. As he turned his head in her direction, Bridget saw that it was Richard, waiting for her on the top step. Holding out his hands, he came down as she ran lightly up toward him, her own arms open.

"I'm sorry I'm late," she breathed as he enfolded her and pulled her closer.

"It's all right," he whispered, his lips buried in the warm spot just behind her ear.

"You didn't have to wait."

"I did," Richard answered without hesitation. "Grandmother would have wanted me to. I wanted to."

"Thank you."

He slid his arm around her shoulders and opened the door to the church; doors that weren't locked to keep her out. The moment she stepped inside, Bridget felt the calm she'd been searching for all day. The music, the flowers, the people in the church, all seemed to make her welcome. Together Richard Hudson and Bridget Devlin walked down the center aisle toward the altar, over which hung a fabulous cross of gold. The priest stood there, smiling at them. Ted and Kathy Hudson moved in the front pew, making room for the younger couple. Nothing could have been more perfect. When they were settled the priest began to speak.

"Today, Maura Kilburn is with us. We cannot see her but she can see us, each and every one. Today, Maura Kilburn can see into our souls because she is home, in Heaven."

Beside Bridget, Kathy Hudson smiled bravely. On the other side of her, Richard squeezed her hand as he bent his head, and Bridget saw a single tear course down his cheek.

Chapter Five

"I'm glad you didn't mind my coming early. I just couldn't sit still a minute longer."

Richard picked up a stick and swiped at a low-hanging branch as they ambled through Golden Gate Park. The sun was out and the April day was warm. Richard's sleeves were rolled up revealing strong forearms covered with soft golden hair. His jacket was slung over his shoulder. By his side, wandering a step or two away now and again, was Bridget.

She seemed like part of the landscape, a chameleon ready to change her ways at the drop of a hat so no predator could find her. Her dress was long-sleeved and the color of the first spring leaves. The cotton knit clung lightly to her subtle curves, accentuating the swell of her breasts and the slightness of her hips. Richard, glancing at her when a comfortable silence came between them, thought he had never seen a more beautiful woman. Others were more physically perfect than Bridget but none more exquisite. In her there seemed to be a calmness he had not encountered in other ladies, or perhaps *serenity* was the word he was searching for. Yes, that was it, for certainly there was a difference between mere calm and the serene.

Watching her stop to pick a flower and twirl it between her fingers, or seeing her shade her eyes so that she could enjoy the sight of children playing down the hill, was a pleasure. Bridget neither cared that he was watching her, nor did she pose to make sure he would. Yet when she turned her attention to him, it was full and interested. Bridget Devlin made him feel as though no more interesting, exciting or desirable man existed on this earth. She was the one he wanted and soon he would tell her; once his grandmother's estate was settled, Richard knew he would bring Bridget Devlin into his family. Once again he raised his stick and brought it down through the trees, making the leaves rustle as though that would calm the excitement he guiltily felt as he looked forward to the meeting with the family lawyer, Brandon Madison.

"I still don't think I should be with you at all," Bridget complained, feeling uncomfortable that she had been asked to the reading of the will.

"But of course you should. Grandmother wanted you there and so do the rest of us."

Richard kicked a pebble, sending it flying. Bridget let her gaze slide toward him, noting again how taut his body was, how anxious the look in his eyes.

"All right, Mr. Hudson, what is it that has you in such a fit? You're as impatient as a lad on Christmas Eve."

Bridget turned in front of him, stopped, and put her hands on her hips. Richard walked right into her, easing his hands around her waist so he could hold her to him. His jacket, which still dangled from his fingers, tickled the back of Bridget's legs, but she said nothing for fear he might release her. Throwing his head back Richard heaved a great sigh before looking at her again.

"You have the most incredibly clear green eyes, Bridget. Did you know that?" He began to rock her, mesmerizing her with both the motion and his words. "There are these little golden flecks that sort of dance around in there. If you look real close, you're never quite sure that you've seen them, you only know that they're there. It's really quite beautiful. Now tell me, what do you see with those eyes? You must see things more clearly than the rest of us."

Bridget brought her hands up and wrapped her fingers lightly about his tie. The silk felt marvelous; a rich and privileged fabric fit for a king. She lowered her lashes, hiding those all-seeing eyes from Richard until she was ready to look again.

Richard was right, she did see quite a bit, but

not as much as he gave her credit for. Bridget felt her shamrock eyes were blind to so many things, but not to Richard. In him, she saw promise. With him, she felt hope and for him, she felt such great affection. Slowly she raised her lashes and looked into his deep brown eyes. She would try to see the present and the future if that was what he wanted.

"I see," she began, "a man who seems to be feeling a lot of things that he thinks he ought not to be feeling, isn't that so, Mr. Hudson?"

"How do you do it?" Richard murmured, laughing softly.

"You forget, I'm trained to notice symptoms. The tick here, the paleness there, the movements that are too quick or too slow. There's nothing wrong with you, Richard, except maybe you're feeling a bit guilty, as though your sadness over your grandmother should last longer. But it doesn't have to. Just because you're looking ahead to more practical things doesn't mean you're not mourning her. Sure I know that she's there in your heart." Bridget tapped his chest, wishing she could spread her hand out over it and follow the course of his well-defined muscles. "I saw how much you loved one another. It's nothing to be ashamed of that now you're interested in what she's left behind."

"You're right, Bridget. But you're wrong, too." Richard moved away from her and immediately she felt a bit lonelier despite the fact he stood only a few feet away. "You're wrong because you're making my confusion seem so heroic. It's not. I'm sorry, but I can't help thinking about Grandmother's estate. That's what makes me feel so really awful. And the worst of it is, I'm sure she wouldn't give this whole thing a second thought."

He turned back to Bridget and leaned against a convenient tree. In the filtered sunlight she thought he looked like a figure in a hunting scene. If only he were in knee breeches, the picture would be perfect. She smiled at him but remained silent as she walked slowly forward and rested against the other side of the oak.

"She and I talked about this many times," Richard went on. "Not her will exactly, but the fact that people must be practical and do what it is they feel is right. Grandmother had very little use for anyone who wore his emotions or desires on his sleeve. She liked strong people. I suppose that's why she liked you so much." He leaned over and ran the back of his hand down Bridget's cheek before pulling a leaf from the tree and twirling it between his fingers. He held it up as though to compare it to her eyes and found the plant lacking. "I don't think Grandmother would have been upset that I was planning for the future now, do you?"

Bridget hung her head and contemplated the ground, wondering what her next words should be. The earth was as spotty as her mind. Part of her thoughts were as lush and green as the new spring grass, so full of promise for a life blossoming with happiness. This was the part of her that believed she had a future with Richard.

Another part of her felt as barren as the dirt under the trees where not even a speck of grass grew. Richard cared for her, of that she was sure. Yet if she pointed out how desperate her situation was, how quickly a decision must be made as to whether she stayed in the United States or returned to Ireland, would Richard feel obligated to make a decision regarding their future without the luxury of time and fair, deep thought?

"Bridget? Are you all right?"

Her head snapped up. "Yes, I'm fine. Just thinking." She hesitated then drew a deep breath and looked him straight in the eye while she hugged the great oak tree, taking courage from its strong trunk.

"Richard, I think your grandmother would have wanted both of us to plan ahead. She always said your future was secure because of your talent for the law. You've no idea how proud of you she was. You chose to work for the Attorney General's Office when you could have easily gone straight into private practice and made your fortune."

"Fortune," Richard scoffed, as though it meant nothing. "I've had money all my life. There will be plenty of time to make more."

"You take so much for granted," Bridget murmured. Then she said more strongly, "But the way you try to pass off your wealth only tells me she was right about you. You're embarrassed that you decided to do something noble like working for the government for so many years. It's as though, because you're rich you don't think you deserve to have strong feelings about what is right and wrong. Of course you do. You're allowed to fight for what you believe in. Now that you've given all the tears you have for her, your grandmother would expect you to look ahead and know what the next step is. She would be the last one to berate you. She loved your decisiveness and your fairness. Sure she wouldn't want you to falter, would she?"

But Bridget faltered. Now that the time had come for her to speak of herself, she found it more difficult than she imagined. Unwelcome tears stung the back of her eyes, and her voice quavered, yet she forged ahead.

"You're not the only one who has been considering the future, Richard Hudson. I've had to do the same. Your grandmother has been my family all these many years. My own da couldn't have been dearer to me. And the only thing Mrs. Kilburn wanted was for me to secure my future, here in this country where there is work. But I didn't do it, Richard. I became so comfortable here, with your mother having me to dinners and taking me shopping. Your grandmother becoming my dearest friend and her home became like my own, home though I've never lived in a house with more than five rooms in my entire life . . ."

A sob broke through Bridget's soliloquy, much to her dismay. She had wanted to sound so capable, as though she hadn't a fear in the world and was only thinking rationally about her situation. Yet now that she had started, now that she had listed all the wonderful, marvelous, comforting things about her life in America, the thought of losing them was almost too much for her. She felt Richard's hand on her shoulder but she pulled away. His touch would soften her resolve, and she must speak her mind.

"No, I've started and, by God, I'm going to finish this up, Richard Hudson. Now, where was I?" Bridget controlled her voice as she moved slightly behind the tree so he wouldn't see the tears still slipping down her cheeks. She leaned against the strong old trunk, her eyes closed.

"Oh yes. So, there was the house and your grandmother and your mother and father all being so kind to me. Then, Lord above, there came you tripping into my life as though you'd belonged there the whole time. I won't apologize, Richard. I love you. There. I've said it. And I love you with all my heart the way a woman should love a man and I want you. And . . . and . . ." with a great effort Bridget finally voiced what needed to be said. ". . . and I don't even know if my papers will let me stay in this country now that she is gone. It's my own fault for not making plans for my future as your grandmother wanted me to. Oh, Richard, I don't know what I'm going to do now, and the thought of having to leave you is just about to rip my heart into pieces."

Wrapped up in her speech, Bridget was crying properly now, all sobs and tears. She pushed away from the tree, not because she had anywhere to go, but because if she didn't move she knew she was going to jump out of her skin. She didn't get very far. Richard was there as though he knew exactly where she was headed. In moments she was wrapped in his arms, her own gathered up in front of her as he held her tightly, his lips burying themselves in her wealth of hair as the breeze kicked up and wrapped them in a soft caress.

"Shh, Bridget, darling," Richard soothed, his voice like cool water pouring over the fire of frustration and confusion she had lived with for so many days.

"But I can't help it," she said against him, sure that his shirt was going to be a mess by the time he let her go.

"I know. I know," he whispered, rocking her slowly. "I've been awfully selfish, not thinking of you in the least. I suppose the surprise of Grandmother's death made me forget that you needed comforting as much as any of us. But you were so wonderful during this entire thing, taking care of the house, tying up loose ends. I suppose I just thought you and I had taken the reins so that Mom wouldn't have to and, until everything was settled, we would just go on being responsible. It was as though you and I were halves of the same whole. I'm sorry, my love, so sorry. It's my fault that you feel so left out. For all the looking out you did for us, we did damn little for you. Bridget, forgive me?"

Richard placed his hands on each side of her head and made her meet his eyes.

"You've never looked more beautiful to me as you do at this moment. Do you know that's the test of a truly beautiful woman? How she looks when she cries? Well you, my darling, pass the test with flying colors, but I wish I hadn't ever made you take the test in the first place. God, I've been so selfish!"

Sweetly he kissed away the tears, then wiped the few that were left with the back of his fingers, searching her face all the while for some remnant of pain that he could clear away. Finally he smiled, satisfied that he would find none.

"Bridget, you needn't worry, you know. Believe it or not I haven't thought only of myself these past few days. You've been on my mind and in my heart since the moment we actually decided there could be something between us. You've got a future here, that I know. But neither you nor I should make any decisions until after we hear the will. I'm sure Grandmother was most generous to both of us."

"I don't want to think about that. If she remembered me, I'll be a happy lass. But it isn't what's important," Bridget muttered absently, drained from her crying and the courage it took to speak her heart.

"No, of course it isn't," Richard soothed knowingly as he lowered his head to hers, draping his arms over her shoulders while they swayed a bit in the cool breeze. "What you care about is Bridget Devlin and where on earth there is a place for her. Don't you worry, there is a place for her."

Bridget, eyes still downcast, said laconically, "But I have neither a job nor the proper papers."

"True," Richard noted, trying to hide the tease in his voice, "that is something to consider. I suppose either my parents or I could swear we intend to continue to employ you."

"I suppose," Bridget murmured.

"The only other way you could possibly stay in this country legally is to get a green card or by marrying a United States citizen. But I'm not sure that that's a viable option for a strong-willed woman like yourself. I mean, a man would have to be pretty brave to tangle himself up with a woman who's as demanding as you are. A lifetime commitment would be a challenge."

Bridget stopped swaying and stood very, very still. She listened to everything carefully: the quiet of the park in spring; a faint echo of city noises somewhere far in the distance; the call of the odd bird anxious to be home before the fog rolled in; a child's small voice calling to his mother; and Richard, dear Richard's voice as he used a word like marriage.

Carefully, unsure of where all this was leading, Bridget stepped back from him. His fingers sliding down her arms until he no longer touched her. Tentatively she raised her hands just a bit. Richard reached for her but changed his mind before he actually grasped her. Instead they stood, fingertip to fingertip, the touch so gentle the breeze could easily part them.

"Do you know anyone who might be willing to take a chance like that?" Bridget's voice was hushed but strong. She wasn't fully convinced Richard wasn't having a go at her.

"I don't know. I suppose there might be a guy somewhere who would be willing to take the plunge when the time was right. I know at least one guy who loves you as much as you say you love him."

Richard pressed Bridget against the tree as he laced his fingers through hers and held them back against the bark. His lips were close, his eyes sparkling in the late-afternoon sun. In that tranquil setting, his voice reassured her with the truth of his affections.

"I know one man who loves you like a lover should, not like a helper or a sister or a friend, but as all of those things. This man wants you to be part of his world when the time is right." He moved an inch closer, his lips only a breath away from hers. "If we weren't standing in the middle of Golden Gate Park—" this time Bridget leaned closer still "—and if we weren't due at Brandon Madison's legal office—" now they were body against body and Richard still held her captive, still wouldn't allow her to lower her arms and let her hungry hands touch him "—I would show you exactly how much this woman is loved by this man."

With only a sigh and a step, they were together, their bodies melding into one another. Their lips met in a kiss so unlike any they had shared. Bridget found within her a moment of sheer surprise, as though she stood in the eye of the storm, before deciding she preferred the tempest outside to the quiet within.

She pressed herself against him, and Richard finally released her hands. Bridget's arms encircled his neck. Ecstatically she abandoned herself to his embrace as he pulled her up and against him. He twirled her round, making her as light as the leaves and as warm as the sun that was already relinquishing its hold, as the fog moved in. Beneath her breast she felt Richard's heart beating wildly. Beneath her hands his body tensed with passion and desire. But both knew this was neither the time nor place for their first union. It was then that their hunger abated. The fire that had blazed was tamed to only a lick of flame, burning gently until they could let their passion

97

run its course. Bridget buried her face in the crook of Richard's shoulder. He held her a bit longer, letting her dance in the sky, before easing her to the ground. The moment, by necessity, was over. The moment, in reality, would always be cherished.

"I love you, Bridget Devlin. God knows where we go from here, but I love you and I want you," he whispered, hugging her to him still.

"I love you, too, Richard. Pray we do the right thing. If this is real, sure don't I want it to last forever, not just a night."

"Never just a night, my love. Never," Richard murmured before losing himself in her once more, his kiss telling her so many things he could not in a minute's time. Finally, unable to put off the inevitable, he held her away. "We have to go."

"I know." Her hand trailed across his hair and down his cheek. "I know, and I don't want to. I don't care about your grandmother's will. She's already left me her treasure—you, Richard."

He laughed, his brown eyes twinkling. "Then humor her grandson. I'm afraid I'm as curious as the cat."

"To be expected from a man who makes his living making sure all the i's are dotted and the t's are crossed. But perhaps we could continue this later. Don't you think we've left a lot unsaid, man."

"I do. And I know just the language it should be said in."

Bridget grinned, "I think I speak the same tongue."

"I know you do," he teased as he draped his arm around her shoulders and Bridget slipped hers about his waist. It was as though they had always walked that way, together, close, with no thought of parting. Bridget finally at peace in her mind, raised her eyes to heaven, hoping Mrs. Kilburn was still on that cloud watching them in their happiness.

"Bridget, come out this minute. You look wonderful."

"Shut the door, Richard," Bridget whispered hoarsely, shocked he would dare to open the door to the ladies' room and call her.

"There's no one in there but you, and I know you're worried about your face. Not a trace of a tear left. Now come on and smile. We're about to find out what our future is."

"All right. One minute," Bridget pleaded.

Smoothing the skirt of her dress and tugging at the satin bow on the collar, Bridget stood back surveying herself as best she could in the small mirror above the sink. Did she seem as though she was ready to face her future? Did it really make a difference what was said in Brandon Madison's office today? Sure wouldn't she love Richard if he were poor just as well as if he was richer than he already was.

"Bridget!" Richard called again, anxious to be in Brandon's office.

"Sure I'm coming. Just now."

Gathering up her things, Bridget took a deep breath and calmed herself. Though she had known Brandon Madison for years, she had never been in his office, and the thought of being anywhere near a legal establishment made her nervous. Her situation, after all, was tenuous at the moment. At least, until Richard made a decision one way or another.

"There you are," Richard said as he stopped his pacing to study her. "And well worth the wait. You look marvelous."

He took her arm and led her to the double doors of Brandon's office. Inside, a receptionist, younger than Bridget but looking very fashionable and sophisticated, led them down a long, softly lit hall and opened another set of double doors. Bridget stepped inside. Richard followed, never taking his hand from her arm. He felt her shiver a bit as she glanced around the well-appointed room. For the first time he saw a lawyer's office the way someone unused to them might. It was formidable. Second nature to high-priced clients, probably terrifying to a lady like Bridget.

He squeezed her elbow a bit for reassurance, silently encouraging her not to be intimidated by the trappings of power and wealth. This was not the bright home of his grandmother. Here legal tomes lined the walls, chairs were high-backed and swathed in dark, rich leather. Even the air hung heavy and oppressive to those who didn't know how to breathe it comfortably. He steered her to a chair in the center of the room, seating her between those already present. As the group exchanged solemn greetings, the lovely receptionist disappeared quietly.

"Mr. and Mrs. Hudson, hello," Bridget said, accepting Kathy's kiss and Ted's hand. She felt her color deepening, feeling the full force of her embarrassment. This really was such a personal thing. It was no place for her.

"Hello, Bridget," Kathy said. "Richard. You've kept Brandon waiting. I don't think that was very kind of you."

"Sorry, Mom, but Bridget and I had a few things to talk about." Richard couldn't help looking Bridget's way.

Kathy, a smart woman, realized that what she had seen coming between those two was now nearing a culmination. With great effort, she hid a smile of satisfaction and sat back down in her chair.

"I see. Well you're here now."

"Nice to see you again, Bridget." Ted Hudson leaned past his wife and smiled.

Bridget returned the gesture. He was such a nice man, and she could see where Richard got his lovely eyes. Thankfully Richard hadn't inherited Ted Hudson's quiet ways. She never had any idea what to say to the man. How he had managed to capture Kathy Hudson's effervescent heart was beyond her. Still she liked him and imagined he really came into his own in the boardroom. A wallflower could never have accomplished what he had. Last Bridget had heard, he was buying his eighth company.

"Hello, Bridget." Brandon Madison was shaking Richard's hand, letting go of it just as he greeted her.

"Mr. Madison."

Bridget inclined her head and gave him one of her brightest smiles. He had always been so lovely to her, but this time his return greeting was different from all the others over the years. It was a smile that didn't quite reach his eyes; it seemed aloof rather than warm and welcoming. The odd light in his eyes was strangely sad. Bridget, fascinated, could not take her eyes off him. He stared at her as though trying to peer right through her and into her heart.

"It's nice to see you again, Mr. Madison," she said quietly for lack of any other way to break this spell. She saw him shudder and pull his shoulders tighter under his fine suit.

"Yes, of course." Looking around the room he composed himself. "Shall we begin?"

Everyone was seated, but each seemed to have one more thing to do before Brandon opened the envelope in front of him. Kathy rose slightly and smoothed her skirt underneath her, Ted shifted in his chair while he unbuttoned his blazer then reached out and covered his wife's hand with his own. Bridget saw him look lovingly at her and wink as though to encourage her, tell her this was the last painful thing she would have to endure. Richard reached for a gold pen in his inside pocket. He held it against his cheek as though the coolness of the fine metal would help him concentrate. Bridget simply folded her hands in her lap, wishing she was anywhere but directly in front of Brandon Madison.

"All right," Brandon began, "I would first like to offer my condolences to all of you, Kathy, Ted and Richard . . ." Bridget raised her head and looked at him quizzically, wondering if he had intentionally left her out of that statement. Realizing he had, of course, since she was not a real member of the family, Bridget relaxed, accepting the strangeness of her reaction. Intently she focused on Brandon, believing concentration the only way she could keep her imagination in check.

"I respected Maura more than I can tell you, and I liked her very much. I can't say that about all my clients. I will miss her greatly."

"Thank you, Brandon. I think I speak for all of us when I tell you how much we appreciate the considerate service you provided her all these years." Ted glanced down the row, at his wife and his son, reserving a kindly smile for Bridget. For the first time Bridget understood his success. His voice was modulated so that everyone turned to look directly at him, waiting for instructions. "We know that she valued your counsel, and we also appreciate the personal attention you provided. That meant a great deal to her."

"Yes, yes." Brandon waved away the compliments, feeling guilty that Ted had even spoken about his counsel and service to Maura. As far as he was concerned, he had failed her. "I appreciate that, certainly. Now. I think it's time we get on with the document. This won't take terribly long. It's all rather straightforward."

"That's just like Mother," Kathy commented to Bridget. "She never did want to fool with a lot of extra nonsense did she?"

Bridget shook her head. "Never. Sure didn't that woman have a mind of her own? Always going after whatever it was she wanted."

Brandon cleared his throat, silencing them.

"Excuse us, Brandon," Kathy said, though her manner indicated that she had every right to reminisce.

"Not to worry. I just think you'd really better hear this now — so you can get on with your day," he added hurriedly.

"Well, of course, I'm sorry," Kathy apologized, believing he had other appointments. "That was inconsiderate of me. Go ahead, Brandon."

He cleared his throat and began.

I, Maura Elizabeth Kilburn, a resident of

*San Francisco, California, do hereby declare
this to be my last will and testament.*

*I have been widowed from my husband,
Sean Kilburn, for thirty years. I have a
daughter, Katherine Kilburn Hudson. I also
have a grandson, Richard Hudson. My son-
in-law is Theodore Hudson. My nurse and
longtime companion is Bridget Devlin of
Kilmartin, Ireland, and my cook and housekeeper is Mrs. Rose Reilly.*

*I confirm that no one has any interest in
community property in my estate. It is mine
to bequest as I see fit.*

*Upon my death my estate should be di-
vided as follows:*

*To Mrs. Rose Reilly, for her many years
of fine service, I bequeath the sum of fifty
thousand dollars in the hope that she will
invest it properly so that she may live off
the interest and not have to deal with any
more cantankerous old women . . .*

Kathy and Bridget laughed while Ted raised his
eyes to heaven. Richard sat back and closed his
eyes, almost hearing his grandmother's voice dic-
tating the bequest. Brandon hurried on

*To my son-in-law, I give the three volumes
of legal text published in England in the
early eighteen hundreds that he has always
coveted for his collection.*

105

To my grandson, Richard Hudson, a dear and smart boy who made me not only proud but happy, I leave the sum of three hundred thousand dollars. This sum is to be used to establish a legal practice of his own or to buy into an existing one. Whichever he chooses, I know that Richard will be a great success because of his talent. I hope that he will always remember that money must be earned through hard work. If given too freely, the receiver can forget that many people struggle for what he has gotten so easily.

Beside her, Bridget felt Richard move in his chair. Chancing a glance, she saw that his expression hadn't changed, only the look in his eyes. There was just a hint of hurt that his grandmother had thought to leave him so little of her vast estate. But Bridget knew he would soon get over that. It was Kathy's after all and wasn't Richard her heir?

To my daughter, Katherine Kilburn Hudson. I leave everything precious to me, to the most precious part of me. My Katherine, I am proud of you as I have never been of anything else. I am proud that you and your husband have done so well. You lack for nothing, not even the most priceless thing in the world, love. You receive it from a hus-

band who would lay down his life for you, a son who adores you and friends who respect you. Therefore, I leave you the house on the cliff to do with what you will, and all the items your father and I acquired and cherished over the years. You may keep them or discard them as you wish. I only ask that you keep the china for yourself or give it to Richard when he marries. I know that my beloved home will be safe in your hands, and that you will use your best judgment regarding these things. They meant so much to me in life, but never more than you who were my life.

"Brandon, I think we should cut through the prose. Could you just give us the bottom line here on the estate?" Ted was getting anxious. Maura's will was not what he had expected. He squeezed the hand that Kathy gave him. Bridget looked to Richard. Richard stared straight ahead.

"We're getting there right this minute," Brandon advised without looking at anyone.

For my family, this is my final bequest. I believe that you might question my will. You may think that this was not the wisest thing to do. But in the end, when your fine hearts and minds have considered this, you will know I have done what I did because I loved and respected you so much. Kathy and

Richard will never want for anything and knowing this I make my last bequest.

I wish the money Sean and I made together to be a gift that will be used to fulfill dreams, not just set aside to make more money. Therefore, the remainder of my estate, stocks, bonds, cash from various accounts, and the land just south of the city. . . .

Bridget leaned forward, her hand almost on Richard's shoulder to reassure him that his grandmother only meant the best for him, when Brandon finished reading.

. . . is given to Bridget Devlin, my nurse and companion, my friend. May she make all her dreams come true with it, both in this country and in Ireland that we both love so well.

Brandon Madison finished reading and raised his eyes just long enough to see that Maura Kilburn had made a big mistake.

Chapter Six

Brandon Madison carefully placed Maura Kilburn's last will and testament on his desk, and laced his fingers on top of it. Richard, who had leaned closer with each word Brandon spoke, was now frozen in this odd position. His face registered neither surprise nor regret. It was perfectly still, quiet and unreadable. The countenance that had so impressed his grandmother now sent shivers up Brandon Madison's spine. Ted Hudson had fallen back in his chair and put his hand to his throat. By his side, Katherine, after uttering a small cry, remained mute, clutching her stomach the way people do when they've been hit hard and fast with a sucker punch. Bridget was silent, too. She sat stiffly in her high-backed leather chair, her lovely lips open slightly, her hands still resting in her lap, her spine rigid as a bar of steel.

In the first few moments after the lawyer finished reading, Bridget felt absolutely nothing. The familiar syllables of her name sounded foreign. Because she had expected nothing, Bridget's mind rebelled against the idea that she had received everything. Her first thought was that Brandon Madison had made a terribly ridiculous error—or he was playing a horrible joke. But in the ensuing silence, Bridget knew he was neither stupid nor cruel.

Stunned, feeling faint one minute and lightheaded the next, Bridget felt as though she could float to the ceiling, where she would have to wait patiently until someone tugged her down. Instinctively her hands went to the arms of her chair, her fingers digging into the supple leather as she realized what Maura Kilburn had done.

She could accomplish so much now. A trip so her da could see America! No, a new house for him, perhaps even a school for Kilmartin and dresses for herself, maybe a car. On and on the thoughts went, one careening off the next until her head was a jumble of what might be and what had been. Only what was, that minute of reaction by the people she loved, escaped Bridget's notice. What seemed like an eternity was only a second before she turned to look at Richard.

Richard, who had so much, would now have a woman his equal. Her darling man who wanted his house to be a home would have it! She would buy anything he wanted—golden tables, crystal lamps and marble beds. There was nothing she couldn't do, and wouldn't do, for him now. And together—why anything was possible.

A small sound bubbled up from her throat, the first note of a disbelieving and amazed protest. Bridget put her fingers to her lips and turned her shining eyes toward the man she loved. Dazed, glowing, her eyes glittering like two emeralds in a bed of pure white sand, Bridget sought Richard's dark gaze and found it before he was ready for her.

Richard turned slowly toward her, poised between giving his attention to her or Brandon. His strong face was pale, his lips parted slightly in astonishment. Bridget thought he had never looked more handsome. In her love for him, her excitement of what they would share, Bridget reached out for his hand. Still unable to speak, her mouth widened in an ever more excited smile. Before she touched him, before she could grasp him, she pulled back and her smile faded in bewilderment.

There, in the deepest recesses of his eyes, Bridget saw something so frightening she couldn't bear to acknowledge it. In Richard there was a hurt so raw even she couldn't put a healing hand to it. Or was it *especially* her touch Richard couldn't bear? Did she also see anger? Did Richard, her Richard, feel betrayed not only by his grandmother but also by the woman who loved him?

Then the moment was gone. Bridget leaned forward another inch, the chaotic rush of those questions quickly smothered in a growing dread and confusion. Richard lowered his eyes and stood. Bridget shivered, suddenly cold, and was about to join him when Brandon addressed her.

"Bridget, I'd like you to stay if you have time."

Unable to find her voice, she only nodded, sinking back in her seat. All around her there was hushed activity. Ted and Kathy stood. Kathy was hugging her lovely leather bag close to her, the golden chain dangling in front. It caught on the arm of her chair. Dazed, Kathy reached down and apologized to no one in particular while she unwound it and tucked it into the corner of her purse.

Ted slid his arm around his wife's waist. Though she wasn't conscious of thinking about it, Bridget's mind registered the slight collapse of Kathy Hudson's body against her husband's tall frame.

"Thanks so much," Ted Hudson murmured putting his hand out toward Brandon. The attorney took it in both of his.

"Of course, Brandon . . . so nice of you . . ." Kathy muttered.

The couple turned to their right and took the first step toward the door. For an instant, just a millisecond, they hesitated and looked directly at Bridget. Reflexively Bridget smiled wanly. Ted's lips twitched as he returned a weak smile. Kathy laid her hand on Bridget's arm. That hand felt cold and lifeless, dry; as though if touched, skin and bones would crumble like an autumn leaf. Bridget's eyes softened with tears of gratitude as she grasped at the gesture, seeing in it exactly what she needed to see.

Instinctively Bridget covered Kathy's hand with her own to warm it, bring life back into it. Bridget was so grateful that Maura's family was with her on this astonishing day. But Bridget's attention was arrested by Richard's hesitant touch. He ran his hand over her shoulder. When she glanced up at him, her heart beginning to beat now at a pace that Bridget feared would burst it, she saw he wasn't looking at her. Rather he was watching his mother intently, his face appearing hard in the subdued light. It was as though looking at Kathy had weakened him, and Bridget was only a support to hold him upright.

"Bridget. I don't know what to say," he muttered, squeezing her shoulder before moving away, going to the door of the office three steps behind his parents. Speechless herself, Bridget found nothing amiss in his comment.

Brandon followed the procession, murmuring his proper goodbyes. Bridget listened to Kathy Hudson's voice. No longer handsomely modulated, it sounded strangely hollow as she spoke. "And you'll contact us with all the paperwork,

Brandon? You'll tell me what needs to be done? You'll . . ."

"Kathy." Ted Hudson silenced her tenderly but effectively. "You don't have to worry about any of that now, darling. Truly. I'll take care of it with Brandon."

"Not now, Mom," Richard reiterated.

Bridget wished she could turn around without seeming like a small child spying on the adults. She wanted to see their faces. She didn't want the tall back of the chair hampering the sights and sounds of a day she wanted to remember in detail. Somehow this impressive office was making the Hudsons' voices sound all wrong. Of course they should be surprised, but why did they sound so sad, all of them off-key and not quite themselves?

Then, as the incredulity of the situation hit her, Bridget realized they had every reason to be a bit stunned. Sure wasn't she? Who would have thought she would be an heiress? Bridget felt her shoulders droop a bit with the weight of the word. She had no idea what it meant to be responsible for a fortune and a dead woman's wish that it be used wisely.

It was a moment, before Bridget realized Brandon Madison was back at his desk. He was looking at her oddly, as if she had done something to hurt his feelings. Bridget pulled herself together, knowing it was terrible to be off dreaming of the fine things she was going to do

114

with what Mrs. Kilburn had left her. A blush rose to her cheeks under his scrutiny. Sighing, he slipped his glasses onto his nose as though with great effort. His voice, businesslike as always, was also tinged with sadness as he spoke.

"I suppose I should get on with this. We can work out all the details later but Maura wanted me to be sure you had access to immediate cash. There's an account set up in your name at Bank of America. The paperwork and some cash will be delivered to you to tide you over until the account is activated. The portfolio will take some explaining, so, for now, let me just give you an overview."

Pulling a file from the top drawer of his desk, Brandon opened it carefully. It was so thin Bridget's heart sank. There couldn't be much in a thing like that. Maybe the fortune Mrs. Kilburn had always talked about was wrapped up in the art in the house, making Kathy the real heiress. That was, of course as it should be.

She was resigned, knowing the streets of Kilmartin might not get paved after all. But Bridget was willing to bet she could at least build her da a new house with her inheritance.

Sitting back, she folded her hands and listened politely. Brandon spent the next forty-five minutes cursorily explaining the information listed on the papers. When he finished, Bridget was pale, her hands were still folded in her lap, back still straight in the high-backed chair, but it was only the power of shock that held her so. Brandon was on his feet, honestly concerned for her.

"Are you all right, Bridget? Perhaps a glass of water?"

Bridget nodded, taking the cup in both hands when he brought it to her. Her parched throat slowly opened until finally she could speak.

"You can't be serious, Mr. Madison?" she whispered in disbelief.

"I never joke about matters like this. The total amount of your share of the estate comes to just under two million dollars, Bridget. Of course only about a quarter of a million is liquid at the moment. All the information is here," he said, sliding the folder toward her. Bridget looked at it but didn't touch it. "You'll want to familiarize yourself with this. The names of the bank, of various stock and commodities brokers, etcetera. Of course, it will be a day or two before I can actually transfer the funds. And there will be the estate taxes, but I think we've been rather creative. You can count on those being minimal." Realizing his mistake, he asked, "But you aren't a citizen of the United States, are you?"

"No, I'm not." Bridget shook her head.

"Then I know you won't have to pay taxes in this country, but you must report this income to the government of Ireland. I'm not familiar with the tax laws there. I can recommend an international attorney if you like."

"Yes, thank you." Bridget took another drink. Her voice sounded so small she wondered if it would disappear completely. How on earth could this be? Not only an heiress—a millionaire heiress!

"Well, then, if you haven't any questions right now . . ."

Brandon left Bridget's side. He stood back a respectful distance waiting for her to collect her purse, rise and attempt to thank him with some degree of poise. To his surprise, Bridget raised one hand to her forehead, rubbed it gently then gazed up at him with the most tragic face he'd ever seen.

"This isn't right, is it, Mr. Madison?" Bridget asked.

Astonished, it took Brandon a moment to decide how to answer her. A lawyer, after all, had at least a dozen answers for any one question, and this one was no exception.

"It all depends on how you view the situation, Bridget," he responded carefully, clasping his hands behind his back. "If you're asking is it legal that Maura Kilburn left you her property and money, then I will tell you the answer is absolutely. Is it proper? Well, that's another question—one I'm afraid is impossible to answer with any certainty."

"But you must have an opinion. Sure you

were her attorney. You knew her as well as anyone."

"And you were her nurse, Bridget. You were with her twenty-four hours a day. I saw her only briefly every quarter unless there was an emergency. Because of your proximity to Maura some might question how freely this bequest was made," Brandon responded.

"Are you saying, Mr. Madison, that perhaps I've done something to ensure my future? That I used my position to make Mrs. Kilburn leave me her money?"

"I'm saying nothing of the sort," Brandon laughed, his voice kindly but his eyes shrewd as though seeing some truth in her statement. Bridget responded to the look in his eyes, not the words from his lips.

"I didn't, you know. By the Virgin, I didn't do anything but be a friend to Mrs. Kilburn. Sure I miss her as much as anyone. I would never have done anything to take advantage of her," Bridget insisted, wounded by the mere thought she could have been so devious.

"I believe you. Unfortunately, it doesn't change the fact that I disagree with what Maura did. I tried to talk her out of rewriting her will."

"Then you do think this is wrong," Bridget pressed.

"I think it's unfortunate," Brandon answered as he rounded his desk and sat down heavily in his chair. Tenting his fingers, he narrowed his eyes and waited for a moment before speaking again.

"Bridget, as an attorney I can tell you that a bequest such as this is a difficult one to swallow for all the parties concerned. Maura Kilburn had a daughter and a grandson, who would have been the logical heirs except for you—a beautiful young woman with no ties to this country, a background accepted on paper but never checked out first-hand. It's the stuff TV movies are made of. On a personal level it's hard for me to conceive of working all my life and not leaving my estate to my children—to blood relatives. Do you understand?"

"Yes, I do," Bridget answered quietly, her brow furrowed with worry. "But, sure none of that applies to me. What you said about being young and not having any ties here, I mean. My references were checked by Kathy and Mrs. Kilburn before I took this position."

"I've no doubt," Brandon interjected, "I'm only saying that appearances can be deceiving."

"Not in this case, certainly," she maintained. "I am who I am. And if anyone thinks any differently, then I'll take care of it this instant. In fact, Mr. Madison," Bridget said, her face relaxing as she leaned toward him, "I know exactly how to take care of this. Much as I like the idea of being an heiress, mind you, I think the best thing to do is give all the money to Kathy.

Sure wouldn't that make me feel better, for right now my stomach is churning like the bay on a bad day."

"I don't doubt that, Bridget," Brandon laughed gently. This was an unusual young woman. Even if she was only paying lip service to such a plan, her intentions were admirable. "I think my stomach would be in a bit of an upheaval if I were in your shoes. And, though I think the sentiment is admirable, I'd like to advise you not to act too rashly. I'm not sure you'd be any happier if you gave all the money to Mrs. Hudson."

"Then I'll give part of it to her. I'll keep just enough to do a few of the things I've been dreaming about for sometime now. That's allowed, isn't it?"

"Anything is allowed, Bridget. You could throw your inheritance into the ocean and it would be all right. But would giving the Hudsons your legacy follow the intent of Maura Kilburn's will?"

"To share with the people I love? I don't think she'd mind. Didn't she love them herself?" Bridget scoffed, surprised an educated man could even ask such a question.

"She did, of course. But Maura was making a statement not just about her bank account, but about her feelings regarding you, Ted and Kathy, and even Richard. Her sentiments were very clear and actually quite logical. I think she may have been a little overly optimistic about the largesse of her family, though. Much as I hate to admit it, Maura knew exactly what she was doing and in doing so, left behind more good questions than acceptable answers."

"I'm not sure I'd know one from the other, Mr. Madison." Bridget sighed wearily. The base of her skull throbbed and her eyes felt heavy. Brandon lay his palms flat as he spoke, looking into Bridget's green eyes without apology.

"The first question people will ask is why did Bridget Devlin inherit a substantial fortune from Maura Kilburn? The real answer, aside from the possible tabloid ones, is Bridget Devlin gave Maura Kilburn seven years of her life as freely as she would have given it to anyone who employed her. But to Mrs. Kilburn she also gave friendship and love. I saw the two of you together. There was no guile, no coercion on your part. There was nothing between you but honest, genuine affection. A fine reason to want you to have something. But to want you to have *everything*, when her daughter and her grandson were alive and healthy? What's the answer to that one?"

Bridget nodded without speaking, knowing the question to be rhetorical.

"Mrs. Kilburn herself addressed that question in her will. Her last wish was that you, Bridget Devlin, receive her real estate and money. She left her daughter the things she felt Kathy needed the most—things that had been collected and shared with her daughter over a lifetime—things that had memories attached to them. The artwork, the statuary, the crystal and silver—these aren't worthless baubles by any means, but they are priceless when one considers their history within the Kilburn family. Maura also knew Kathy's marriage is solid and, together, the Hudsons are very wealthy. So Kathy has no need of money. Nor is it likely she will find herself divorced.

"But what about Richard?" The lawyer continued gravely. "Well, he is a rich young man in his own right. His grandfather's trust, his own work, and the probability that he will inherit from his mother and father doesn't exactly dim his future prospects. In short, Richard Hudson will never have to slave to make a living."

Seeing that this assurance did not dim the pain in Bridget's eyes, Brandon went on.

"Yet Maura also wanted Richard to have the satisfaction of building and managing his own fortune. She realized his life has been one of incredible ease. Even Richard acknowledges that. I sometimes find it amazing he has turned out as well as he has given the privilege of his background. But Maura saw the danger in advantage. She wanted Richard to stand up on his own and truly work for what he gets. She left him enough so he would never want for anything, but not so much that he could forget work is part of life's equation.

"And, finally, there is the question of what you will do with all this money. Maura spelled that out quite clearly. She hopes you will help those less fortunate in a country you both love. Why she didn't feel Richard or Kathy could do that I'm not sure. Perhaps she felt a kinship to Ireland through you. I don't know.

"But these are the questions and answers as I see them. I don't think Mr. and Mrs. Hudson or Richard would expect you to give them your legacy, but that's not to say that they aren't confused at the moment and probably a bit hurt. But money is just that—money. There are no memories that make it any more special than the money the Hudsons have in their own right. Giving your inheritance to Kathy Hudson or to the poor, while you continue working as a nurse, is not what Maura Kilburn wanted. Her intention was that you enjoy a life of greater ease than you've had, that you determine how you can best help Ireland, and that you be happy as a reward for all the happiness you have given her. I also happen to know that Maura Kilburn imagined your inheritance might, one day, be mingled with Richard's money. I had understood that was not a farfetched idea."

Bridget lowered her eyes and smiled for the first time since Brandon had begun their private interview.

"I don't think you were misled, Mr. Madison," she answered, raising her eyes to his. Certainly her feelings for Richard were something she was proud of. "I'm just surprised that Mrs. Kilburn anticipated so much."

Brandon laughed even though he would lay money Maura's hope had a slim chance of becoming reality after today.

"Maura Kilburn never anticipated anything. She always knew exactly what was going on around her even when the parties involved didn't. I'll be delighted if things work out."

"Let's hope that's the case, Mr. Madison. But sure I'm not counting my chickens, if you know what I mean. My da always said that was bad luck." Bridget smiled softly, thinking of her father and how happy he would be for her, when he heard the news.

Oh, if she could just run out of this place and into his little house, how wonderful that would be. Sharing this news in front of the fire over a cup of tea at her da's home with Richard by her side would be heaven. But she wasn't in Kilmartin, she was alone with Brandon Madison. He had been kind enough to spend this time with her and put any doubts she had to rest.

"I appreciate what you've told me, Mr. Madison. I see now that we've all gained greatly from Mrs. Kilburn's life and now each of us has something important from her in death."

"Yes, I believe you all have. Whether or not

the Hudsons will agree with you, though, Bridget, is another matter," Brandon cautioned, unable to find the words that would make her understand what lay ahead of her. He prayed her faith in the Hudson family was justified. Perhaps the Hudsons were the antithesis of snubbed heirs. For this young woman's sake, he hoped all of them had hearts as big as Maura Kilburn's.

"I can't see why they wouldn't. And if they don't, I'll simply explain to them the way you explained to me. Still, I do think I should at least offer a part of this inheritance to Kathy. It will make me feel all that much better, Mr. Madison."

"As you wish," he conceded, knowing it was a full but useless gesture.

"Mr. Madison," Bridget ventured, confident that all was now well, "I wonder if there's anything else. I imagine Richard is outside tapping his toes, and I don't want to keep him waiting. I'm sorry for all the time I've taken up and I dearly appreciate the help you've given me, but I must remember too that I'm only Bridget Devlin. I still have things to do at the Kilburn house. Not to mention that Richard and I are going to dinner. 'Tis getting late in the day if I'm to do all that."

Brandon cleared his throat. "Of course. We should have been done with this an hour ago. Now I simply need to know if you would like me to continue administering the investments. If not, I suggest we complete the paperwork and hand over those duties to someone else by the end of the business day, so we don't jeopardize your holdings," Brandon suggested, almost sad to get back to business.

"Please, Mr. Madison, you take care of things. Or . . . well . . . let me think." Bridget was on her feet instantly. "Just a moment. I shouldn't make these decisions on my own. Can you wait a wee bit, Mr. Madison, while I fetch Richard and Mr. Hudson? They'll know what to do."

"Bridget, they may not . . ." Brandon began, half rising and putting out his hand.

But she was already out of the office, headed down the hall. Brandon knew he should have stopped her, but he was not about to go chasing a young woman down the halls of his own law firm. The junior partners would have a field day with that. All he could do now was hope his worst fears weren't confirmed. Bridget Devlin had a pretty easy time of it, from what he could tell, a real clear-eyed lass all right. Pain and suffering didn't seem to have a place in her life — until today. Brandon wondered how long those green eyes would remain so crystalline now that she'd come into this money. If the Hudsons didn't break her heart over it, there was sure to be someone just around the corner who would.

Tipping his head, listening for the sound of her voice, Brandon knew the hurt Maura Kilburn's money brought with it was going to start right about now. Hearing Bridget in the reception room, Brandon couldn't make out the words but he knew exactly what she had found.

Bridget was back in his office a few minutes later. Brandon saw that her step wasn't as light as it had been going out, but she wasn't dragging along, either. He looked at her, a question in his eyes.

"They've gone home already, Mr. Madison." There was a catch in her voice that she tried valiantly to hide. She smiled bravely, taking in a tremulous breath. "Perhaps another sip of water."

Brandon handed it to her over his desk. "I suppose we have been in here awhile. They must have been tired of waiting. It's been a long few days."

"I'm sure it was something like that," Bridget agreed bravely. "Perhaps Mr. Hudson had an appointment. Or maybe they thought we'd be much longer. Because you see, Mr. Madison, your lady out front said they left immediately. I'm sure they had a very good reason." Her voice was husky, laced with bewilderment.

"Of course they did," he agreed gently, knowing their good reason was one Bridget Devlin could not yet accept nor understand. In fact, Brandon was a little disappointed in Richard himself. Kathy he could at least understand. "You look tired, Bridget. We'll leave things as they are for today. Maybe you'd like to go home. Or possibly you could call someone to come get you."

"Oh, no, thank you so much," Bridget said as brightly as she could. If Richard wasn't here for her, there was no one else she wanted.

Tears stung the back of her eyes but Bridget pulled her shoulders up and squared them. Heiress or not she was still Bridget Devlin a proud lass of Ireland and she would not be feeling sorry for herself until she found out why she had been left alone. Best to get on back to Mrs. Kilburn's and wait for Richard there. They had, after all, made a date. Richard would never be so ungentlemanly as to leave her without a word.

"Well, then, Bridget. It's been a pleasure. I hope we'll be doing business for a long while to come.

Brandon put out his hand. She took it gratefully.

"Sure I hope I'll count you a good friend for a long while, Mr. Madison," Bridget responded.

"I know that won't be a problem. But Bridget, I must warn you, my first loyalties are with the Hudsons. In this matter, should they choose to question your legacy, I cannot help you."

"There'll be no need to test the truth of that,

Mr. Madison. The Hudsons have been like my family. You won't be compromised."

"I sincerely hope not," he said more gently now. What he didn't add was that it was for her sake, not his, he hoped all would be well.

"Goodbye, then. And thank you. This has certainly been the most extraordinary day, Mr. Madison."

"Yes, my dear, it has."

With a final shake of his hand, Bridget walked out of Brandon Madison's office with her head held high and rode down the elevator alone.

Outside the sun was setting on San Francisco. Bridget paused a moment as though confused to find herself in the middle of the teeming rush hour. People were pouring out of the high-rise office buildings. It was after five, but just. The spring sun was ablaze on the horizon, giving the skyline a flamingo-pink backdrop on which to etch its handsome profile. On the streets traffic zigged and zagged, each automobile anxious to move, even though there was precious little place to go. Cable cars whizzed by on their tracks. The air was crisp, cool and refreshing. It parted, gently caressing Bridget's face as she began to walk. Unsure of her destination, her heart and mind in turmoil, Bridget couldn't seem to focus on any one thing. She desperately wanted something familiar to cling to. More than anything else Bridget wanted to be surrounded by reality: Mrs. Kilburn's house, her own room and, please God, Richard.

Quickly now she moved on, her feet picking up speed as though in panic. Bridget clutched her purse closer to her and kept her eyes down, warding off the feeling of dread that was beginning to encompass her. She was almost at the corner, ready to turn toward the bus stop when a hand grabbed her arm and a man's body pressed against hers. His other arm slid around her waist. He fell in step with Bridget just as she turned frightened, then relieved eyes his way.

"I thought you'd gone," Bridget breathed, her body curving into Richard's the moment she recognized it was he who was holding her so close.

"Was that wishful thinking or disappointment?" Richard asked, his voice low and strangely even.

The next moment he steered her off the sidewalk and into a coffee bar. Small and intimate, it was filled with young, well-dressed men and women. Richard released her and took her hand firmly in his, pulling her quickly toward a quiet table in the back of the establishment before Bridget had the presence of mind to stop and force him to face her. Irish up, green eyes blazing, Bridget demanded.

"Explain yourself, Richard Hudson, before I go another step."

Chapter Seven

"Bridget, please, this is not the place to make a scene!" Richard said, his voice losing that frightening coldness.

"Then that was no comment to make to the likes of me," she informed him. "I'll have you know that my heart was broken when I found you weren't waiting for me at Mr. Madison's office. I . . ."

A man and woman pushed peevishly by them but neither Bridget nor Richard gave ground.

"I'll have you know I was worried to death about you. So many ideas were going through my head I couldn't even imagine one that might be the truth. Lord above, Richard, wishful thinking! Do you imagine for one minute I was kicking up my heels, grateful that you weren't around to share in my good fortune? Maybe you thought I'd go out and find me a lad who would paint the town properly?"

"Don't be ridiculous. Of course I didn't think that," Richard scoffed when indeed he'd entertained a fleeting thought that Bridget might now wish to leave everything old and familiar behind, including him. God, how that had hurt and how unfair an assumption it had been.

"Then explain yourself, if you please," Bridget demanded, the anxiety of the day falling in on her. Now that Richard was beside her she was more confused than ever. Why wasn't she in his arms listening to his words of congratulations, his plans for their future. Why wasn't she. . . .

Before she could ask herself one more question or speak another word, Bridget wasn't thinking at all. Instead, she was transported to that place of sheer ecstacy; the world where Richard's kiss and the feel of his flesh were the only things that mattered. Every fibre of her being melted until she didn't care if they were standing in the middle of Grand Central Station and the pope himself was watching. Richard's fine lips were silencing her, the feel of his body pressing into hers was exciting her, and the smell of his skin mingling with her own scent drove any questions from her mind.

"Bridget, I'm sorry. It was a thoughtless and stupid thing to say. I'm not sure why it popped out of my mouth," he whispered when he finally relaxed his hold. "Now, if you can manage to calm the storm in those beautiful eyes of yours and tame the torrent of words from those fabulous lips, can I take you to a table where we can start this all over again?"

Bridget nodded, sure her lips were crimson with the memory of his kiss. Richard wound her hand beneath his arm and led her past the crowded tables. The women watched her with envy as she passed, the men with desire. Bridget Devlin and Richard Hudson made a beautiful couple. As Richard passed her gently into the booth it appeared to everyone that these were two people made for each other.

A waitress appeared magically, taking Richard's order for two Irish coffees. Though Bridget craved something cool, she didn't contradict him. Instead, she waited for him to speak. But his comments were long in coming. Richard sat quite still, his back straight, his hands laced on the table in front of him. Suddenly he leaned forward as though a great weight was put upon his shoulders. He smiled still, but it wasn't Richard's smile of hours ago. This one was strained, incredulous, almost sad.

"I suppose I should say something." He laughed self-consciously. "But the thing of it is, Bridget, I don't know quite what to say."

"Nor do I. Sure wasn't I shocked when Mr. Madison read my name."

"Then you had no idea Grandmother was planning this?" Richard asked, knowing his motives were selfish but unable to help himself. He had seen how shocked his mother was, watched her tears of hurt begin to fall. And, if he were truthful, he felt. . . . Well, what he felt was nothing to think about right now. Richard would concern himself first with his mother and Bridget, then he would worry about himself.

"Richard," Bridget breathed, "of course not. Had I known, I would have certainly put my foot down. What does a woman like me know about two million dollars?"

Richard moved in his seat, then found himself almost paralyzed, forgetting Bridget, but not the shock of her words. "I didn't know her holdings were that extensive."

"I'm not sure I even thought about it," Bridget said, letting a quiet come between them again as she contemplated that which seemed incomprehensible. "But now that I've received such wealth, well I think I must make some decisions, don't you?"

"Of course. Naturally. I think we all have decisions to make."

Richard grabbed the straw she held out to him. He wasn't thinking straight, but he knew now what he'd only suspected as he'd rushed back to Brandon's office to find her: he needed space and time away from Bridget Devlin until he could sort out his own feelings and help his mother with hers. It was even difficult to listen to the voice he loved so much as Bridget talked of plans. Plans with his grandmother's money—money that represented a life on this earth that first belonged to her family, not to outsiders. Richard shook his head. He had never considered Bridget an outsider—until now.

"I'm sorry, Richard, I'm not sure I understand. Is there something you or your parents must do, before I can go ahead with the work your grandmother wanted me to do?"

He shook his head. "No, nothing like that. Actually, Bridget, it's a bit difficult to explain."

Curious now, sensing that all was not right with Richard, Bridget said cautiously, "Whatever it is you must explain, I hope you'll do it now and honestly."

Finally, for the first time since they were seated, Richard looked directly into Bridget's eyes. Though so close to her he could see the golden flecks dancing there, he felt more removed from her than if he had flown to the moon. Desperately, gently, he picked up her hands in both of his and brought them to his lips.

"You are so trusting, Bridget. You are so easy to love. Because of that it would be so easy to lie to you. But I can't. I can't sit here and tell you how happy we are for you. And I won't make up some story about why I need to be away from you."

Bridget gasped. There was a tightness in her chest. Richard squeezed tighter as he felt her hands begin to shake. He forced himself to hold her gaze, though the hurt in her eyes was almost beyond bearing.

"What are you saying to me, Richard?" He

brought her fingertips to his lips before he answered, and kissed them. Bridget found no reassurance in this gesture, so she asked again. "Richard?"

"It's hard to believe that you honestly aren't aware of what a blow that will was to my mother. But believe it I do."

Richard sighed and laid Bridget's hands on the table in front of him, keeping them covered with his own as though to tether her and keep her from running away.

"Bridget, my mother is devastated that you inherited the bulk of her mother's estate. She can't understand what has happened here, and it's going to take her a while to sort things out in her mind."

"Oh, Richard, sure if that's all then I've already taken care of everything. I told Mr. Madison that I should be giving back most of this to your dear mom. I only want to keep enough to do some fine things for Kilmartin the way your grandmother wanted. So you see, there's no need for her to feel bad."

"Bridget, this had nothing to do with money. My mother has more than she'll ever need," Richard scoffed, truly amazed at Bridget's naïveté.

"Then what is it, Richard?" Bridget persisted, taking her hands from under his. Suddenly she felt hot and anxious. She wanted to walk. She wanted to be back in the park the way they were earlier, but Richard showed no signs of moving. He sat back when the coffee came and smiled a wan thanks to the waitress, allowing Bridget a moment to really study him.

Something had changed—his sparkle, his confidence. It was no more than a fleeting feeling reinforced by the way his eyes wandered away from hers for a second or two, the way he moved his shoulders not toward her but back as though putting a barrier between them. Then his attention was hers again.

"Bridget, I honestly don't know what my mother is feeling. She asked me to come to the house. All I know is that she's devastated. I can make a guess, but I don't want to speak for her."

"Then guess, Richard," Bridget pleaded. "Sure don't leave me like this, wondering what it is that's made you so sad. Or is it angry you are? If that's it, I'll give back every cent of the money."

"Bridget, I told you," he snapped wearily before his tone gentled. "It's not the money. This has to do with expectations. Do you understand? Sometimes when something doesn't happen the way it normally would, people are disappointed. Mom is devastated, and I'd like to find out exactly what it is I can do for her and what it is she's feeling."

"I wouldn't expect you to do anything else," Bridget answered quietly, forgiving him for his curtness, and a little frightened by it, too.

"I mean that it may take a while, Bridget. I probably won't be seeing you for a few days. Perhaps longer . . ." Richard let his hands slide off the table just as his voice slid away.

"How long do you think?" Bridget asked, her eyes downcast as though that might help him decide in her favor. Looking at him as the tears welled behind her eyes might tip the balance in favor of lengthening the time apart.

"I really don't know. Let me talk to my mother. Let me understand the situation a little better. Because until Mom can come to grips with all this, our relationship will never be the same. Let me work things out with her. I promise I'll do what I can and call you as soon as possible. But for now . . ."

He never finished his thought. Instead, Richard reached into his pocket, pulled out a few bills and put them on the table.

"I've got to go. I love you, but I've got to go."

"Yes," Bridget nodded, wondering why on earth she wasn't begging him to stay. Thankfully this seemed so unreal, Bridget was sure she must be dreaming. Of course she would wake up and find everything as it had been.

"Can you find your way home?"

She nodded again.

"Ah, Bridget," Richard breathed, as he put his lips to her cheek and his hand in her hair,

"I love you so. I love you so and I'm sorry it has all come to this."

Richard was at the door by the time Bridget raised her eyes. She watched his strong, straight back until she could see it no longer. Sitting stiffly as her coffee cooled and the door remained stubbornly closed, no sign of Richard walking back to her, Bridget wondered if indeed this was all about Kathy or was it truly about Richard himself.

Finally, pushing herself from the booth, Bridget stood and smoothed her skirt. Her mind was a maelstrom, realities twirling about until one was just as surreal as the other. Two hours ago Richard had said he loved her. Two hours ago Richard had promised they would be together and she would never have to worry about her future again. Now her future was secure and Richard wasn't sure he could see her much less think about marrying her.

Exhausted and confused, Bridget left the coffee bar without looking right or left. Outside, the evening crowds were still thick, the air was cooler, and Bridget had no idea what she was about. The great chasm Richard had created in her heart had swallowed her reason and her joy. Seeking direction, she found it in the clang of the cable car bell.

Drawn to it, Bridget ran as the queue of working folk and lost tourists began to move. Quickly, unaccustomed to her high heels and unsure of where she was going, she stepped over the tracks and made it to the other side just as the car started moving.

Her senses dulled first by the shock of the will then by Richard's abandonment, Bridget was not thinking clearly when she reached for the pole. Her hand grasped it, wrapping itself around the shiny metal, but her feet were out of sync, and the hop she had anticipated would get her to the platform only made her falter. Feeling herself falling, her hand slipping as the metal afforded no traction with the car picking up speed, Bridget heard a collective gasp of horror rise from the other passengers. Her own wail of despair joined the rest as she realized she could neither let go nor bring herself up. In her mind's eye she saw herself crying for Richard to come save her, pull her out of harm's way. In her mind's eye he reached down for her, his strong hands winding around her arms and. . . .

And then hands were there, clutching her arms, and she was being pulled up. Bridget felt light as a feather, moving through the air like a fairy, before suddenly being deposited on the floor of the moving cable car. A sturdy arm was wrapped about her waist and her body was squashed rather awkwardly into that of a very tall man.

"Are you all right? Did you hurt yourself?"

"Forgive me. Sure I don't know what happened. I thought I had caught it before the car started," Bridget babbled, terrified now that she saw the ground disappearing so quickly beneath the rushing car.

"My fault. I was in your way . . ." The man began.

"I feel so stupid . . ." Bridget spoke over him, raising her face but not her eyes.

"Miss Devlin?"

Finally Bridget looked up. All the way up past a lovely broad chest swathed in a fine sweater of pearl-gray cashmere, past a charming scarf lying casually around a long neck. It was Michael Payne looking every inch the man-about-town, and nothing at all like the local pharmacist.

"Miss Devlin! How very nice to see you."

He laughed delightedly and adjusted his hold on her so that now she was truly pressed against him in the most unsaviorlike manner. Bridget didn't move as Michael Payne continued to smile down at her.

Chapter Eight

"Sure I'm thinking I'm fine now, Mr. Payne, thank you very much."

Michael released her. Bridget stepped back, steadying herself as best she could in the crowd.

"You're sure you're okay? That was a pretty nasty fright you had."

His hands were still held toward her in readiness should she need his assistance again. He thoroughly hoped she would. Seeing her dressed as she was he realized the uniform she usually wore did not do her justice, nor had the dark dress she'd worn for the funeral.

"I'm afraid I would have been fodder for this cable car if you hadn't acted as quickly as you did."

The bell rang and the car jerked just before it headed down the steep incline of California Street. Gravity insisted Bridget follow suit. Involuntarily she leaned toward Michael. Grinning, he placed his hands on her shoulders to steady her.

"I would have hated to see you chopped up

under this thing. You look far too marvelous out of uniform. If I had known you took this line I would have ridden the cable cars ages ago, waiting for you to need help."

"Sure that's a lovely thought, but I'm afraid it would have been a waste of time. I hardly ever take them since I'm usually headed home on the bus. But today . . ." Bridget spoke quickly and politely, wanting nothing more than to be alone. But looking ahead she realized things didn't look quite right. "Oh, dear Lord above! I don't think I've done this correctly at all. Am I headed toward home or away from it? Surely this looks very much like I'm going the wrong way!"

"You're going toward the Bay. Isn't that what you wanted?" Michael asked.

Looking over his shoulder, Michael grinned at what he considered the most marvelous sight in the world—the city of San Francisco—sitting contentedly on all those hills. It was so wonderfully busy and rich, full of people making money, creating art, decking themselves out in all their finery for opening night at the opera. He loved it. San Francisco had such style, and he loved every expression of it. Michael Payne sampled the best the city had to offer every chance he got.

"I was going back to the house. Mrs. Kilburn's house. I suppose I was in such a state after everything that happened today I didn't really look where I was going. This is a pickle, isn't it, Mr. Payne?"

Michael chuckled, the comforting sound of it

almost drowned out by the screeching of the cable car's brakes. People moved all around them, pushing Bridget and Michael this way and that as they tried to get off and another wave of humanity clambered to get on.

"I couldn't hear you!" Michael called, his marvelous eyes lighting up behind wire-rim glasses. Reaching over the head of a woman in a hat too big for the close confines of a cable car, Michael grabbed Bridget's hand and tugged until she let go of the pole she had latched on to. "Come on. Hurry. We'll have to ride all the way down to the Embarcadero if you don't go now."

Cheerfully Michael Payne jumped down leaving Bridget no choice but to follow him. Hurrying, yet mindful of her high heels, he grabbed her hand and jogged them across the busy street, dodging a car or two that registered its displeasure with a long lay on the horn. Bridget was breathless and baffled by the time she reached the safety of the sidewalk, but her cheeks were flushed and she couldn't help the skittish laughter that bubbled out of her.

"Don't you think that was a bit foolhardy, Mr. Payne?" Bridget groused.

"Not at all. Most people won't take that much of a risk," Michael snapped his fingers and grinned. "I like to live life to the fullest. Hell, I spend my entire day dispensing medicine. When my day ends I want excitement. I want to appreciate every bit of life. The less sane the better."

"I suppose that's one way to live, though I

don't know how long you'll be on this earth to enjoy it all," Bridget muttered.

"I'll worry about that later," he laughed. "Now, two things you must remember." Michael steered her to the left. Though Bridget followed, she continued to scan the neighborhood trying to get her bearings, her main objective to find her way home. "First, where were you headed if not downtown and second, will you stop calling me Mr. Payne? My name is Michael, or have you forgotten?"

"Bridget. In case you forgot," she sniffed.

"Better," he said.

"As for the first part of your question, I was going home. I need to get back to the house, I've been gone all day and I . . ."

Bridget faltered and finally stopped trying to explain. Almost forgetting Michael was with her, she slowed her step. Michael, too pleased with the day, himself and his companion, hardly noticed she was deep in thought.

"What on earth are you going back for? Certainly Mrs. Kilburn has relatives to put things in order? It isn't your job."

"No, of course I didn't presume to put her things in order," Bridget said testily, picking up her stride again, wanting only to be alone to lick her wounds. "I suppose I don't really know what I was going back for, other than because it's a habit. I've come to think of it as my home. You know, I was nurse to her for seven years. We lived a very quiet life, but I loved it. I suppose we were the kind of people you despised. The kind who won't take that much of a risk." Bridget snapped her fingers under his nose and kept walking.

"Oh, wait." Michael stopped and held up his hand to halt her progress. A wisp of baby-fine, straight hair fell over his forehead and he shook it back without a second thought. "I didn't say I despised those people. I only meant to say I'd like to wake them up. I want to let them know that life is worth living." His voice softened. "There is nothing more wonderful in the world than spending a quiet evening with someone you like. If it lasts one night or seven years, that's by far the most fantastic and productive way of spending any time of your life. People can learn so much from each other. Most don't listen to the lessons, though. But you can also lose by thinking that's all there is to experience."

Michael looked deeply into Bridget's eyes. He, like Richard, saw the enormous depth of them, the beauty of their color. She was a lovely woman and easy to talk to, if he could get past her distraction. Michael was not insensitive. He saw the pain and confusion, the conflict in her and, liking to deal with neither, he chose to cheer her up.

"Sorry," he apologized, "it's not like me to get so serious or so unfeeling."

"Not at all," Bridget said breathily, as caught up in the interesting planes of his lean face as he was in her eyes.

"I really am sorry if I gave you the wrong impression," Michael murmured.

"Well, I do have my rather dull side. I'm afraid I'm not terribly adventurous," she admitted.

"Then be tonight," Michael urged, waving his hand merrily in front of him as his mood picked up again, hiding the touch of sympathy in his tone. "You have absolutely nothing to go back to that house for. Fate has put you on the wrong cable car and thrown you into my arms after all these years of filling prescriptions for you with a counter between us. I say we throw caution to the wind and accept what destiny has decreed. How about it? Dinner at this little place I know tucked away in Chinatown. If I ask real nice, they'll still whip me up a few pot stickers, maybe some chou sui bow or a little parchment-wrapped chicken? There's nothing like dim sum even if it's for dinner. How much more tempting can I be?"

Exhaustion suddenly claimed Bridget. She needed Richard and reassurance, and because of that she'd been rude to a man who had saved her from injury. Looking in Michael's marvelously open face, Bridget felt more than a twinge of guilt. He was trying so hard to impress her, and he didn't even know she was no longer simply an Irish nurse caring for an elderly patient. She smiled genuinely now.

"I haven't the foggiest if that's tempting or not, Michael, since I've never had any of those things," she answered softly.

"Then, my lady, this is your night! I will introduce you to the exotic dishes of the Orient right here in your own backyard. If you say no, I might have to take back everything good I've been thinking about you and assume you are dull and mean-spirited, after all."

"Jesus, Mary, and Joseph, a fate worse than death," Bridget cried, almost caught up in Michael's joi de vivre. He was right. There was nothing to go home to. "I'm at your disposal, sir."

"Then let's begin. The evening is young, yours, and there's time for everything. Onward to Lee Ho's for the most fabulous dinner you have ever had in your life. I promise, this is one evening you'll never forget."

"It already has been," Bridget murmured under her breath. "Unfortunately."

"Watch out, Bridget. That rock over there is loose. No, go to the left. Oops! Ahh!"

"Michael, are you okay?"

"Couldn't be better, for a man who has just taken a fall on a piece of concrete. I saved the bottle of wine, but I think my posterior is going to have quite a nice bruise. I may need a nurse to tend to it in the morning."

"Don't be silly. Good grief, I've ruined my stocking with all this climbing. At least stand up and let me know where you are. It's awfully dark here."

"Dark but splendid, don't you think?"

Bridget paused to peer through the darkness. His voice and the moonlight had guided her until now, but the moon was gone, hiding behind a cloud, and Michael decided to remain uncharacteristically silent for a minute or two while he nursed his bruise.

Balancing herself on two large rocks, Bridget looked around her. The edge of the Bay was close, she could hear the soft slap of water washing up against shore. Behind her and to her left was a stand of trees, twisted and gnarled from years of buffeting by the sea wind. To her right, the way she had come, was nothing but rock, boulders, and pebbles all mixed up together. Just ahead of her she could make out a shape, something flat and angular like a stage in the middle of nowhere. Through the blackness she could see a number of stationary shapes and the faint blur of something moving. That had to be Michael, but all she could make out was his arm holding the bottle of wine high.

"Talk to me again, Michael, at least until Mother Moon decides to show her face," Bridget pleaded, unsure of how she'd managed to get this far without turning back.

"As you wish," he called. "Let me see. Ah-ha! I have it. 'Happy the man and happy he alone,/ He, who can call today his own:/ He who, secure within, can say,/ Tomorrow do thy worst for I have lived today!' "

Bridget reached him as he called the last word, his rough voice falling to a baritone as he lifted the still-unopened bottle of wine to the moon. Bridget sank down beside him, tired from the climb over the rocks in the dark. He looked at her, quite pleased with himself.

"The poet Dryden. Like it?"

"Sure I haven't the foggiest. I don't know anything anymore, except that you are perhaps the strangest man I've ever met in my entire life." Bridget's teasing complaint only seemed to stir the playfulness in Michael.

"So true. Too black for heaven and yet too white for hell. Why is it," he asked, popping the cork on the wine and pouring it into two plastic glasses, "that Dryden sticks in my mind after all these years out of school. Sometimes I dream in Drydenese. I remember it was Mrs. Folks who pounded it into my head in seventh grade. A hell of a thing to saddle a seventh-grader with, don't you agree?"

Gallantly he handed Bridget a cup of wine. She accepted and took a sip, trying hard to retain her feigned irritability so Michael didn't continue to think he was utterly charming.

"Sure isn't it thanks to Mrs. Folks and seventh grade that you have at least a bit of the civilized about you, Michael?"

"Oh, come now. I promised you an adventure, and aren't you having one?" He prodded.

He had no idea how grateful Bridget was for his good humor. He had treated her as extravagantly as a new heiress should be treated. Though she wished it had been Richard toasting her with plum wine, Richard who kissed her cheeks and gazed at her with captivating amazement, she knew it would not have been the same. Richard, still divided in his heart, would never have captured the proper feel of the evening. He could never have acted with such verve, such genuine excitement. Now, looking through the dark, Bridget realized she owed Michael for making this a very special evening.

"I suppose. But it would be a much happier adventure if I knew where we were," Bridget said, pouting through her smile. The night had turned cold and she was without a jacket.

"You're sitting on a bit of history, my darling Bridget. This huge thing—" Michael half turned and slapped the giant piece of concrete "—is one of many bunkers constructed during World War Two. San Francisco was going to be prepared when the war landed on our doorstep. But the war never came this far, and San Francisco was left with a bunch of unused bunkers. And now people like you and I come here and watch the Bay and listen to the fog horns and gaze at the stars and the moon when the clouds give way long enough. We look one way and we see the lights of the city. We look another way and we see the blackness of the great, deep sea. I should have been a poet, Bridget," Michael said drowning his lament in his wine, perfectly content with himself and the situation.

"You should have been something other than a pharmacist. How on earth do you stand it? All your energy, all your flights of fancy, and you spend your days putting little pills in little bottles."

"I like what I do. I do it well. It is but a means to an end. And the end is—"

"Living your life like a page from a magazine." Bridget threw her arms wide and grinned.

"True," Michael agreed, toasting her. "But I enjoy it, and that's all that counts, isn't it?"

"Sure I can't say that's entirely true," Bridget said, her attention distracted. "Oh, look what's happened. I've ruined my shoes too, coming over all these stones."

"Let me see."

Michael was up, scrambling over to her. She could make him out clearly as he bent over her feet, examining the damage. It gave her a moment to study him once more. She had been doing it all evening, trying to figure out exactly what it was that made him handsome.

His eyes were plain, not deeply set or widely spaced, but they had a liveliness about them that made them seem exceptional. His face was long and, if he turned his head just so, his very vogue, shingled haircut made him look less than attractive. Yet when he looked at her full-face, honestly interested in what she was saying, when his glasses caught the light just right and his full lips parted just a bit, she thought he was the most handsome man she had ever seen—next to Richard. Michael had that long, lanky look of a male model. He could have been a blond Italian playboy or a count of German extraction. Whatever he was, though, the true Michael Payne was hidden by the roles he played, and Bridget was sure he preferred to keep his true self well hidden. He would be an easy man to adore, but a hard one to be in love with. Not that it mattered, since it was Richard she loved.

"Ah, I see what you mean. You're right. The shoes are scuffed beyond repair. So, we simply take them and do this."

With one swift, sure movement Michael slipped the heels off her feet and threw them into the Bay.

Aghast, Bridget was on her feet, her arms flailing helplessly by her side. Michael's charm quickly disappeared.

"How could you! How could you! Those were my best shoes, man!"

"And they were ruined. And, as you told me over dinner, you are now an heiress. Start thinking like one. Start acting like one." Michael slid his arm around her shoulder, his hand running down the side of her arms to quiet her. "Look out there. That is only part of the world. You can have that or anything else you want. You are a millionaire, Bridget Devlin, and that means that you can buy new shoes anytime you want. You can buy twenty pairs with a snap of your fingers. Think big, Bridget. Think like a really rich person. Close your eyes and tell me the first thing that comes into your mind. Don't forget to think rich."

Bridget obliged, her eyes shut tight, her lips pulled together in a thin line. "I'm thinking my feet are cold, Michael, and all the money in the world won't bring back my shoes to keep them warm right at this moment."

"Oh. Yes." Michael took one step back and assessed the situation. "I suppose that was a bit excessive on my part, wasn't it?"

"A fine time for you to realize it. I'm chilled to the bone as it is, and now I have no shoes."

"I'll remedy all of that in a second," Michael insisted.

"Ah, Michael, I don't know. I think maybe I'm tired and would like to go home. I've had a wonderful time, truly I have. But it's going to take a while for the new Bridget Devlin to surface. The old one feels tired and wants to go to sleep before midnight."

"Okay. If that's really what you want. But come here. Let's sit for just a minute. I've got this marvelous wine, the best money can buy. We have this great, quiet place, and I'll keep your feet warm while we celebrate your marvelous news and drive the longing for that cad Richard from your heart."

Bridget grasped his hand and allowed Michael to lead her toward the bunker roof. There she sat sideways, her feet tucked under Michael's long legs, his cashmere scarf slung over her shoulders. Michael stared at the water while Bridget stared at him, wondering what was going on in his mind now that he was silent and she wasn't listening to him verbalize every single thought. He raised his head, held high his cup and spoke softly and purposefully into the night.

"To Bridget Devlin and her newfound fortune. May she see to it that every penny is spent as she wishes it to be spent, wisely or frivolously, it doesn't matter. May her life be filled with all the good things—the kind that money can't buy and the kind that only money can. And, to the muses above who have the power to do anything at all about her guilt complex, may you squash it now before it gets out of hand. May you know that love means accepting your lover's good fortune and bad without question." Turning his attention to Bridget he added, "You are a beautiful woman in so many ways. Enjoy what you have. Don't waste one minute of your life trying to second guess the reasons for this good fortune. Enjoy it, share it, use it properly. Life is very short even when you live as long as Mrs. Kilburn did."

With that, he raised his drink toward Bridget. She did the same, and their cups met in a toast. The moon, fully out now, shone down casting a sparkle on the white wine. When Bridget raised her glass to her lips and lowered her eyes, she thought she was drinking a cup of liquid diamonds.

Lowering it again, she thanked Michael before looking out to sea. She didn't feel as chilled any longer, nor did she feel so alone. Michael Payne had injected a bit of frivolity and a large dose of celebration into a day that had left Bridget shocked and dismayed. For that she would always be grateful to him. But as she sat in the dark, surrounded by the trees and the water, it was Richard she longed for, Richard's voice she wished to hear, his congratulations she wanted to accept. For the first time in many hours, Bridget allowed herself to wonder where he was and what he was doing. Had he tried to contact her? Was he frantic because she couldn't be found? In her heart of hearts she hoped he was, she wanted to find him on the doorstep of the Kilburn mansion, cold and anxious.

"What are you thinking about?"

Startled by Michael's voice, Bridget was jolted back to reality. Richard wasn't here, but her friend was and he deserved her attention.

"I was thinking that I've never had a more lovely toast. Thank you so much. I promise to live up to the responsibility of my newfound wealth."

"And the fun of it, too," Michael reminded her gently.

"And the fun of it," she reiterated. "But now I must go home. Sure I'm almost frozen, Michael, and it has been a big day. Do you mind terribly if we leave now?"

"Not at all. As long as you promise to come back with me some sunny afternoon. I promise not to throw your shoes in the Bay again."

"Then I vow to come back with you," Bridget said, laughing.

Leaving the half-full bottle of wine for the

next adventurers, Bridget allowed him to lead her gingerly back to where they had started. Shoeless, she walked with Michael until they found a cab. It was almost eleven by the time Michael kissed her breezily on the cheek and left her standing at the all-too-familiar door of Maura Kilburn's house.

When he was gone, the cab speeding off into the night as though it knew Michael Payne could not stand to go slowly, Bridget looked up at the dark structure. This house that had been her home for seven long years seemed ominous now, so black with not a light shining.

"Richard," Bridget whispered, though she was sure his name had only come into her head and had not been spoken. He should be here to walk into this black and empty place with her.

Inserting her key into the door, Bridget stepped across the threshold and immediately turned on the foyer light. Closing the front door, she leaned against it until her eyes adjusted to the brightness. Everything was as she had left it. The house was spotless, the artwork straight, the furniture impeccably turned out. She was back where she belonged, but it felt no more like home than the cold concrete of the bunker. Without Maura Kilburn sleeping upstairs, without Mrs. Reilly listening to her television in her room, this was just a house filled with beautiful things. If Richard were holding her in his arms as they planned their future, knowing that they could do anything and be anything they wanted thanks to Maura

Kilburn, then life would be perfect. But surrounded by the hollow silence of the house, Bridget Devlin just felt incredibly, desperately lonely.

Heading to her room, she resisted the urge to pick up the phone and dial the Hudsons' residence. Richard would call soon enough. But now she needed someone who loved her to listen. Quickly she climbed the stairs to her room, sat cross-legged on her bed and dialed a number she knew so well. An old sleepy voice answered on the third ring.

"Oh, I forgot what time it was!" Bridget said. "Oh, Da, it's Bridget. I'm sorry to wake you. But, Da, I've so much to tell you. So much . . ."

Chapter Nine

"I'm sorry I couldn't get here sooner." Brandon apologized the moment he stepped through the door. "I had five court appearances in the last two days. By the looks of you I think you should have told my secretary it was an emergency. If I lacked tact, I'd ask who died."

"Tact is the last thing we're concerned about." Richard, looking tired and not at all happy, spoke as he led the way through his parents' sprawling home in Marin.

Unlike Maura Kilburn's home, the Hudsons' taste was eclectic. The modern, one-story structure was deceiving from the outside. It looked architecturally modest, set on two acres of forested land at the edge of the Bay. But once past the front door a visitor was treated to an exquisite journey through rooms created almost entirely of glass.

Light poured in from every direction. Artwork of every imaginable sort was scattered throughout the house, statues in bronze and stone peeked out at a visitor from the oddest places or were frozen in their stride in the middle of one of the enormous rooms. Furniture was sprinkled lightly about. Some pieces were antique, the warm woods and tapestries in stark contrast to the modern art. The floors were thickly carpeted in places and bare bleached wood in others so that, as Richard and Brandon walked in silence, the sound of their steps were alternately echoed and muffled throughout the house.

"This way," Richard murmured. He stepped to the side, and Brandon found himself in a familiar and favorite room. Three walls and the ceiling were glass.

This last room in the house jutted out slightly over the Bay so that by sitting at one of the artfully arranged groupings around a fireplace in the center of the room, a guest might feel as though he or she were floating in the air, hovering over the sea. Brandon had always felt this was a lovely room for contemplation, as though by simply moving through the doorway and taking a seat, all the worries of the day would be dispelled. He liked to joke to his wife that if all the leaders of the world had rooms like this one there would never be wars or prejudice or any of the hateful things in the world. He would have to remember to tell his wife that he had been wrong. Anger, perhaps hatred, flourished even here.

"Brandon, so good of you to come this early in the morning. I'm afraid Ted and I, and Richard too, couldn't wait another moment to confer with you."

Kathy Hudson, stunningly dressed in a simple

cat suit of bright red that showed off her flawless figure, sat as though she was knotted up. Her arms were crossed at waist level, one leg crossed over the other, her ankles entwined. Her face was pulled into a concentrated mask of control. Ted stood, his back to the bank of glass, looking sadly at his wife. Kathy, Brandon noted, threw glances at Richard now and again as if she wanted him to confirm something he would not, or could not. Richard never looked her in the eye. Finally she gave up and focused her complete attention on Brandon as he took a seat opposite her.

"Coffee, Brandon? Or tea? Perhaps some breakfast?" Kathy asked, trying her best not to let her irritation show and failing miserably. Brandon declined.

"Well, since we can't offer you any refreshment we'll simply get right to the point," Kathy said, taking a deep breath before continuing. "We want to know . . . that is I especially want to know . . . if there is any way we can contest this will that Mother has left. This is in no way meant to cast aspersions on you or the work you did for Mother. And, I suppose, I should be seeking outside counsel to look into this question. But you wrote that will, Brandon, and you, of all people, should know how to break it."

"I see," he said quietly. Richard spoke before Brandon had time to formulate his answer.

"I've told Mother that I doubt you would conveniently leave a loophole, not to mention the

161

fact that I believe the will was made in good faith. Much as Mother may dislike the terms, Grandmother knew exactly what she was doing. Bridget is Grandmother's monetary heir."

"I won't accept that," Kathy spat. "Bridget did something to Mother and cleverly covered it up. There is no other explanation. Now, Bran—"

"Mother, that simply isn't so. We've known Bridget for years," Richard cut in. But Kathy stared at Brandon without acknowledging her son and continued with her thought.

"Now, Brandon, if you would be kind enough to answer my question."

He sat forward and rested his arms on his knees as he spoke to Kathy, and only Kathy. He had read Ted's face well enough. He didn't want his wife hurt, but he had obviously exhausted all the arguments against pursuing this. Richard. Well, Richard looked pained and perplexed. He obviously didn't know what to think, but he was having a hard time condemning Bridget despite his loyalty to his mother. Kathy, though, always one to run when she should walk, wasn't going to spend one minute considering anything. She wanted action.

"Richard is right, you know. Bridget had nothing to do with this. You would be wasting both your time and your money if you tried to contest that will. It is airtight."

"But, Brandon, it can't be. You must understand . . ."

"I don't think I could understand. No, that's

not true. I do understand how unfair you think Maura was. What I can never do is feel the way you feel about it. That is something so personal I wouldn't even begin to guess at how awful it must be. But you must remember something. Your mother was in her right mind when she made out that will. She was as lucid as can be. She and I talked at length about the step she was taking and she made a whole lot of sense. If called upon in a court of law to swear to her state of mind, I would have to tell them exactly what I told you."

"But, Brandon, there must be something. Bridget! She must have done something we weren't aware of. Don't you understand that?"

Kathy Hudson's voice was rising, headed toward hysteria, when Richard stepped in and placed a hand on his mother's shoulder.

"Mom, please. You know Bridget even better than I do. You've' watched her work, you've brought her into your home, you treated her like a daughter. If she had been aware of what was in Grandmother's mind, I'm sure she would have put a stop to it. I can't imagine that you don't see that, too. You can't possible suspect her of anything underhanded when she's never given you cause in all these years."

"I have to agree with Richard," said Ted, coming forward reluctantly. "We've known Bridget so long. She's sat at our table. She cared for your mother like a friend, not an employee."

"Kathy, I'm afraid we all agree. There isn't anything legally that can be done, and I don't think there has been a moral transgression on Bridget's part. Bridget Devlin is your mother's monetary heir. That's all there is to it."

"Excuse me, Mrs. Hudson?"

Lilly, the Hudsons' housekeeper, stood respectfully in the doorway of the glass room. She was young and not used to the somber faces and sad voices in this house usually filled with Kathy Hudson's plannings and goings on.

"Yes, Lilly." Kathy acknowledged her without taking her eyes off the three men who opposed her.

"It's Miss Devlin again, asking for either you or Mr. Richard."

Looks were exchanged. Kathy Hudson's face tightened and closed, so that Brandon Madison could only guess at the depth of emotion hidden behind her expression. Richard moved toward the door.

"I'll take it, Lilly," he said quietly. But Kathy's harsh command stopped him in his tracks.

"We're still out, Lilly. Please just take a message from Miss Devlin until we tell you differently." Her eyes blazing a challenge to her son.

"This is uncalled for, Mother," Richard said softly.

"Are you still my son, Richard?" Kathy responded icily.

Richard matched her unwavering look. Logically, lawyerlike, he weighed the evidence before him. His mother was pained, reacting without thinking. Bridget was confused, but confusion could be banished with an explanation. Pain had to be nursed. He would help his mother, then he would decide what to do about Bridget. That seemed the logical thing to do.

"Mother, we'll have to come to an understanding on this. I am not going to feed on your anger or accept your vindictiveness as my own," Richard said evenly, hoping his forthrightness would shock her into a more sensible attitude. But Kathy looked past him and spoke to the maid.

"Until I tell you differently, Lilly, we are out to Miss Devlin." The young woman disappeared and Kathy Hudson muttered to the maid's back, "I'll never tell you differently."

"Mom, please," Richard pleaded ineffectually. He had seen people in this state a hundred times; people who wanted justice. But what justice could there be here? No one would win no matter what the outcome. Turning away from Kathy, he rolled his eyes to the ceiling of glass and the sky beyond.

It was a beautiful clear day in Marin. Across the Bay the city was lying under a light fog that he knew would burn off by noon. He should have been over there whisking Bridget off to a picnic, kissing her in a darkened booth in his favorite steak joint. He should have been making plans with her, loving her, rejoicing that their life was going to be so full of the best that money could buy. Instead he was here, not quite sure he knew what he was feeling about her, his grandmother or this damned will.

"Please, Richard, you tell your mother. You're a lawyer. There just isn't anything to be done." Brandon spoke just to fill the icy silence in the room.

"I'm a criminal lawyer, Brandon," Richard said, his voice controlled and steely, "and the one thing I can assure my mother is that nothing criminal is going on here. Nothing. We're going to have to trust you, Brandon. And as far as I'm concerned, there's another person who has earned our trust years ago, and I don't think we should be taking it away from her blithely, no matter how we feel about Grandmother's legacy."

Kathy didn't twitch as her son spoke. Ted turned back to the window. He had spent himself, trying to convince his wife that she should simply let this whole matter go. Cut Bridget Devlin from their lives if she must, but don't begin a bitter vendetta. Brandon, more uncomfortable by the moment as emotions ran high and bewilderment became palpable, decided there was nothing more he could do. He spoke as he stood up.

"I'm sorry, Kathy, I tied up every loose end. It will do you no good to pursue this. You'll simply spend a lot of money trying to do the impossible."

"If only you'd said something, Brandon," Kathy pressed, her tone making the statement sound more like begging. No one in the room understood that had even been an option.

"Kathy." Ted stepped up to his wife and took her chin in one hand. He looked at her with such love Brandon was impressed. "It's business, Kathy. If you don't cut your losses this will eat away at you until it's all you think about — changing the unchangeable is all you'll want. It's a no-win situation."

"This is not one of your mergers," Kathy muttered, moving out of her chair so quickly the men were startled and couldn't react. "None of you understand a thing. You think this is about money, and it's not. I could talk myself blue in the face, and you two lawyers, you Richard and you Brandon, would sit there with those grave looks on your faces telling me that nothing can be done. And you, my husband who is suppose to support me in everything, you think I should just write it off like a bad debt. I won't have it. I won't."

Frustrated by a vocabulary that couldn't convey what was deepest in her heart, Kathy Hudson wheeled away from the men. With her back straight, her head held high, she left the room with purposeful strides. Neither Brandon, Richard, nor Ted saw the tears that were streaming down her cheeks.

"I'm sorry, Ted," Brandon said quietly.

"I understand. She'll get over it. You must admit, it's not as though we're hard up for cash. Still, there were plans, if you know what I mean."

167

"Of course. That was only practical," Brandon said.

Ted shrugged as though to say that *practical* was no effective bandage for the hurt his mother-in-law had caused. He had no explanation for it. He had always thought things were perfect between her and her daughter.

"Goodbye, Richard." Brandon shook the young man's hand.

"Brandon," Richard nodded as he shook the older man's hand. "She's just going to need some time."

"I know that. Your mother is a smart woman," Brandon acknowledged.

"Smart enough to figure out in the end that there are more important things in life."

Brandon pressed. "And what about you, Richard?"

Honestly taken aback, Richard looked curiously at his professional peer. "I'm afraid I don't understand the question."

"Stop me if I'm being too personal, but Maura led me to believe you were quite serious about Bridget. Have you been able to deal with your own feelings here?"

Richard laughed outright now, but the sound was hollow. "I'm afraid the only feelings I have for this situation are sadness for what my mother is going through. Believe me. I still feel exactly the same way I always felt about Bridget."

Brandon nodded, gave Richard's hand another quick squeeze and said his goodbyes. As he got into his car he looked back at the house, thinking about Ted and Kathy and Richard Hudson. It was going to be a long haul for all of them. He started his car, thinking that no matter how hurt Kathy was it was going to be easier on her than Richard. At least Kathy was honest about her feelings.

Everything was spread out on her bed: a request for address information from her new bank so they could print her checks; a letter of welcome from both of the brokerage houses; and a great deal of cash that had been gladly handed over when she went to the bank that morning. In the midst of all this paper lay Bridget.

Facedown she cradled her head in her hands and sobbed as though she hadn't a friend in the world. Two weeks and not even a note from Richard. She was being treated as though she were a floozy from town come to marry the widowed miller to get his fortune.

Finally, through her tears, Bridget laughed at herself. What a dramatic girl she was! Wouldn't her da chuckle if he could crawl in her head and hear what she was thinking. Ashamed, Bridget sat up and wiped her eyes with the back of her hand.

This was no way for a lady of means to act. It was high time she took matters into her hands and not wait for everyone else to come to their senses. First she would call her da just to hear a loving voice again. She only hoped she could

169

keep her plans for Kilmartin a secret. It was more and more difficult each time she spoke to him. Then she would get dressed and go find Richard. Together they would work through this or they would. . . .

Bridget stopped her cerebral list-making and sat very still. Way down at the bottom of the stairs she heard a sound. Small though it was, it couldn't have been a heaving pipe or the house settling. Bridget knew all those noises. Cautiously she eased herself off her bed, wincing when the springs gave a little creak. As carefully as possible she stepped toward the door, flattening herself against the wall to peek out. All was clear on the stairwell.

Bridget was positive she had not only locked the front door but activated the alarm, too. Without a key and a code there was no way anyone could get into the house without the alarm going off. Straining to hear, Bridget leaned forward, hoping she wouldn't detect another sound. To her dismay she heard it again, faint but definite. There was someone downstairs!

Fear shot through her like wildfire and burned itself out just as quickly. Next came apprehension, but that lasted only a second and was replaced by a blazing anger that shot up and consumed her. First Richard leaves her to her own devices, Kathy Hudson hasn't the manners to return her calls, and now some stranger is coming in here to do God-knew-what to her and this house. That was the last straw. She had enough. Bridget Devlin was a woman who could take care of herself, and pity the poor creature below because he was going to find out just how well she could manage.

Silently Bridget backed away from the door of her room. Keeping her eyes on the hall she reached for the phone by the bed, dialed the police and whispered the address.

Hanging up, Bridget looked for her shillelagh. Sure she hadn't used that sturdy stick since she'd been in this country, but it was heavy and just the thing to take care of the intruder downstairs. Riffling as quietly as possible through her closet, she wrapped her hands around the stout club.

"Here we go now, straight and sure if I have to use you," she whispered to the thick piece of carved wood just before she gave herself a quick cross over her heart.

Feeling a confidence she shouldn't have, Bridget worked her way down the long flights of stairs. With each step the sounds became clearer, more ominous because of their casualness. The intruder picked up a vase and put it back. Bridget had heard that sound a hundred times when Mrs. Reilly cleaned. A drawer was opened, silver was riffled through, crystal tinkled. The horrid person was taking his own sweet time about deciding what he wanted.

Shifting the club so it was now raised over her head if she needed to bring it down quickly, Bridget stood on the last step, said a small prayer to St. Bridget and jumped into the doorway to confront the trespasser.

"All right, you. Stand where you are and put your hands in the air. The police are on their way!"

In front of her, a woman in a winter-white suit and diamond earrings the size of peas jumped in a most unladylike way, her free hand fluttering to her breast in surprise. When she saw Bridget her expression changed, settling into one of refined peevishness. In an instant the only sign she had been startled was a scarlet tinge just above the collar of her suit. She eyed Bridget as though the young woman was a creature from space.

"You really shouldn't do that," she said, reprimanding Bridget, "it's hardly seemly." The woman in white eyed Bridget more closely and waved her hand, silently insisting Bridget lower her weapon. "You must be Miss Devlin. I certainly hope you haven't called the police," she said coolly, replacing the Boehm statue she had picked up as she jotted something on the clipboard she held.

Slowly Bridget lowered the shillelagh without a second thought. Few thieves favored sling-back pumps, their hair done just so and a clipboard in their hand. She also wasn't a friend of Mrs. Kilburn's. After all these years Bridget knew every single one of the ladies Maura Kilburn called friends. Yet this woman knew her name and was not at all surprised by Bridget's presence in the house.

"You're Miss Devlin, are you not?" the woman

demanded again.

"Y-yes," Bridget answered, taking a few steps toward the woman. "I am," she said more forcefully. "Who are you?"

"You've called the police." The woman sighed, quite put out as she realized what the situation was. "Perhaps you should call back and let them know there's no reason to be alarmed."

The woman pointed regally to the phone as though Bridget were her servant. This was not a wise thing to do considering Bridget's mood.

"I'll call them when I'm convinced there is no need for their help. Please be so kind as to explain what you are doing in this house, handling Mrs. Kilburn's things." Bridget responded curtly.

"Actually, I think I should be the one doing the asking," she answered in that lazy haughty manner Bridget was coming to despise. "I was assured by the new owner—" she checked her clipboard—"Mrs. Katherine Hudson, that you, the tenant in this house, would more than likely have left the premises by now. I'm here to take inventory so Mrs. Hudson can decide what items she wishes to auction and which she wishes to retain.

"Now, if you have a problem with that, I suggest you take it up with her. I really have no authority here other than to complete this inventory. I can't possibly discuss your lease. Mrs. Hudson seems like a reasonable person. I'm sure she'll give you an extension on your agreement if you explain whatever circumstances have kept you here. You really should call her. I believe the locksmith is coming tomorrow. Then, as I understand it, the house is to be closed until decisions are made."

Losing interest in Bridget, the woman in white resumed her work. Stunned, Bridget watched her stroll about the room jotting little notes to herself, picking up the pieces that had been so precious to Mrs. Kilburn, then putting them down as if they were no finer than a pot she'd found at a jumble sale.

If Kathy Hudson had walked into this house and slapped her, Bridget could not have been more devastated. Her first instinct was to cry; her second was to force herself not to. She had shed too many tears, first for Mrs. Kilburn, then in frustration over the past few days as she had realized the Hudsons' affections were not as keen as she'd imagined. The first tears were deserved; Bridget was beginning to regret the rest.

"I think that's exactly what I'll do. I'll go see Mrs. Katherine Hudson myself," Bridget muttered as she stormed out of the living room. "Tenant indeed!"

It would seem the new landlady had obviously lost either her mind or her heart, and Bridget was determined to find out which one it was. First, though, she would call the police and tell them there was nothing they could do here, and that was the understatement of the decade. What was wrong in this house might be beyond repair.

Chapter Ten

"This the place?" The cabby cocked his head toward the Hudsons' home forcing Bridget out of her preoccupation.

"Yes, this is it," she told him quietly.

The driver was out of the car in an instant, opening her door as though it were a can of sardines. Bridget slid out of the back seat, fully aware that he was admiring her long, sleek legs. Standing straight, Bridget resisted the urge to tug at her short skirt, while berating herself for giving in to the urge to follow the fashion, when she and Michael had gone shopping together.

"Can you wait?" She asked in a manner that left no doubt she wanted to complete her business, not show off her legs.

"I don't know," he shrugged. "How long are you going to be? I gotta make a living, you know, and you already got forty-five bucks on the meter. Marin ain't exactly hoppin' with fares back to the city this time of the day. I mean, lady, this waiting stuff ain't exactly kosher, if ya know what I mean."

The man raised a hand to his cap, tugged it off and scratched his head, while he considered Bridget. He'd seen better-dressed women with no money and worse-dressed with a ton of it. This one he couldn't figure out. Pretty, nicely dressed, no attitude, kind of sad or mad, he couldn't tell which. It was a tough call, trying to figure if she was good for the fare and a wait.

"I understand," Bridget said quickly and, surprisingly, she did. Everything was crystal clear to her as the man stood bouncing from one foot to another, not really saying what he meant. She grinned at him gloriously as it dawned on her that she, Bridget Devlin, had the power to make him stay and wait. "Sure and isn't it an inconvenience for you to be stuck out here in the middle of nowhere. I should know whether or not I'll be a while after I talk to my friend. Could you wait ten minutes or so? Here."

Bridget snapped open her purse. Her wallet was in her hand magically. Fumbling with it just a bit, she pulled out two new bills. They felt surprisingly nice between her fingers and a quick glance reassured her there was more to be had if she needed it.

"Here, can't you wait for ten minutes, please? Wouldn't that be enough?"

Replacing his cap, the cabby fingered a fifty and a twenty. Ten-minute wait paying half of what it cost him to take her all the way across the bridge? He could even be nice for that.

"Sure, miss, I'll wait." He grinned, too. They were fast friends now. "How about if I knock on the door in a few minutes, just in case you get to gabbin'? Not that I want to mess around when you've been so generous, but—" he shrugged—"I'm makin' a livin'."

"Certainly. You do that. Come right on up and knock. Ask for Bridget. But I won't forget you're here. I promise."

She gave him a little wave. Bridget was already halfway up the long walk, vanishing behind the wall of greenery, by the time he got back in the car and shut the door.

She had rung six times and knocked as many, yet still no one came. While she stood alone on the doorstep, she made excuses for Ted, Kathy, and Richard, then discarded them one by one. There was always someone in the house: the maid, the cook, someone. Obstinately she put her finger to the bell and left it there, jumping back when the door was finally opened furtively, and Lilly stepped out, half closing it behind her.

"Miss Devlin, please, the whole neighborhood can hear you!" she shushed, obviously unnerved.

"I'm sorry, Lilly. You must have been terribly

177

busy not to come to the door. I've been here ringing almost five minutes," Bridget said as evenly as she could.

"It's a very big house, Miss Devlin," Lilly answered. "I was in the back. I couldn't get here that fast because I was putting away the laundry and . . ." Lilly was wringing her hands, wishing Bridget would say something and save her from this terrible drama. Lying did not sit well on her.

Bridget felt sad that Lilly had been put in this position. She had always felt a kind of kinship with the maid. But before she could call upon that feeling the door opened slowly. Lilly was gently moved aside as Richard put his two strong hands on her shoulders. Then he was the one facing Bridget, and her eyes softened almost to tears when she saw the look of longing in his.

"It's all right, Lilly. I'll talk with Miss Devlin."

Richard remained silent. Bridget assumed he was waiting for Lilly to leave before asking her in. Instead of admitting her to the house, he stepped onto the wide porch.

"I'm surprised to see you," he said softly, "but I'm glad, too. You look wonderful."

"It's been so long since we've talked. I didn't know what to think. You said you'd call."

"Things here are a bit more complicated than I thought. I'm afraid Mom is still very upset."

"Then it's a good thing I'm here, Richard. I've got to talk with her. Things are so strange now. I don't understand . . ."

"Bridget, please. I know you want things to be the way they were, but if you insist on pushing Mom to talk to you, they'll never right themselves. She just needs me and my father. She needs family to talk sense into her."

"But, Richard, my darling, I'm the only one who could do that. Sure doesn't it make more sense for me to sit over a cup of tea with her and just talk about your grandmother?"

Richard reached his fingers out and put them over her lips. This woman was so beautifully optimistic and so tragically honorable. To her the solution was simple. Unfortunately there was nothing simple about the way Kathy Hudson felt. For that matter, there was nothing simple about the way he felt. Only now, his fingers touching her velvety lips, his eyes drinking in every inch of her, did Richard realize how much he had missed her, how desperately he cared about her and how strangely necessary it was for him to remain away from her so he wouldn't have to acknowledge other deep and disturbing emotions.

"Bridget, please go home and I'll call you later tonight. We'll have dinner. We can talk then. But don't press Mother. It's not going to work no matter how good your intentions."

"Richard, if you care about me at all, you

must let me into this house. It will do us no good to love each other if her anger is always between us. You said that yourself. Let me try, at least."

"Yes, Richard, let her try." Behind them a voice as cold as ice broke into the conversation. Richard whirled, his face hardening as he faced his mother. Bridget's expression was hopeful, open with anticipation. "It's all right, Richard. Let her in. I'll see Miss Devlin."

Richard stepped between the two women and addressed his mother.

"No, I don't think you have anything to say to Bridget that she needs to hear. Not now at least. Maybe in a few weeks." He moved closer, lowering his voice. "Haven't you hurt her enough by cutting her out of your life?"

"Richard," Bridget said, pushing around him, "I think now is as good a time as any since your mother is willing."

"You have no idea what you're getting into. I don't think this is wise."

Kathy snorted. "Let the woman think for herself, Richard. You can't protect her from the bad things in life. She already has all the good things. Come in, Bridget. Richard, I think I'd like this to be a private conversation."

Agreeing, Bridget slid her arm from Richard's restraining hold and followed Kathy through the house into the glass room. Suddenly wary and uncertain she remained at the doorway watching

Kathy as she gazed out toward the Bay. The silence between them lengthened until finally Kathy turned and faced Bridget.

"You're here. You've been trying to get to me for days. Say what you have to say. Then I think it best if you leave."

Surprisingly, Kathy found she couldn't look at Bridget. As much as she wanted the young woman to see her hurt and anger, Kathy knew it was only pain Bridget would see in her eyes. And her voice, far from furious, sounded tired and sorrowful. If she heard it, then Bridget did, too, and the last thing Kathy Hudson wanted was sympathy from her.

Kathy needn't have worried. Standing far away from the woman she had always regarded with love and respect, Bridget felt even more isolated than she had when she was standing alone, knocking on the door. Kathy's abandonment was as real as if Bridget were a child left at the convent for the sisters to take in. Bridget attempted no bravado, she didn't square her shoulders nor did she raise her voice. Instead, her words came from the heart, as did the catch in her throat and the softness of her plea.

"I don't know what I've done, Kathy." Bridget began, then stopped abruptly. This was a beginning, and there was so much more, but she had no idea how to tell Kathy Hudson everything without sounding selfish. How could she demand to know why *she* wasn't loved any longer;

why *she* wasn't welcome where arms had always been held out to her? Taking a deep breath, Bridget tried again. "I feel as if I died along with your mother. One minute my life was so full of color and wonderful things, marvelous people—full of love. You and Mr. Hudson treated me as though I was part of your family. Mrs. Kilburn, your mother, never questioned my feelings for her or our friendship. And I was in love, Kathy. Richard and I, we were caring so much for each other that I thought, truly, I would be part of this family sooner than later. Sure and I thought I would be your real daughter."

Bridget took a tentative step or two into the room. Her hands held out, raised gently toward the woman, were ignored as Kathy lowered her head and turned away from Bridget.

"In one day it was gone. No—" Bridget shook her head adamantly—"in one minute it was taken away. The minute that man, Mr. Madison, said my name in his office, all my happiness was destroyed. And I don't know how to get it back, Kathy. I've come to ask you what it is I can do. I want my life back and, sure 'tis, I need you to be my friend again. Just tell me what to do."

"There's nothing you can do," Kathy answered flatly, hoping it would be enough to stop Bridget. It wasn't.

"There must be something."

Bridget moved around the sparse furniture, ignoring the statuary, unwilling to go too close, but wanting, at least, for Kathy to look at her. She was sorry when Kathy obliged. Kathy Hudson raised a tight face to her, her eyes armed against sentiment, her heart fortified with grief against love.

"There is nothing you can do, Bridget. My mother elected you her heir, and that is all there is to it. I find it difficult to live with her decision. Therefore, I find it difficult to live with you as part of my life. I think that's about as clear as I can make it."

"By the saints I never asked for her money, Kathy. Never once did we even discuss it," Bridget persisted, unable to sway Kathy.

"That's supposed to make me feel better?" The older woman scoffed. "Even if you told her you didn't want her money, even if you offered to turn it all over to me, it wouldn't make any difference. She left it to you. *You* and not me. Not even Richard. That I would have understood. He's younger, he has more years to enjoy it. But you? A young woman who was taken to heart by this family, but were not a flesh-and-blood part of us. That hurts, Bridget. I can't believe you're so insensitive as not to see that."

Kathy whirled away from the glass as though trying to escape and realizing the route was not behind her. She took a few steps and placed her hand on a beautiful bronze. One hand slid down the statue's naked leg, her eyes following its progress as though determining whether or not her hand was functioning properly. She had dressed for the day in charcoal-gray leggings and a white chiffon top fashioned after an artist's smock. The voluminous garment and her short, short hair made her look a bit like a cosmopolitan Peter Pan. But the expression on her face was far from that of a never-to-grow-up sprite. On every inch of Kathy Hudson's countenance Bridget saw misery like she had never seen before, and it broke her heart in two.

"Bridget, the point you seem to be missing here is a very simple one," Kathy continued quietly. "My mother obviously thought more of you than she did of me. Period. It is that easy. Now my mother is dead. I have no way of asking her how it was I failed, yet I'm slapped with the realization that I did. I'm fifty-nine years old, Bridget, and some say I look forty-five. Given my mother's longevity, I'll probably live another thirty years. How do you think I'm going to enjoy them knowing that I, my mother's only child, was replaced in her affections by a woman she had known only seven years?"

The question rang in Kathy Hudson's perfect house. It shot off the walls and assaulted Bridget from every direction. Overwhelmed by Kathy's heartache, Bridget looked away, not knowing if she would be able to answer. When she did, she hoped her voice was composed; she hoped she didn't sound as though she were lecturing. Bridget prayed she sounded like a friend.

"Ah, but Kathy, it had nothing to do with how she felt about you. Your mother, rest her soul, loved you like I've never seen anyone love another human being. Truly, that's the case," Bridget insisted. Kathy snorted in disbelief and gripped the statue knowing that she would have to hear Bridget out before she would vanish from her life.

"But 'tis true," Bridget protested in vain. "She loved you so dearly. With her heart the way it was, that woman wouldn't have been in this world past seventy years if it hadn't been for you and Richard and Mr. Hudson. It had nothing to do with me, at all, I swear."

"And that's why you are now sitting on a rather sizable fortune that my parents sweated for."

Bridget responded immediately, wanting to keep the dialogue going, knowing that at least in communication there was hope.

"I'm sitting on that fortune because it was your mother's wish I could do something with it, improve someone's lot, make myself worthy of your son. I know she understood how much we were coming to mean to each other, and it entered her mind that Richard and I might one day wed. But more importantly she and I shared dreams of Ireland and how sad that lovely country had become with so many people needing so much. I believe she thought I could make a difference with her money."

"And I couldn't?" Kathy railed, almost yelling but controlling herself just in time. She lowered her voice more than necessary to compensate as she insisted, "I could have done anything she wanted me to do and more, Bridget. All she had to do was specify what it was she desired, and I would have done it."

"Sure and it wouldn't have been the same, Kathy," Bridget soothed gently. "Your mother remembered Ireland. She remembered living there and how the air smelled and the wind felt on her young face. She remembered falling in love and how hard it was to leave the place. Sure and Ireland was my home, too, so we had memories in common. We both of us knew first-hand what the people there were like and what they needed. But you've never lived in Ireland. You're a USA lady through and through, there's no denying that, is there? You wouldn't have understood what it was she was thinking about if she left you a bunch of instructions on a piece of paper. I'm not even sure what it is she wanted me to do back there. But one thing I do know — Mrs. Kilburn wanted an Irish heart to do it."

Bridget took a small breath, encouraged that Kathy hadn't cut her off. She seemed to be listening, praise God, so on Bridget went, forging ahead quickly as her mind grasped at anything that might make Kathy Hudson understand what Bridget Devlin still did not.

"She left you the house and all her lovely things because she wanted you to have memories, to have the things she had touched." Bridget hesitated. She looked around the incredible room in which she stood. The sofa alone cost more than she had made in a month working for Mrs. Kilburn. The artwork was museum quality. The view was the stuff of which dreams were made. Bridget chose her words carefully. "And sure it was your dear mother knew you had every material thing a body could desire on this earth. It was your heart she concerned herself with. Didn't she understand, now, that if she left you her money it would simply mean you would be wealthier. She wanted you to have more than a new bank balance, Kathy. The house, her home, those are the things that matter."

"You're wrong, Bridget." Kathy moved quietly and calmly away from the statue, interrupting Bridget's speech.

It was at that moment Bridget knew she had lost. But she wouldn't admit it. "I'm not wrong. I can't be. Because if I am, then that means love and money are the same thing and, sure, if that's the way 'tis, I'm not sure I like this world very much."

"Then you'll live in an imperfect world because love is equated with passing on everything that one acquires in this life. I would no more dream of cutting Richard out of my will than I would cut off my arm. He is . . ."

"But you weren't cut out," Bridget wailed, exasperated by her defeat.

"I might as well have been," Kathy snapped, "because Mother succeeded in cutting out my heart." Controlling herself she went on. "So, you see, under the circumstances, I don't think we could continue with the relationship we once had, Bridget. It wouldn't be possible — for me."

"Excuse me, ma'am."

Lilly interrupted the two women tentatively, much as she hated to. The air was so thick with confused emotions she could feel it closing in on her, the minute she stepped through the doorway. And when the two women snapped their eyes her way, she wished she could have shielded herself from the intensity of their gaze.

"What is it, Lilly?"

"The cab driver, ma'am. He wants to know if Miss Devlin is ready to leave."

Kathy looked slowly and surely back to Bridget, their eyes locking for a long while. Bridget held her breath, swearing she had seen the older woman's eyes soften, but it was only a trick of the light.

"I think Miss Devlin is ready to go, Lilly," she said without taking her eyes off Bridget. Kathy's gaze lingered a moment longer before she walked away without looking back.

Bridget's shoulders sagged. Her heart was so heavy she wasn't sure she could drag it with her. Until now she hadn't understood the meaning of the word *anguish*. Now the definition was crystal clear, every nuance of its meaning something she felt now. She raised her head, watching Kathy's straight, proud back clothed in all its perfection. She couldn't leave things this way. Bridget called out.

"Wait. Kathy. Please," she beseeched.

Surprisingly, her back still to Bridget, Kathy paused.

"Richard?" Bridget asked apprehensively. "He doesn't feel as you do, but he couldn't love me while you hate me."

Slowly, deliberately, Kathy Hudson rotated toward Bridget. Her body tensed, her hands clenched into fists by her side as though she couldn't stand hearing her son's name on Bridget's lips.

"Richard's feelings are his own. We haven't discussed you, and I doubt we will," Kathy informed her quietly.

"I could refuse the money," Bridget said, even though she knew such a gesture would mean nothing. Frantically trying to keep Kathy in the room long enough to figure out what would stop this horrible pain for both of them, she added, "I could tell Mr. Madison I didn't want it."

Kathy shook her head sadly. "You just don't

understand." She sighed, her lashes lowering. "The damage is done. She chose you over me. I thought of contesting the will, you know." Kathy raised her eyes, now shining with flinty anger. "But I'm not going to."

"Then you can't be that angry . . ." Bridget said hopefully.

Kathy spoke over her, effectively dashing any hope that a shred of affection was left for her. "But I finally realized that will was put together by a fine attorney. It's airtight. It can't be broken even if I wanted to try. Face it, Bridget. My mother loved you more than she did me. Goodbye, Bridget. I don't think we'll be seeing each other again."

Kathy Hudson turned her back on her mother's nurse and disappeared, seeking refuge from the misery she felt in aloneness. Left behind in the room of glass, the statues and paintings mutely witnessing the moment, Bridget Devlin's heart broke in two.

Chapter Eleven

Aware that Lilly watched from a corner of the room, aware the cab driver had scurried out of the huge house, aware that her body was trembling with shock and despair as though it might shatter at any moment, Bridget fled, running from the glass house. Her breath came in big gulps, yet still she couldn't seem to take in enough air. Every nerve in her body quivered as her senses were sharpened. Each bird that called, every leaf that rustled, every sound from the Bay was heightened to such a point Bridget thought she couldn't stand to listen any longer. How could she take in such beautiful sounds when she still heard so clearly the ugly words she and Kathy Hudson had exchanged.

Clutching at a tree that shaded the walk, Bridget laid her forehead against her hand, vainly attempting to calm herself. She knew she sobbed, she could feel it and hear it, such a foreign sound in this beautiful place. Closing her eyes against the light, Bridget fought back tears of despair and tried not to think of the pain she had caused a woman she cared so much for or the wound Kathy had opened in her heart.

Just as Bridget raised her head, shaking back her heavy hair, two hands fell lightly on her shoulders. Richard turned her into him and wrapped her body safely in his strong arms.

"Richard! Oh, Richard!" She cried, clutching at him, thankful for his strength and his warmth. To be in his arms at that moment was like coming home. He at least was honest enough to show his true feelings. Freely she let her sobs come now, not thinking it strange tears did not accompany them. For a long while she stood that way. Too long it was before she realized that, while Richard held her tenderly and kissed her hair gently, he was speaking no words of love to ease her pain.

With a final, controlled whimper, Bridget stood away from him, wiping at her dry eyes, her lips still trembling, her emerald eyes searching his dark ones for a sign of love. He reached up and cupped her face while she tried to read what was behind his eyes. She saw love for her there, deep down behind the golden brown orbs. But it was a tired affection, unable to shine through his own distress that sprang to the fore. Raising her trembling fingertips to her lips, she backed away a bit though he tried to hold her. Bridget whispered, "Oh, no, Richard. Sure you can't possibly believe as your mother does?"

"Bridget," he whispered gently, taking her fingertips in his hand and away from her stricken face, "I don't believe as my mother does, I only understand what it is she feels. I know how hurt she is. How hurt we all are, including you. This has been a terrible time for my family." His voice was deep and soothing, but the best of it was held back from her, so she received no comfort.

It was Bridget who slid away from his touch. She saw the pain in him when she did this, but she couldn't be near until everything had been said. "But Mrs. Kilburn didn't love me better. Not better than your dear mother. She didn't," Bridget protested, trying so hard to make him understand.

Richard sighed and shook his head. "She loved you dearly, but what she did was like slapping my mother in the face. Her emotions are extremely complicated. In her entire life her mother never denied her anything. Now, with her mother's death, she is denied that final vote of confidence from a dearly-loved parent. Bridget you must understand her feelings, and then you must understand why it is that I have to stay away from you until my mother comes to her senses. I will not be the second person in this family to disappoint her, and I will not run around behind her back like a teenager to see you. We both deserve more than that, Bridget."

He stepped toward her as though to wrap his arms around her again.

"We loved each other, Richard, there's no shame in that." Bridget's eyes were wide in amazement. He was abandoning her pure and simple. Pulling back from him, she felt how easily he turned her loose. Narrowing her eyes, she looked into his. "Sure and maybe I've just hit upon the truth of the matter. *Loved* is past tense, Richard. You cannot find it in your heart to stand by me. You believe her feelings to be truer than mine. Is that it, Richard? You think I stole something from your grandmother, too. Oh, not her money. All of you think I took something more precious from you — you think I took her love away from you."

"Don't be absurd," he said evenly, "I think nothing of the sort. In fact, I'm getting damned tired of everyone telling me how I feel about all this."

"Maybe, then, somebody should be telling you, since you can't seem to work it out yourself."

Bridget turned half a step away but continued to watch him, seeing him in a new light. There was a chink in his perfect armor, and she had unwittingly found it. "There would be no need for secrecy as you suggest, would there, Richard? Our love isn't forbidden, you've only chosen to treat it as though it were, because you're angry, too."

194

Bridget waited but he said nothing in his own defense.

"Sure isn't it a convenient excuse, using your family the way you are. If you were an Irish lad, you'd have the decency to be straight with both your family and me. But you've not got that decency. Education and money have made you beautiful and confident, Richard, but they've also given you the means to run when you want to. Hide behind your money and your sense of righteousness, it will make no difference to me, man. I love you still. I loved you through my pain and my anger. I love you even though you aren't taking me up in your arms and telling me that together we can make your mother understand she's wrong to banish me the way she did. I love you despite all that."

Richard looked toward the forest of landscaping his parents had created around their home as he buried his hands deep in the pockets of his gray slacks. Squinting into the filtered sunlight, he seemed starkly pensive and never more handsome. At length he returned his gaze to Bridget, who stood expectantly in front of him, her pale skin fairer than he had ever seen it. He wanted so to reach out and caress her, to draw his fingers down her cheeks where he swore he could see the tracks of too many tears.

Richard imagined one touch bringing back the lovely blush to her cheeks. He wanted to be magic and make all this doubt and pain go away. But he wasn't magic and neither was she. They were only two people with feet of clay. He was only a man torn between the woman he loved, the pain of his mother and an inexplicable something deep in his own heart. Loving her still, Richard knew it was no longer a pure and whole love he had to give her.

"Bridget, I will only tell you this once," Richard said evenly. "I do love you, with all my heart and my soul, but I will not stand here and take this from you. This is not your precious Ireland. You can no more wish me an honest Irish lad then you can stay the same woman you were. Already you've begun to change. We have to decide if we'll continue to love each other as our situation changes. But don't lay this at my feet, Bridget. In the end it boils down to the fact that your presence in my family's life both enriched us and tore us apart. That's just the way it is. Now you can wait until things calm down so that we can begin seeing each other without this pain between us or you can go on your way. But I will tell you one thing. I have nothing to hide. I will not abandon my mother, and I will not indulge you by creating my own insanity so you can cure it like the Florence Nightingale you are."

Bridget stiffened, her eyes hardening as she looked into his with new understanding. When she spoke again her voice was cold and lifeless.

"I see. Sure I see so well how much I mean

to you. All your fine words can reduce me to one thing or the other. But in your heart you know the truth of the matter. You cling to your mother's pain because you can't face whatever grief you're living with."

He shook his head in disbelief. "You can never know what I feel about this."

Bridget held up her hand. "At one time I would have known, because you were true and honest and satisfied with who we both were. Now you don't know either one of us, and I don't want to know anything more from this family. 'Tis amazed I am that a woman as constant as your grandmother could have been surrounded by such fickle actors. Sure it is money that makes you all run no matter how your mother protests it's love."

"You're talking nonsense," Richard objected, but she laughed, harsh and loud.

"Aye, is it? If that wasn't true you would all love me still, and it would be a true and happy love. You would have listened to all of your grandmother's last words instead of the ones directed to me. Or have you forgotten as well as your mother? Have you forgotten what she said to your mother in her will? She called Kathy the most precious part of her. She talked about how loved and fortunate your mother was. Sure didn't your grandmother ask how could Kathy have anything more from life than she didn't already have?"

Richard bowed his head, hearing again in his mind those exact same words, his heart unable to accept them.

"And you, Richard," she threw out his name as though it was now distasteful to her. "Ah, it's not worth the words. Mine aren't so logical as yours. I just hope someday you have the courage to look into your own heart honestly."

"And you, Bridget?" he asked, looking at her under hooded, steely eyes. "Will you ever understand that your pain is not the only one that matters? Will you ever offer Mother the same assistance you would offer anyone else who hurt? Give her the healing of time, please. You don't know everything in our hearts. Your honesty can just as easily be labeled cruelty. You give yourself too much credit, thinking yours is the only way to look at this situation."

Bridget's shoulders slumped. He said so many true things. But the one misery, the one horrendous hurt she could not bear was that Richard, who had always been so just and able to see both sides of a question, could not do so now. She turned her face away, hearing the cabby honking on the road. It was time to go.

Much as she wanted Richard to stop her, much as she wanted to hear him say the magic words that would wipe away all the hurt, leaving only the deep, never-ending love she still felt for him, Bridget didn't hesitate. She turned on her heel and walked purposefully toward the yellow car. With each step she expected him to come after her, but he stood his ground, certain of his righteousness. When she opened the door and settled herself, when the engine gunned and the car began to move, Bridget lowered her head, burying her face in her hands. In her heart the joy of loving Richard was a memory. Now all Bridget knew was the pain of loving him.

By the time the cab crossed the Golden Gate and drove into the city, Bridget knew where she needed to go and it wasn't home.

A wry laugh slipped through her lips. Home seemed an extremely amusing term at the moment since Mrs. Kilburn's house had been quite effectively put off limits. She should have asked Richard what kind of justice there was in that? One week to get her things out! She would have been due more courtesy if she'd been renting storage space. Kathy hadn't bothered to calculate how long it would take to pack up her heart and move it away from the only home she had known in this country. Kathy Hudson couldn't give her enough time for that project.

"Damn," she muttered, exhausted with the unfairness of the situation, crushed by Richard and Kathy's rejection of her, vexed that what should be the happiest days of her life were being turned into long hours of misery and self-doubt.

Pulling back her shoulders, sniffling a bit, Bridget gave directions to the cabby. Soon she was headed for the one person she knew who would welcome her with open arms. Michael Payne would make her laugh. Michael would make her feel like the luckiest woman in the world. And wasn't that what she was? Lucky in everything but love.

Chapter Twelve

"I think it's marvelous, Bridget. You just have to get used to it! Come on, get into the spirit of things."

"I don't know, Michael," Bridget said with a pout, hands on her hips as she turned in front of the wall of mirror.

Certainly she looked different, right out of a magazine, she did. During the last week everything about her had changed. Michael had taken her in hand quite nicely, thank you. Resisting at first, not wanting her life to change, Bridget had rebelled finally and done exactly as Michael insisted. In many ways Bridget was happy he had. The changes gave her something to do, something to admire in herself, when the last thing she felt was admirable. For how could she be when Richard could cut her off so easily?

"Nothing better for a woman's spirit than a new hair-do," Michael informed her, once again bringing her back from the brink of self-pity.

"But, Michael, I like my hair," she wailed clapping her hands over her shoulder-length tresses as though that would stop him from his devious scheming. It hadn't. She was marched off to one of the most expensive hair dressers in the city. When he was done with her, Michael raved. Though the stylist had hardly done anything but snip here and there, Bridget saw and felt the difference. Her hair was still long yet it seemed fuller, to almost have a life of its own as it feathered around her face and stood in saucy wisps at the crown.

"That's the difference between a seventy-dollar haircut and a ten-dollar one," Michael told her with an authority she had stopped questioning. "It's the same difference as a couturier gown and one off Macy's rack. Come on, I'll show you."

And he did. Her new hair-style bouncing sexily around her face, Bridget followed where he led—straight into Neiman-Marcus. It was Michael who tumbled through the racks of clothes, piling his choices atop the arms of a delighted saleswoman, who dutifully placed them in the dressing room. When Bridget tried to carry her own choices after the lady, Michael plucked them out of her hands, holding them out, hangers clattering, as he discarded each and every one.

"Bridget, no, no, and no. Look at this—small floral print, high-necked, long-sleeved. This is not taking full advantage of your new status in life or that indecently beautiful figure you are so intent on hiding. Look." He came up behind her and held the dress close to her body, his lips just inches from her ear. She could feel the warmth of his breath as he whispered. "Look at your face with that marvelous mass of newly cut hair. You are an exotic creature, always have been. Little flowers and a white collars? Never again."

He kissed the lobe of her ear lightly before sending her off to the dressing room where, much to her chagrin, Bridget had to admit he was right about everything.

The pillar of red cashmere was exactly the right shade to complement, rather than fight with her hair. The sweater dress started at her chin, curling into a high turtleneck before falling to the floor, outlining the high swell of her breasts, dipping into her hand-span waist and hugging her slender hips as it cascaded down to the floor. A thigh-high slit was evident only when she walked. Over it Michael slung an elongated cardigan in red, white, and blue, shot with gold threads. For the opera, he explained, and she would be buying the tickets. For day there were leggings in every conceivable color, blazers for tailored hours in the city, huge sweaters that snaked off her bare shoulders, and oversized blouses for at-home wear. A suit of white suede for the bank. Shoes and boots, purses in leather as soft as a baby's bottom. Huge earrings that peeked out from beneath the feathering of her hair, bracelets that cost more than her da spent in a year on clothes.

Now Michael was at it again, and Bridget had to admit his taste was absolutely perfect. She was beginning to look like the heiress she was. Somewhere inside her was the instinct to carry herself taller, make her movements freer, reach into her wallet more frequently without batting an eye. And it was this last that made her frown at her image in the mirror.

"I don't think you like it," Michael groused as he sat splayed in a tiny little chair in the couture department of Neiman's.

"I do. I love it. But, really, man, where on earth will I wear a silk trench coat with a gold paisley print?"

He shot up, anxious to utilize the opening she had given him. "Anywhere you like, naturally. That's the superb thing about being wealthy. You can do exactly what you want."

Bridget sighed and loosened the belt at her waist. She slid the coat off her shoulders, ignoring the mirror, not wishing to be reminded that, in the black wool jersey cat suit, she looked more sexual, more sensual, more sophisticated than she ever would have imagined she could. Silently she handed the Versace coat to the waiting saleswoman. It was the last item she had chosen to try. The woman disappeared while Bridget joined Michael, collapsing in the chair next to him.

"You don't look like you're having fun, Bridget," Michael complained.

With a wry smile she cast him a sidelong glance. "You are, though. Sure don't I think you enjoy spending my money more than I do."

Bridget pushed herself out of her chair and wandered around in a tight circle, her fingers touching the garments so tastefully displayed in this quiet section of the exclusive store. Stopping, Bridget leaned against a table facing Michael, sharing the place with an emaciated mannequin who seemed perfectly happy wearing her Laura Biagotti mandarin-collared cashmere coat indoors.

"I'm not sure this is fun. I don't know what I need all these things for. Sure I do love the new me for the most part," Bridget reassured him.

The last thing she wanted was for Michael to feel as though she didn't appreciate his help. Without him she would simply have packed up and gone back to Kilmartin to lick her wounds rather than wait until she could return to her home whole and energetic. Without him she would still be nursing a bleeding heart rather than one that seemed to be on the mend. Now, at least, she was burying her hurt and confusion under the excitement of shopping trips, dinners, and meeting Michael's friends, not to mention the preliminary planning she was doing regarding her dreams for Kilmartin. Thankfully everything of immediate concern was taken care of. The long-term care of her heart that still longed for even a word from Richard—that was another matter.

" 'Tis just that I don't think this is exactly what Mrs. Kilburn had in mind when she left me all her money. Don't you imagine she meant for me to do something with it. Something real and vital."

"Yes, she did," Michael told her. "She wanted you to have the kind of life she had. And she wanted you to make your dreams come true. Now if that means sending some of your bucks to Ireland for a new road, then great! Do it! I know you've been drawing up lists and checking them twice. But why go through all that work? Why not send your dad a big check and let him give it to whomever you are supposed to give it to? That's all Mrs. Kilburn wanted, Bridget. She didn't want you to be Mother Teresa. From what I saw when I picked you up for dinner the other night it looked like Mrs. Kilburn enjoyed the finer things just as much as anyone. I think she'd be awfully pleased that you're blowing out a bit, after all those years of watching after her."

"I suppose you're right. 'Tis just that I never thought, after a while, that shopping could become so . . ." Bridget searched for the right word and found it instantly. "Boring. It's almost as though I have to work at it."

"Oh, my God." The back of Michael's hand hit his forehead with a thunk. "I never thought I would hear anyone say anything remotely like that. This is just too incredible. But speaking of work, I think tomorrow, maybe for a few days, I'm going to have to leave you completely on your own. My substitute is feeling as though the pharmacy belongs to her. Some of us do actually have to labor for a living."

"And some of us have to worry about where we'll be living. Or have you forgotten what day tomorrow is?" Bridget collected her purse, silence hanging in the air as though to underscore the sadness of her plans.

"Oh, Bridget, I'm sorry. I did forget. You're moving out of Mrs. Kilburn's house tomorrow. Are you positive you don't need any help?" Michael asked with less enthusiasm than he showed for shopping.

"Of courses not. Your friend was kind enough to leave everything in that apartment, down to an extra tube of toothpaste," Bridget reminded him.

"Sublets can be wonderful," he quipped, peeking in the mirror to check his perfectly knotted tie. "So all you have is your clothes?"

Bridget laughed. "I wouldn't pass that off so lightly with what I've acquired in the past few days. But yes, I can put the cases in a cab. It will take me a while to get settled and comfortable. Then I have an appointment with the man who is going to try and explain the stocks to me. After that I want to stop into a construction site I saw on Divisadero. I'll be needing some advice on my da's house. I tried to find out what kind of house he'd like when I spoke to him the other day, but he just grumbled at me. That man could do with a bit of the gift of gab."

Bridget smiled, thinking of her father's grunts that passed for conversation. With a sigh she brought herself back to the here and now. "Then, Michael, I think I'll take a long walk and figure out what I'm going to do with the rest of my life. Rich or not, I cannot go on as I am."

"No, I suppose you can't," he admitted, putting his hand gently on the small of her back, pausing before he ushered her out of the store. "Bridget, is it getting any better, missing the way things used to be? Missing Richard?"

Bridget looked up at her tall, handsome companion. She leaned into him ever so slightly, holding herself erect as she did so. Michael had become so dear to her, Richard even dearer. Honesty is what she gave to both of them, and it was Michael who accepted it without complaint. She owed him something more than that, so this time her lie was white.

"A bit, Michael. A bit."

"I'm glad."

With a grin he slid his hand around her waist and out they went, walking right by the saleswoman who had assisted Bridget during the past two hours. Neither Michael nor Bridget said a thing to her. It was she who murmured thank you, though they hadn't bought as much as a scarf. For the first time in her life Bridget Devlin walked past a human being without noticing they were there. Michael had been right. The rich did things differently.

Bridget gazed out the window as the car drove on. Michael was in a rare, contemplative mood. This cabby was quite gentle, easing the auto over the hills and around the curves. The ride had been pleasant after their dinner of carpacio and pasta and Bridget didn't really want to see it end as they headed down the road toward Mrs. Kilburn's home.

She trembled with the regret that filled her heart. This would be the last time she would be driven down this road, the last time she would sleep under that roof. Kathy Hudson hadn't called to mend the fences broken between them. The house would be closed with a coldness that belied the warmth and love of so many years. Bridget's eyes fluttered shut. In the few moments it took to bring her and Michael to the front door, she visualized all the wonderful moments she had spent there.

She imagined Richard, seeing him again for the first time, her golden man at the end of the rainbow. She saw herself sitting in front of the fire playing chess with Mrs. Kilburn, talking about Ireland and the dreams they both had for their homeland. Bridget envisioned Kathy flitting about the house as though she owned it, happier then than she was now that it was indeed hers.

When Bridget opened her eyes again, they were dry. Funny how that Irish sentiment, that emotion worn on her sleeve, seemed to be diminishing now that she was learning to live like a lady of means. Perhaps this feeling of emptiness had nothing to do with the money. Perhaps, Bridget realized, she was just now learning that the world was full of things that made one want to cry. But tears could not be shed on every single one of them. By St. Patrick, she had been sheltered all those years, living first with her da in that little village of Kilmartin, then in the nursing dormitory and finally with Mrs. Kilburn. Twenty-seven was high time she put a sharper edge on herself.

"Keep the change," Bridget heard Michael say. It was enough to snap her out of her daydreams. Sliding out of the cab into the dark, Bridget walked across the drive to the lower door, somehow unable to bring herself to climb the steps to the front entrance.

"Thank you," she said as Michael joined her. She adored his insistence on treating her like any other woman he might date, paying for the cab and dinner, never asking her to foot the bill for their evenings out. Much as he liked helping her spend her money, Michael never once led her to believe he wanted anything for himself.

"You're welcome," he said with great courtesy.

Bridget walked up to the door. "Last time." She held up her key for him to see.

"This is it." Michael shrugged.

Bridget inserted the key and heard the familiar click of the lock. For a second she stood there, not wanting to take the key out, not wanting any of this to end.

"You didn't mean it did you, Bridget?" Michael moved up behind her, his hands on her shoulders. He asked the question suddenly and with such urgency it surprised Bridget. She turned toward him, the key sliding out, locking the door again as she did so.

"Mean what?" she asked quietly, taken aback

at his earnestness.

"In the restaurant. That bit about going back to Ireland, going back home. You must know that's impossible."

"And why is that?" she mocked prettily, knowing full well it wasn't the going back that might be impossible, but the returning.

"Because I would miss you so much." Immediately Michael saw the apprehension in her expression. Hurt once, Bridget was one to guard herself against another. "Oh, don't worry. I'm not ready to declare my undying love yet. I'm not a pushover for a gorgeous lady with a ton of money. But—" he shuffled his feet a bit, the porch light catching the golden highlights of his fine hair as he settled against the wall of the house "—I'm not sure I'm ready to have you go before I can figure out exactly what it is we have here, if anything."

"Oh, Michael, dear man," Bridget breathed. "That is so sweet of you."

"Sweet? Hah!" He stuffed his hands in his pockets, his fingers pushing the pleats of his herringbone slacks out so they billowed around his long legs. "Sweet has nothing to do with it. Selfish. I'm selfish. I know it. I admit it. And I don't want you to go."

"But I have to, at least for awhile. I want to see my da. He was so happy for me when I called him with the news. Now I want to go back home and start doing all those things I dreamed about doing someday. Of course, it will take a while to plan. I must learn a bit about what it takes to reconstruct a village and I must talk to a lawyer about returning to America. I don't know that they'll let me back in. It's been forever since my working papers expired, and I've no green card."

Now Michael did laugh, hard and with the utmost delight. "Bridget, me darling," he said in his horrible imitation of a brogue, "you must be joking. No one, and I mean no one, is going to ask you for your green card." He stepped up close to her, wrapping his arms lightly around her so they rested on her hips. Bridget's open face tipped up, and he saw again how marvelously unclouded those emerald eyes of hers were.

"Bridget," he said more softly, "you have so much money you'll never have to work another day in your life. Our esteemed government is only worried about letting people in this country without proper documentation who might end up on welfare or take advantage of our social systems. You they will absolutely love. You're here to spend money, not take it away from a hard-working American lass or lad. Of course you should get your visa in order, but with your money I don't think you'll have to hurry."

"No. Truly, Michael?" Bridget asked, hardly able to believe what he was telling her.

He nodded enthusiastically. "Of course. You can come and go as you please. In fact, you'll probably have some bureaucrat knocking down your door asking you to become a citizen, so they can tax the ever-living daylights out of you on a regular basis. I'm not sure of the specifics, but I'm sure all you'll need is a visitor's visa. Or, if you're thinking of something a bit more permanent, I'm sure immigration will be happy to fix you up with the right documents."

"You aren't joking!" Bridget squealed gleefully as she threw her arms around Michael's neck. His encircled her waist tightly as he twirled her about, astounded that she hadn't known this. "Michael, but this is wonderful."

"I gathered you thought so," he said with a laugh, dancing in the dark cool air with Bridget's feet off the ground, her cheek against his.

"You have no idea," she said softly, arching her back so she could look at him. His face was aglow with delight, his eyes sparkling as he gazed at her. Bridget had never met anyone who took such happiness from the good fortune of others. Moved by his unselfishness, Bridget's fingers wandered into his hair as her lips lowered onto his.

Her first tentative kiss was meant to be one of thanks and relief. Yet soon it became one shared by two passionate people. They had wandered past the sometimes confining bounds of friendship, but were frightened of the wider universe of love. They were caught, straddled between the two relationships, knowing that, indeed, there was something in them that longed to prove deeper and more committed but somehow missed the mark.

Pulling back, Bridget lay her hands on either side of Michael's face. Looking at him she felt a deep sadness. He was offering so much, and had already given more than she expected. But this wasn't right.

"It's not going to work, is it?" Michael whispered. Bridget shook her head sadly. "I don't know what it was about that guy but he sure got under your skin, didn't he?" Bridget nodded, sadly again. "Well, you can't win them all."

Michael set her down gently, his eyes never leaving her face. Bridget could see his disappointment but she also realized it wasn't the kind to last a lifetime.

Then, just as he pulled her close and kissed the tip of her nose in understanding, they were caught in the glare of headlights. Their faces turned in surprise and apprehension toward the car that pulled into the drive, screeching to a stop only a few feet from them.

For a long moment their breaths held. Slowly, very slowly, Michael released Bridget from their embrace while keeping a protective hold about her. Bridget, her arm around his waist, clung to him, her heart frozen as the silence lengthened and they squinted into the brilliant beams. They could see nothing in the glare. Whoever was in the car was taking their own sweet time about making his identity known.

Finally the car door opened, hard shoes hit the pavement and a man emerged, silhouetted in the night. The headlights stayed on.

"Bridget?"

Michael held her as he sensed her knees weaken. He looked from her to the unknown caller. Then he heard her say, so softly it sounded like a moan:

"Richard."

Chapter Thirteen

Richard doused the lights, leaving the three of them to stand in the moonlit darkness, the salty sea breeze blowing through the shocked silence. Startled, Bridget jumped when Richard slammed shut the door of his car, her arm tightening around Michael's waist just before she distanced herself from him. Michael trailed his fingertip over her shoulders, wanting to keep Bridget next to him, yet sensing she didn't want anyone or anything to touch her.

He could almost feel her pulling into herself, steeling herself against any emotional harm. There was nothing he could do to help. Michael focused his attention on Richard Hudson, who was walking toward them, illuminated by degrees as he stepped into the light cast from above the downstairs door.

Michael smirked, almost feeling sorry for the poor guy. Bridget would certainly give him a piece of her mind now and the boot a minute from now. But Michael was wrong. One glance at

Bridget's face told him there were not going to be any Irish fireworks in the California night. In fact, as far as Michael Payne was concerned, it looked like the evening was over. Bridget, despite her defensive stance, only had eyes for Richard Hudson.

"Bridget I . . ." Richard began, his eyes sliding to Michael, ". . . I didn't know you'd be busy."

"It would be hard for you to know," Bridget answered, a slight quaver in her voice. "It's been a while since we've spoken. Sure and the last time we did speak I believed it was our last?"

Michael rolled his eyes. Bridget should have let him have it. Instead, she sounded like she was soothing Richard's hurt feelings.

"Bridget?" Michael said under his breath, reminding her he existed.

"Oh, I'm so sorry. Michael Payne. Richard Hudson." The men nodded. Bridget never took her eyes from Richard so she didn't see the hurt in Michael's.

"I suppose I'd better come back tomorrow," Richard suggested, hoping Michael would take the hint and leave.

"I won't be here tomorrow." Bridget raised her chin proudly as though she hadn't a care in the world, but Michael was close enough to see that it was trembling.

"What do you mean you aren't going to be here?" Richard asked harshly. "Where are you going?"

Michael stepped in, almost between them.

"Bridget, you don't have to tell him. He should have known, anyway. It just shows how little he cares about you." Turning to Richard, Michael's eyes glittered with disdain. "Why don't you go home and ask your mother, since it's all her doing."

"Excuse me," Richard moved forward, his hand touching Michael's sleeve as if to push him away. Michael didn't budge, so Richard's voice lowered threateningly. "I think that's for the lady to tell me. I don't know who you are, but if Bridget wants me to know where she's going, then I don't see that you have much to say about it. And you don't have any right to talk about my family, especially with that tone."

Michael lowered his eyes, looking at Richard's hand with contempt. Though Michael was taller, Richard was by far the stronger. Even in the dim light Bridget could see the flex of his muscles as he tensed for the confrontation. Thankfully there was none. Richard let his hand drop away, stepping back as if baffled, his eyes searching Bridget's face for a clue regarding her feelings for this man. She raised her hand ever so slightly toward Richard, but Michael stood his ground resolutely, unwilling to move until he had said his peace.

"I have a say in what goes on here because I helped Bridget find a place to live after your mother decided to throw her out. Your *mother*," Michael drew out the word derisively, "didn't even have the courtesy to tell her to her face. Some artistic census taker was sent in to drop the bomb without even a how-do-you-do. I took up the slack because the people Bridget depended on let her down. I think that gives me a right to say anything I want, don't you?"

"Michael!" Bridget intervened, her hand sliding around his wrist. She could feel his tension and appreciated his attempt to protect her. Yet no matter how immeasurable her hurt, she could not have Michael assume it for her. Deep inside she felt a swelling of emotion and wondered whether this was a rise of love or simply gratitude for his friendship. Looking to Richard, Bridget realized that, indeed, he had no idea about her eviction. Kathy had spoken truly when she said that Bridget was not discussed in the Hudson house.

"Bridget, please, we have to talk," Richard insisted, his voice tight, his eyes trying to hold hers so that his gaze alone might banish Michael Payne. "I'm sorry. I didn't know. Otherwise, I would have stopped it. This is your home. It always has been."

"Think you might have taken a bit of time to find out what was going on with her?" Michael interrupted, unwilling to let Richard attempt to make amends.

"Michael, please. Stop," Bridget begged softly. He turned his eyes on her. She looked earnestly into his. "Please."

Michael lifted a hand to her face knowing what she wanted, knowing he must oblige, but hardly able to bear the accommodation.

"You'll be all right?" he asked. She nodded, her eyes closing for emphasis before she smiled her assent wanly. "Okay. But one step out of line from this guy, and I expect you to call. You don't have to take anything from him anymore."

"I promise. I promise on St. Patrick's staff." She reassured him with a peck on the cheek before she addressed Richard. "We do have some things we must sort out."

"I'll go, then," Michael growled, looking Richard up and down, angered that Bridget would want to subject herself to this guy's special brand of selfishness.

"Let me call you a cab," Bridget offered, aware that Richard had yet to take his eyes off her. She felt an intensity from him she had never experienced before, as though he was taking her apart and assessing her inch by inch. Bridget had forgotten she had changed. In her eyes, the new, sleek version of her old self was the one that had always existed. But to Richard she looked unique, almost frightening, in her perfection. He couldn't help but search for the old Bridget, the one who at least gave the appearance of vulnerability. Where was the Bridget who flowed so easily and quietly into his life and became a part of it, rather than this woman who stood formidably on her own?

Michael glanced quickly at Bridget and lowered his voice, "That's okay. The walk to find one will do me good. But promise me that you're not going to do anything stupid."

"Sure and aren't you the one to be talking about stupid, the man who throws shoes into the Bay." Bridget teased him uncomfortably, whispering as she tried to make light of the situation. The concern in Michael's eyes cut her short. She sighed and took both his hands in hers. "I promise, I won't."

"Thank you. When will I see you?"

Bridget looked over her shoulder. Richard finally averted his eyes as he judiciously examined the paving of the drive. Facing Michael again, she lifted her shoulders in a little apologetic movement.

"Okay. I won't push. Just be careful," he warned.

Truly surprised, Bridget raised her eyebrows. "Of what, may I ask? Richard would never hurt me."

"Of course not," Michael drawled sarcastically. "Just like your friend Kathy Hudson wouldn't. Just like he hasn't hurt you with his silence." Without missing a beat, Michael squeezed her hands, pivoted on his heel and walked down the drive leaving Bridget and Richard alone.

Collecting herself as best she could, Bridget watched him disappear into the night. Key still in hand, she walked to the door. Richard followed in silence. Once again Bridget tried to insert it into the lock. Under Richard's unnerving gaze she missed the jagged hole.

She could have blamed her ineptitude on the dim light from above, her fatigue, the embarrassment of Richard finding her in Michael's arms. Instead, she admitted the truth. The fault for her bungling lay squarely on Richard's shoulders. He stood too close. She could smell the clean scent of his after-shave and hear the soft cadence of his breathing.

They stood so closely Richard was aware of the scent of coffee and her perfume mingling with the cool night air. From the corner of her eye, Bridget could see Richard's hand balled into a fist and shoved deep into his pocket. She could sense his anxiety, confusion, and desire as they churned in his mind and brought his body to the breaking point of need. And of all these emotions Bridget knew it was the confusion that must pain him the most. Her dear man who loved — no needed — to control his world must hate the uncertainty of this situation.

Indeed, it was turmoil Richard Hudson felt, standing so close to this woman who had claimed not only his heart but his soul. To touch her would be excruciating, to hold her would be unthinkable until it was only love he felt and not anger or resentment. Yet if she didn't move, Richard knew he couldn't be responsible for what might happen. She had turned his life upside down, first with her good cheer and innocence, then with her surprising inheritance, and now there was another part of the equation. It was this last that drove him to distraction.

His body tensed with anticipation. Unsure if it was confrontation or sweet welcome that awaited him, he took a few hard steps away from her. Realizing he could wait no longer, he spun back toward her.

"Who in the hell was that man, Bridget? He acted like you were his personal property."

Bridget whirled on him, the key forgotten, entry denied them as if Mrs. Kilburn's spirit refused such anger in her house.

"Sure and what business is it of yours, Richard Hudson? I wouldn't have thought you cared whether I went with an alley cat. In fact, it was my distinct impression you didn't care whether I lived or died. I believe you made it quite clear your affections lay with your mother."

"You know that's not true," Richard shot back, stepping farther away from the door, away from her. The desire to reach out and grab her, shake her until she thought of nothing but him was intense. He put a hand to his forehead as though to clear his mind. Never in his life had he felt such rage of emotions. It unnerved him. It frightened him. Desperately he controlled himself. He was a lawyer, used to clear thinking. He was an educated man, aware that emotional response was never the answer to a problem. Carefully he whispered, "I never said anything of the sort."

Bridget followed him, her low heels clicking on the brick drive, baiting him because her hurt had been held inside too long. It needed, no demanded, a voice. Now she would give it one.

"No, of course you didn't, boyo. Easy enough

just to beg the question. Last we saw of each other you just stood there and let me break in two from the pain of loving you. Not a word did you offer, not a hand did you hold out, not even a simple embrace of understanding did you offer me. Instead, you gave me logical reasons why I should be the one to slink away with my tail between my legs like the village dog."

Bridget's chest rose and fell with the effort of anger. Richard could see the firm outline of her breasts, the length of her legs, so shapely, encased in pants that fit like a second skin. In the night, under the moon, her angora sweater looked like the haze around the north star. The white fluff had slipped off her shoulder, baring the skin Richard so longed to touch. But it was the flush in her cheek, the flashing of her eyes that both shamed him and excited him as she advanced.

"Let me tell you something, Mr. Hudson. I loved you and you gave me nothing in return because you think I stole something from your mother. Well, here is the reality of it, Richard. Your grandmother's money meant nothing to me. It was your love that made me rich. You and Kathy could have had every last cent back. Do you understand that? But you killed my heart and all the feeling in it, so now your grandmother's bequest is all I have. Her money and my friend, Michael."

Richard flung himself away, knowing the passion he felt could hardly be contained any longer.

But Bridget lunged for him, grasping his arm. If he wouldn't face her, then she would face him. Still clinging to him, she brought herself in front and dug her fingers into his arms with both her hands now, forcing him to look at her.

"It was Michael that made me feel the happiness of my good fortune. Sure it was he who celebrated the wonderful life your grandmother led by toasting the thoughtfulness of her legacy. What a wonderful woman, Michael said, to leave everyone just what they needed to live as they should. That's what my friend said."

Richard tried to push past her. Bridget moved back a few steps straining to keep him from leaving. She would have no more of this indecision. He had sought her out. He had opened the wounds again. She wouldn't let him pour salt on them by popping in and out of her life as he wished. She was an Irish woman, strong in her love and strong in her righteousness. Richard could have had the first. Since he threw it away she would give him the second.

"And my friend, Michael saw to it that I didn't wallow in my self-pity. He made sure I didn't waste my mourning on the likes of you. He showed me that I had grieved and shed my tears for the one who deserved it, Richard. Michael showed me how to live without you."

"Oh, I see." Richard drawled knowingly, stopping his struggle against her surprisingly strong hold. His eyes narrowed, throwing a hard mean light her way. "Now it's clear, Bridget. This wonderful man, Michael, has been showing you how to live. New hair," Richard flipped her long tresses, hardly able to keep from burying his hands in the silky mass, "and the clothes. Clothes that you would never have worn in a hundred years except for him. He showed you a new Bridget Devlin did he?"

"Yes, he did. He showed me I could be more than I was," Bridget answered, her anger faltering under the chill of his words.

"Did he show you how to make love the way the fast crowd does, Bridget? Is that what your new apartment is for? And just how much did you have to pay him to create the new you, to pay court to you? Just how much of Grandmother's money did it take . . ."

Bridget, hardly knowing what she did, raised her hand open-palmed. Horrified, she realized that she wanted to hurt him for all his words—all his hateful, rational, mean words, all his words that weren't of love. Slowly, lamentably, she realized she wanted a physical outlet for her anger, to stop his terrible accusations. Ashamed they had come to this, Bridget buried her face in her hands and turned away.

"Oh, my God, Richard. How could you think such a thing? How could we do this?" Lowering her hands, refusing to look back at him, her body trembling, Bridget walked back to the door. "Go home, Richard. Go home and forget about me and what we had."

"I can't," he whispered. It was a tortured

sound. Bridget stopped, unable to move forward. She felt him behind her. He had taken a step closer but stopped before he came alongside of her. The air between them vibrated with their unresolved passion. "I'm so sorry, Bridget, for everything. My heart is breaking, and I don't know what to do about any of this anymore."

Suddenly Bridget heard only the anguish beneath the words. Richard had lashed out because she had, because both of them hurt and could not heal without the other. An instant in Brandon Madison's office had changed them. Both wished that instant gone from their lives — an impossibility, so they must learn from it, live with it, if they could.

Bridget waited, knowing there would be more. Richard, had isolated himself, trying to figure out what it was he felt, wondering how he could regain what was lost. In the same way, Bridget had thrown herself into a whirlwind of shopping and dinners and exploration of a new friendship. Now it was time to rest and breathe deeply. They needed to stop running from their feelings and each other.

Bridget walked back to the door, this time turning the key with ease, and held it open for him. Without a word, Richard moved into the darkened kitchen past her, his eyes straight ahead as he walked toward the living room. In the foyer he stopped. Bridget had followed him and leaned against the wall watching.

The entrance was dimly lighted, the illumination evident only in the halftones of gray that played across his face. Richard turned. He held out his hands like a mendicant as his voice softened.

"I apologize for what my mother has done. But that's not why I'm here. You were right the other day. I wasn't being honest. For the first time in my life I was afraid of the truth. I've never had to fear the truth because my way has always been right. Can't you see that? The world I thought I had conquered I haven't even seen. I may have been places, but, in reality, I never stepped out of the confines of my safe world. My parents' admiration, my wealth, my grandmother's love surrounded me and made a marvelous haven that I ruled. No one ever questioned my role in that world. I'm sorry for the way I feel, Bridget." The utter desperation in his voice pierced her.

"And how is it that you feel, Richard?" Bridget murmured, her voice quavering but her head held high, as she waited for the answer. Nothing he could say to her would be worse than the silence she had endured over the last weeks. Even Richard's anger was welcome because she was with him to hear it.

"I feel betrayed, Bridget," he moaned, ashamed to have said the word to her.

She slumped against the wall, defeated. "I didn't betray you."

"I know that." Wearily, half turning, his hands moving as if searching for something to hit or hold on to, Richard struggled to find the right words to tell her about the turmoil inside him. "I know that. I feel betrayed by Grandmother, and it makes it worse because she chose you as her instrument."

"No." Bridget moved a step forward, but he stopped her with a look and a word.

"Please, don't. Not until I try to explain. It's so hard to sort through. Before this, before Brandon read the will, everything was so clear to me." He raised his eyes, taking a deep breath as though what he saw was a vision of utter happiness. "I had the world on a string, Bridget. I was smart. I was confident. I loved you. And, most importantly, I was loved. Good Lord, I was so secure in the love my family had for me, so exhilarated by the new dimensions of love I found with you, that I believed nothing would ever hurt me. Then there was Grandmother's death, and I understood what sorrow was. Then there was the will, and I felt pain because she had always made me believe my mother and I were the most important people in the world to *her*. So you see, it's not the money. Heaven knows I have plenty of that. It's that she put an outsider in the same position as me. In fact, she raised you above me by thinking of you first and last in her will. I've told myself my feelings aren't logical, but I don't think any amount of logic can make me feel differently. I'm hurt and, yes, I'm angry that the rules of family and loving have changed."

His dark eyes snapped back toward her. Happiness was fleeting, and he'd been left with the image of it, but he wanted more; Richard wanted to recapture it.

"Aye, you were loved, Richard, by all of us. You still are." Bridget told him softly. "And, yes, you loved me. I felt it every time we were together, in every look and every touch, with every word you spoke. So, tell me, my darling man, what has changed? If we were to wed, you would share your grandmother's inheritance. But that isn't the way you want it to be.

"You could only be satisfied if you controlled my importance within your family. You could love me and bring me into the family, but your grandmother was wrong to force me into it. Is that what you're saying, Richard? The way you talk, it sounds as if I am only acceptable to you if you choose when and where and how I become a part of your life. I can only be loved if I must rely on you for my worldly wealth. Being independent through your grandmother's inheritance, you are no longer able to love me? Is that what's changed?"

Richard shook his head, his fine features looking ever more beautiful as he moved over to the stairs and sat down heavily, his arms on his knees, his hands dangling between his legs in frustration.

"Loving you is, perhaps, the only thing that hasn't changed. But what good is loving you if I no longer know who I am? Would you want a man who has suddenly realized everything he be-

230

lieved about himself isn't real?"

"Stop, Richard." Bridget was in front of him in three paces. She slid to her knees, daring to put her hands on either side of him, capturing him in a cage of adoration and love. "Stop it this instant. I won't have it. You're talking nonsense."

"Am I?" He raised tortured eyes to her as though that would send her away, but she remained. "Think about it, Bridget. There must have been some way I disappointed my grandmother. It's as though, after all these years, I wasn't enough for her. It's as though you were a missing piece to make this family whole, and I just can't accept that. We were whole and happy before. You were a wonderful addition to that family but, Bridget, *I* should have made you part of the family. With the stroke of a pen my grandmother took away my standing, my place in line and raised you above me. That hurts, Bridget. It makes me question my very existence." Richard closed his eyes and continued.

"You know how children go through that stage where they wonder if they're adopted? They rummage through all the old pictures making sure there's one of their mom holding a little baby. When they find it they can sleep again. It's a fear lots of kids have. But you know, I never once even thought about it. I never searched for the pictures." His eyes opened again and there were tears behind them. "But Grandmother decided to send me on that search. Now I have to find the pictures of my life and wonder if maybe I wasn't as much a part of her life as I thought."

"Richard, you are more wrong than you know," Bridget assured him quickly, unwilling to let his thoughts run away with him. Her heart was breaking as she watched him struggle with these new emotions of doubt and distrust. "Just as your mother was wrong to feel she wasn't loved. Your grandmother adored you. She only wanted you to earn your place in this world. In her heart you were first always."

Bridget tipped her head, daring now to put a small smile on her lips as she saw his eyes soften, watched some of the pain go out of them. Bridget pressed her advantage, her voice lowering, soothing, lulling him to believe.

"Ah, Richard. Your grandmother loved you and she loved your mother and she loved me. But I was always one step away from that true and perfect love because I wasn't blood. But your grandmother had another love, one she never forgot though she was away from it for most of her life. It was Ireland, Richard. I'm just an instrument to help her act on that love. She chose me to bestow her legacy on that country. Don't you see that? I understand how hurt you both are, now that you've said what's on your mind. It's no sin to feel this way. You can be angry and hurt and wonder why I've got the strings of such a big purse. But, Richard, to doubt yourself? How can this have happened to you? The Richard of old would simply have said this is they way things are, let's deal with them. The Richard I loved had

232

the world by the tail and knew exactly what he wanted and where he was going. The old Richard would have accepted his grandmother's decision because he respected her and loved her.

"We can't undo things. They are as they are. There is nothing you can do about what has happened, so can't we learn to live with it? Your mother nursing her pain and striking out at me isn't going to bring back your grandmother to explain what was in her deepest heart. You not loving me or yourself isn't going to change things."

"I don't want anything changed, Bridget," Richard sighed in exasperation. "I want everything as it was. A week ago our world was secure. Now it's shattered. My mother feels abandoned. You want me to love you as though nothing has happened, as though you are still that sweet, confident woman who nursed Grandmother. But you're no more she than I am the man with the golden touch. How can we go on loving the way we did?"

"Richard! Loving one another is the answer. Don't you see how much I care about you? Don't you see that loving can make all the difference in the world? I could make that hurt go away. Not with your grandmother's money but with my own dear affection for you, Richard. I could make a difference because no matter how our lives went, each day brings new and different things into our lives."

"Not like this it wouldn't," Richard said and Bridget knew he was right. If they could weather the pain Mrs. Kilburn's bequest had brought, nothing would threaten them again.

Richard gazed into Bridget's hopeful, adoring eyes, knowing he could lose himself in them. If he looked hard, he saw himself as she did; a man to love and respect. Perhaps with Bridget, loving her as he did, he could put his hurt away, pack it up and tie the box tight. In time the questions that had plagued him since the reading of Maura Kilburn's will would be forgotten. Tonight, in the silence of his grandmother's home, surrounded by the things she loved, Richard felt once again the fondness she had for him. Over and over again Maura Kilburn had demonstrated her love, without asking anything in return. For that minute of remembrance, Richard stopped questioning and accepted the love being offered to him now, in this house where it had always been given so freely.

With both hands he cupped Bridget's face and studied it. She didn't move, didn't blink, knowing that in the next instant Richard would decide which controlled his heart—love for her or anguish over what he believed was his grandmother's betrayal. Bridget held her breath, hoping the beating of her heart would not disturb him, praying he could look inside her and see how much she cared. Silently she begged him to understand that nothing meant more than her love.

Bridget felt his hands tighten as they slid into her hair, slipping slowly down her neck until his fingers rested lightly at her throat. Gently Richard massaged her velvety flesh before allowing his palms to roam over her shoulders then down her back, fingers spread wide as if probing the boundaries of her; farther to encircle her waist, almost crushing the breath out of her before deciding, before acknowledging, what he had really known all along.

Pulling her into him, Richard overwhelmed Bridget. He lowered his mouth to hers, devouring her lips, forcing them open with a power he had never felt before, tasting her in a way he had never done before. Bridget grasped him about the neck violently, pushing her body into his, as the long-dormant flame now blazed fiercely in them both.

They were falling, falling to the floor. Ever so gently they rolled over each other, murmuring and biting and touching, each unable to get enough of the other. Skin was caressed and marveled at. Their hearts bonded as their minds pushed every real and imagined hurt away, they banished everything but their desire.

Richard's mouth was on Bridget's shoulders as his hands ripped her fine new clothes away. His lips slid over the swell of her breasts as she writhed beneath him, begging him not to stop. His hands were everywhere, then nowhere. His fingers were feathers falling indiscriminately against her naked body before they became tools of power clutching her. He caressed her until Bridget's mind had nowhere to turn but toward oblivion, and only her body's pleasure became real and urgent.

Then, just before he took her, just before Richard gave her the love she so desperately desired, he looked at her with such long and searching scrutiny Bridget thought she would cry out from her deprivation. His lips opened and he breathed her name, but she silenced him, guiding him into her as though they had been lovers for years rather than the first and only lovers that night.

Richard acquiesced, bowing to her demands, her warmth overwhelming as he loved her gently yet surely. Gone were the frantic demons that at once drew him away from her even as they threw him back, making him unable to live without her.

And when it was over, when they lay in each other's arms, the only sound in the house of Maura Kilburn their exhausted, satisfied breathing, Bridget Devlin gathered Richard Hudson to her and whispered "I love you" in a manner he had never heard before. Those few words were so heartfelt, so magical, he closed his eyes and pulled her tighter against his broad chest so she couldn't whisper them any longer.

Chapter Fourteen

From high above the bed in Bridget's apartment, through a window shaped like an icicle, a ray of silver-gray light fell gently across Richard's bare shoulder. Unable to help herself, Bridget reached out and touched it, wondering if indeed his shoulder was warmer for it. Lightly her finger traced the indistinct outline of the shadowed muscle.

She had propped herself on her other arm, her long hair falling over the hand under her head. Naked, too, Bridget stretched her legs carefully before curling them toward Richard, taking in just a bit of the warmth that radiated from his sprawling body half-hidden under the huge down comforter.

In his rest Richard moved, mumbled, then slumbered deeply again. Gently Bridget laid her hand fully on his arm, closed her eyes as though only that could make her fully appreciate the feel of him, then gently she lay back trying to wait patiently for him to awaken. She turned her head once so she could watch the rise and fall of his back as he breathed. Reluctantly, realizing how early the hour was, Bridget closed her eyes, too, and tried to sleep. But the sandman was toying with her. He had given all his magic dust to Richard, and she was forced to both wakefulness and thought.

Languidly her mind roamed over the past days and weeks. A month was gone now since that night in Maura Kilburn's house. A month of tentative talking, of passionate lovemaking, of waking to each other until finally neither one mentioned Bridget's inheritance. A month of joy. Yes, joy, Bridget told herself. She would entertain no other thoughts, she would accept no other conclusion.

Even when Richard was lost in thought, studying her as though with a heavy heart, Bridget was able to rationalize the bit of sadness in his eyes. He had been working hard, teaching her so many things about investments, about living in his world. Richard, she assumed, was exhausted from the negotiations he had entered into with a law firm interested in taking him on as a partner. He was determined that the final closing of his home be done properly. Once more Richard was in command of his universe, and Bridget put off any unusual exhaustion to the many facets he attended to in his life. Never did Bridget consider that his fatigue sprang from a still-saddened soul. She refused to see questions in his thoughtful gaze. Instead Bridget banished that odd melancholy look with a kiss or a hug or a word whispered in his ear.

And she surprised him. There on the end of the bed was her first present to her lover. A fabulously luxurious black robe with a crest of gold above the breast. He loved it. She adored being pulled into his lap, the robe wrapping about both their naked bodies, their hair smelling fresh from their showers. Bridget simply adored everything about Richard Hudson, and she would not let him be sad or angry or uncertain—ever. Sure wasn't all that pain ebbing away the more they were together, the more she loved him? Bridget knew she cared enough to banish it completely.

Not wanting to think of the remnant of heartache that might still haunt her lover, Bridget rolled into him. Sleep wouldn't come, the morning was getting older and the hour not so early any longer. Sweetly she curled her naked body around his, pressing her breasts into his back, winding her arms around him so her fingers could run down his marvelous chest, tease his flat, hard stomach.

Caught as he was, halfway between sleep and arousal, Richard stirred, unsure if he should smile and give in or swat Bridget's busy hands away. The decision was not terribly difficult. Richard, his eyes still closed, captured her roaming fingers in his own large hand, held them briefly to his chest before bringing them to his lips for a kiss. Finally he rolled over, warm and inviting as he slipped one arm under her shoulders, pulling Bridget toward him.

"Umm," he grumbled, nuzzling into her so his prickly beard rubbed against the cheek she raised for a kiss.

"Sure is that any way to say good morning?" Bridget whispered, completely satisfied just with his presence, having no need of his words.

"Umm," Richard mumbled again. This time Bridget laughed outright.

" 'Tis manners we'll have to be teaching you, my love. This is the way you wish me good morning. With a small kiss, just here," she pecked his cheek. "And here—" her lips briefly touched the tip of his nose "—and here." They found their way to his lips where Bridget kissed him, then leaned away as though to inspect her handiwork, then bent to peck him again. But Richard had enough. The sandman relinquished his hold. Fully awake, completely able to take advantage of the situation Bridget presented, Richard smiled wickedly.

Deftly he pulled her into him, easing her down onto him as he kissed her properly. Bridget needed no invitation. She was ready to love him grandly, passionately or gently, as she would be ready every morning or evening for the rest of their lives.

Understanding that the gray light in the

whitewashed room set the mood for gentle loving, Bridget abandoned her teasing and laughter. A whisper from the bed springs, a rustle as the sheets were thrown away, a sigh from her slightly parted lips were the only sounds that could be heard in the silence that filled the room to bursting.

With one final gesture that brought total satisfaction to them both, Bridget and Richard arched against each other before sinking into the womb of the feather bed beneath them. For a long while they lay quietly, Bridget stroking Richard's face, his hands clasping the gentle swell of her hip. It was Richard who spoke first.

"We have to get up one of these days," he murmured.

"Umm," Bridget answered, then giggled.

"Didn't we just go through this?" He pulled his head back and looked at her testily. But Bridget knew it was a ruse, and she kissed him once again.

Richard smiled, shaking his head slightly on the pillow. With a contented sigh he rolled to his back, his arm loosely around Bridget still. She gave no thought but let her body follow his. She lay over him, her hair spilling over his chest. Absentmindedly Richard's hand stroked and twirled her lovely copper tresses.

He knew he must speak and searched for words. If he wasn't looking at Bridget, then he had to talk to her. In all these weeks Richard found those were the two things that continued to keep his doubts at bay. Hearing her voice, losing himself in her green eyes, admiring her lithe figure or watching her cook dinner, that was what kept his heart filled with love, his mind empty of confusion.

"We've got to meet Jerry today," Richard reminded her. Bridget moved petulantly into him.

"Not today. Sure I'm tired of hearing about rates of return," Bridget complained, knowing full well she would be sitting in the stock broker's office exactly at two just as they planned. But she was frustrated by theory, tired of seeing her money as an entry on paper. Bridget wanted action, and it was time she took a hand in getting it. "Today I think we ought to really be talking to that nice man from the construction company. The one who was going to start pulling together some preliminary figures on building a schoolhouse in Kilmartin. He also said paving the streets wouldn't be a problem at all. A simple job."

"Bridget, you can't possibly think that man can do what he says. I'm amazed you even spoke to him in this much detail."

Richard slid out of bed and into his robe. Glancing behind him, he saw Bridget leaning her chin on her two balled-up fists. She looked utterly fabulous with the billow of the feather bed beneath her, the cloud of comforter lying

242

across the small of her back, and the swell of her breasts just visible between her crooked arms. He shook his head. Love was a misery. Why on earth she had to be so stubborn was beyond him. She was bounding headlong into this building thing like a bull in a china shop. Richard looked away, feeling that unreasonable peevishness rising again. If only she would listen to him.

"Of course I believe him," Bridget informed Richard, unaware of his exasperation. "Sure wasn't he the one that built that beautiful building just down on Divisadero? Don't you think he isn't a wonder when it comes to making things work?"

"Bridget, listen to me," Richard said patiently, controlling his annoyance as he sat on the edge of the bed. "It's impossible for him to give you a clear idea of what anything is going to cost in Ireland. You have to remember, he's going to estimate based on labor and materials cost in the United States. He hasn't got a clue what labor and materials will run in Kilmartin. Nor does he know anything about permits, geology or any number of things over there. He's out to make a big buck, and he's going to make it from you. Either take him over there to check things out or contact someone in Ireland. But don't do this backward. In fact, I don't think you should be worrying about any big projects right now."

"But I wanted this all to be a surprise to the

village. I want to get there ready to build, not tip my hand by dragging a contractor over there with me. 'Twon't be much of a surprise if I have to do all the preliminary work once I get there. I want to spread the plans out in front of my da and the village and show them what wonderful things we can do now." Bridget flipped her hair over her shoulder and snuggled deeper in the warm bed, thoroughly pleased with her plan.

"But you're going about it all wrong. It will cost you a fortune," Richard cried, exasperated.

"Sure isn't that what I have?" she asked teasingly.

To her surprise, Richard pushed himself off the bed, expelling a frustrated sigh. Bridget pulled the covers over her naked breasts as she sat up to watch him.

"You're right," he said curtly, "that's exactly what you have. A fortune. And you have grandmother's express desire that you do something wonderful in Ireland. You have everything you need. You certainly don't need my advice."

Swiftly Bridget reached out as he rounded the bed. "But I do, darlin'. That's exactly what I need. I just want to begin something, the way it was intended, if you know what I mean. I get so tired of hearing about all these investments and such, Richard."

"I know you do, honey," he answered, his eyes softening, his fingers touching her chin briefly. How very simple all this would have been if his grandmother had entrusted him with her fortune. He would have given Bridget anything she wanted for her homeland. As it was he had no control over her wheeling and dealing. She would run Maura Kilburn's fortune into the ground — Irish ground at that.

"I know this is confusing. But you've got to remember that Grandmother had her money invested and diversified for a reason. I don't think she ever meant for you to completely liquidate. If you begin to understand how that money is working for you, then you can go ahead with your plans and do something that will really make an impact. But first, try to understand, you do have limitations."

"But I don't," Bridget rejoined.

"But you do," he said sweetly, chucking her under the chin, "and so do I. I've got a few errands to run first thing, then an appointment with my tailor at ten. I'll be back to get you and we'll head off to Jerry's by two. Bridget, you're going to have to take my word for it. Money will work for you, but you have to pay attention to the rules."

Moments later Bridget heard the shower. Peevishly she flopped back into bed wishing Richard had a bit more of Michael's enthusiasm for the happiness money could bring and Michael a bit more of Richard's reserve. If she could put them both together, she'd have the perfect man.

Bridget was long over her pout by the time Richard, showered and shaved, reappeared looking absolutely wonderful. Over his shoulder he had slung his gray suit with the pale blue pinstripe.

"Will this be all right for the party at the gallery tonight?" he asked.

Bridget eyed him carefully, looking for any sound of sarcasm, any sign of antagonism. Finding none and appreciating Richard's effort to please her by attending Jennifer's party, knowing it was Michael who had invited them, Bridget smiled.

"Sure won't you be the most handsome man there." She grinned.

"Maybe the most handsome, but I doubt the best dressed," Richard drawled. "Michael has that honor hands down. See you later, sweetheart." He headed toward the door, his mind obviously not with her any longer. He seemed anxious to be away and start his day.

Bridget stopped him. "Richard?"

"Yes?"

"I just wanted to thank you. I know Michael isn't your favorite person, but you've been very nice about him."

Richard remained silent, looking at Bridget a moment, thinking how lovely she was, tousled from sleep and lovemaking. She was almost too beautiful with her new hairdo and her long, polshed nails. In a way he wished she would cut those nails and buff them to their natural sheen. That had been one of the things he found so endearing about her before . . . well, before everything. He shook his head. Bridget's nails looked beautiful, polished or not. He had to stop zeroing in on what had changed about her and concentrate on what remained the same. She had, after all, done him the courtesy of loving him with energy and openness. But then Bridget was an exceptional woman. She was also the one who had two million reasons to feel confident. Richard smiled at her.

"I'm glad you've got a friend, Bridget. I never realized how lonely you must have been at times with grandmother."

Bridget shook her head. "That's not what I meant. Sure I only meant I'm pleased not to give up a friendship because I love you so much."

"I'd never ask you to do that. I know how hard it is to give up something you believe in or someone you care about. Now," he insisted, "I've got to get out of here."

"One more kiss," she begged with a pretty grin.

"That, my darling, is not a problem."

He swooped down on her, his lips covering hers for a blissful instant before he was out of the room. A few minutes later Bridget heard the front door close. Now she had two choices. She could snuggle back in bed and hope she woke up at a reasonable time, or she could get up shower and begin the day. Finally deciding to do what she had never done before in her life, Bridget went back to sleep not caring a fig when she woke up.

Richard Hudson, by contrast, was fully awake and anxious to be done with what lay ahead of him. During the short drive to the marina, he held on to the vision of Bridget lying in bed, gazing at him with such love. Perhaps it was a more worldly look now, a more cosmopolitan woman who gave it, but the love was true and it was an emotion he both needed and wanted only from her. Consciously he called up his feelings for her. He could no more leave her than he could cut off his arm, especially now that Maura Kilburn had elevated Bridget to membership in the Hudson clan by virtue of her will. Deftly he parked the Porsche, locked it and went to the café where his mother waited as she had every Saturday for the past month. All the cajoling in the world could not get her to set foot in the apartment he and Bridget now shared. All the logical arguments could not assuage her anger. Kathy Hudson had made it clear that Richard was not to mention Bridget Devlin's name. And he hadn't. But that was all about to change.

Pushing through the glass door, Richard heard the tinkle of the bells that announced his arrival. The two other patrons didn't bother to glance his way. Marcia, the Saturday waitress, smiled and cocked her head.

"Morning, Mr. Hudson. The usual?"

"Just coffee, thanks," Richard said, giving her a grateful smile and going right to his mother's table.

"I was beginning to think you weren't coming." Kathy said, raising her cheek for a kiss. Richard obliged before settling himself on the chintz-covered chair to her left.

"I was late getting up."

"We'll have to get you a better alarm," Kathy teased.

"The alarm worked just fine, Mom," Richard said, hoping this might be the opening for their conversation. Perhaps she might just mention Bridget. But his hopes were dashed in the next second.

"Then it's time you get back to work, if you've become so used to sleeping in that you ignore your alarm," Kathy chattered, her smile broad and happy but drawn a bit too tight. Marcia appeared briefly and set two steaming cups of coffee in front of them. "I absolutely adore this little ritual, don't you, Richard? Coffee every Saturday morning. Just the two of us. It makes me feel so special."

"It makes me feel sad, Mom," Richard answered, pushing aside the floral cup as he crossed his arms on the table and leaned close to her. "Mom, I want you to listen to me. It makes me very sad that we've put ourselves in this position."

"I don't know what you're talking about," Kathy replied, shaking a packet of sweetener and carefully opening it. Richard put out his hand and stopped the motion. He wanted her to look at him.

"You do know what I'm talking about, and I have a feeling you're as tired of this charade as I am. I'm talking about clandestine meetings because you won't acknowledge the woman I love and live with. This isn't normal, Mom. This is childish. You should be doing what you always did when grandmother was alive. You should be popping in to see us any hour of the day. You should be ringing us up and telling us we're expected at dinner. And I should feel free to call you whenever I feel like it, to invite you to my home. As it stands we're not living. We're walking on eggshells because you're holding a grudge against Bridget that's unfounded."

Kathy, who had been staring at Richard's hand while he spoke, now turned her wide, beautifully-made-up eyes his way. His heart sank. Nothing he said had made an impression. Her eyes were hard as flint, an optical wall erected between emotion and reason.

"Okay, Richard. You're right. This is absurd.

I never thought I would be limited when it came to seeing my son. I don't like this hour or two we have every Saturday morning, as though I only have visitation rights. But I'm not the one who created these circumstances, if you recall."

"I recall very well. I also remember that it wasn't Bridget who created them. It was Grandmother. Bridget offered to give all the money back and you wouldn't even listen. I defended you then. I tried to explain to Bridget why you had every reason to be hurt. I hid behind your pain and didn't acknowledge my own for too long. In fact, had I waited another moment to tell Bridget that I, too, felt betrayed in many ways, I would have lost her."

"Wouldn't that have been too bad," Kathy drawled, taking her hand from under Richard's. Suddenly his hand felt heavy and warm.

"That's enough," he whispered heatedly, flinging himself back in the chair in frustration. "I've really had just about enough of this vendetta against Bridget."

"This is no vendetta. These are honest feelings, Richard. But then it doesn't surprise me at all that you can't accept that," Kathy responded coolly.

"What is that suppose to mean?" he blinked, truly amazed by this tack.

"It means that you aren't even honest about your own feelings, so you'll forgive me if I don't take your little sermon too seriously."

"Mother," Richard said evenly, "you realize this is absurd. I'm not the one who has flung Bridget out of my life after years of embracing her. I'm living with the woman. I love her. She is honest and true. She is kind. And, on top of it, she's nobody's fool."

"But she suffers them. If she were as intelligent and wonderful as all that, don't you think she'd see through you, Richard?" This time Kathy reached out for her son. She lay her fingers gently on his arm as her voice pleaded and her eyes softened. "I don't like to hurt you. And I don't want to disillusion you any more than you already are. I know how you feel. It's as though your grandmother remembered a foundling's birthday and forgot yours. I'm not stupid, either, Richard. I know you hurt and for different reasons than I do. Mother forced Bridget into our family, into our world, without even consulting us. But, Richard, don't compound the problem. You're living with a woman you couldn't possibly love. Be honest with her and yourself."

"I have been, Mom, and I resent the implication that I haven't thought my relationship through properly with Bridget."

"It's not an implication. It's the truth. Believe me, Richard, if you don't face your real feelings now, the rest of your life is headed toward disaster."

"Don't be silly . . ." Richard scoffed, but

Kathy stopped him.

"I'm not. Just listen to me. Deny, if you will, that it hasn't occurred to you that a relationship with Bridget means Mother's fortune remains in this family and under your control. Isn't it entirely possible that those growing feelings you had for Bridget became very serious when you realized that she was your grandmother's heir? Would you really have been this serious, this quickly, about that young woman if she were still a duty nurse?"

Richard was up in a flash. The lovely little chair he had sat in toppled to the floor with a thud. He towered above his mother, who looked him full in the face. He loved her more than he ever thought possible for a grown man. In her he saw so many things he admired—strength, commitment, determination. What he didn't see was the one thing he adored. Kathy Hudson's sense of fun and fair play had flown out the window. She had reduced her logic to a simple equation, and it didn't add up for Richard.

"Yes, Mom. I would. I would love her if she was a maid. That isn't the point."

"I didn't say you wanted her because she was rich," Kathy said, sniffing.

"I know. You only said that there was an added incentive to loving Bridget. If I married her, I would control Grandmother's fortune and keep it in the family. Well, you know what? Bridget has her own plans for the money. I

doubt whether I could control that money ever
if I wanted to. I'm advising her, yes. Controlling
her, never."

"There's a thin line between advice and control, Richard," Kathy noted.

"And I haven't crossed it. I love Bridget, and
I intend to make her my wife. I came here today hoping you would understand that I've
found the same thing with Bridget that you and
Dad found so long ago."

"I'll never understand that," Kathy whispered,
turning her eyes toward the window, not wanting
to see the truth of Richard's words.

"That's not true. You can understand it, you
simply won't. And you know what? That's a
terrible loss, Mom. I never knew you to be prej-
udiced, to be small-minded or mean. I was so
proud of you because of your openness. When
other kids' mothers gossiped, you put your nose
in the air and didn't pay one iota of attention.
When I made mistakes growing up, when I was
struggling with ethical decisions as a young lawyer, you never once told me how I should act,
react or feel. I never heard a disparaging word
pass your lips. And now you condemn and criti-
cize a woman who has done nothing to you.

"You're not really hurting her, Mom. Nor are
you hurting us as a couple. Bridget is secure
with my love as I am with hers. You're hurting
yourself. You've pushed away people who love
you dearly. And for what? Money? Bruised feel-

254

ings? It's so little when compared with what Grandmother actually left you. Priceless vases, paintings, chandeliers from French chateaus. Sell everything in that house and you'll have enough money for three lifetimes. But look at everything in that house, touch it, and you'll see Grandmother left you a wealth of memories. She left you custodian of all that she loved.

"But perhaps the saddest thing is that you've betrayed yourself, Mom." Richard's voice shook, almost breaking, with the effort of so painful a discussion. Quickly he controlled it, knowing if he didn't, the unfairness of the choice he had to make would overwhelm him. "If you don't take a real hard look soon you're going to lose everything that made you such a special lady. I'd hate to see that, but I'd also hate to live my life dwelling on the unfairness of this situation. I have a life to live, and I'm not going to do it by sneaking out to meet you on Saturday mornings and trying not to talk to Bridget about you. That's the way it is, Mom, and that's the way it's going to stay. I've made my decision. I hope you can live with it. If you can't, then you're going to live without me."

Slowly Richard bent down and righted the chair. He kept his head down, but from the corner of his eye he was aware that his mother sat rigidly staring straight ahead. He looked at her, hoping she would return the favor. She didn't. Softly he spoke once more.

"I love you, Mom. I'm trying to put my own hurt behind me. Don't give me a new one to deal with. I'm not asking you to love her the way you once did. None of us can love the way we once did. I'm asking that you try to understand and forgive Grandmother's decision and come back into our lives."

Richard waited, his fingers tightening over the back of the chair. He heard the tinkle of the little bells above the door but didn't turn to see who had come or gone. Every bit of his concentration was directed at his mother. When she remained silent, Richard sighed, his sorrow worn on his face for all to read. But Kathy Hudson didn't want to look.

"Goodbye, Mom. We'll be waiting to hear from you. Both of us."

Still silent, Kathy Hudson didn't flinch when Richard rounded the table to kiss her cheek. He was out the door before Kathy allowed a tear to slip down her cheek.

Bridget had been terribly lazy. Lingering over tea after sleeping until eleven was not her usual morning routine. But she had, and now she was paying for it. Quickly she cleaned the apartment and finished by one. Stepping into the shower she realized Richard would, as usual, be punctual, and she had to be ready at two if they were to make their appointment with Jerry. Her hair was just dry, her sweater still unbuttoned when the bell rang. Bridget ran to answer, thrilled he was more than fifteen minutes early.

"Sure did you forget your key, man?" She called happily as she opened the door, still buttoning the pearls on her cashmere sweater.

Bridget's smile faltered, her fingers stopped moving. Almost paralyzed with astonishment, she clutched the front of her sweater closed as she faced her visitor.

"I imagine you were expecting Richard," Kathy Hudson said quietly.

Bridget nodded, mute with surprise and apprehension. All the horrible words they had exchanged came flooding back to her. Kathy turning her back on her, banishing Bridget from her life. The tears. The pain. Now Richard's mother, looking every inch the San Franciscan matron, stood at Bridget's door neither angry nor vindictive. Instead Kathy's face wore the expression of an invalid, one who has known great illness and is determined to be well again.

"Y-yes, I was," Bridget stammered, suddenly all action as she made herself presentable. "I—"

"It's all right. I've known you two were living together for quite some time. Richard and I have been seeing each other every Saturday for breakfast, so I know what's been going on."

"I didn't know," Bridget said quietly. "I'm sorry you had to meet that way. You should feel free to see Richard whenever you like."

"Yes. Well, it just didn't work out that way, did it?"

"Not because I didn't want it to," Bridget insisted, feeling her heart icing over again. Determined not to let Kathy Hudson ruin the goodness that had finally come out of all this, she raised her chin in defiance and waited.

"I know you didn't. Actually, Bridget, I've known for a long while that you really were never to blame for anything. I simply didn't want to acknowledge that you were blameless. I've been so angry with my mother, with myself for feeling the way I did. I think you became my proverbial whipping boy. I didn't want to believe I was capable of such anger. I've been selfish and vindictive. Richard, it seems, was far more reasonable than I. He at least could admit that he continued to love you through his own hurt. I wouldn't even give you the courtesy of that admission. Can you forgive me?"

"Oh, Mrs. Hudson," Bridget whispered, "I think so. This has been a hard time for us all. Maybe we could start again. Wouldn't you like to come in and begin now?" Bridget stepped back slightly, a blush rising to her cheeks. So much had happened between them it was difficult to open her heart again.

Kathy shook her head, lowering her eyes to contemplate her handbag as though in it she would find the right words to say.

"No, thank you. Bridget, I came to tell you something. I came to tell you it was difficult for me to continue to hate you the way I did initially. I was blaming everyone in sight for something, when no one was at fault. It wasn't my place to determine what my mother did with her estate. Nor was it my place to judge her. I realize now that Mother was doing exactly what she thought best. I also remembered that my mother proved how much she loved me every day of her life.

"But all that anger took a lot out of me. I'm ashamed to know that I have the ability to hate so deeply. I never thought I was that kind of person. When I realized I didn't like the person I had become, when I realized Richard could overcome his own hurt and still love you, I had to search my soul for some answers. That was a terribly painful process."

"Please, Mrs. Hudson, come in." Bridget reached out and touched Kathy Hudson's hand. The other woman smiled listlessly.

"No, really. I'm not ready yet. I only came because if I didn't come now I would lose myself and Richard. I would even lose you and I'm not sure anymore that I want that.

"Things can get out of hand, Bridget. I'm glad Richard made me realize that. There are things I need and more money isn't one of them. I need the happiness I used to have, the excitement of living, the peace of mind. And it was the people I loved who gave me energy. Now I'm in danger of losing all of that affection. I hope we can start again, Bridget. I hope you'll let me try to make up for what I've said and done."

"Oh, I can't think of anything that would make me happier than to have things the way they were," Bridget said softly.

"Never the way they were. Remember that today is made up of an awful lot of yesterdays that aren't forgotten. It's never as simple as one would hope, but then it's never as lamentable as it might seem, either."

"I'll remember that, Mrs. Hudson. Surely I will," Bridget said quietly.

"Good. I'll look forward to us becoming fast friends again. Oh, and Bridget?"

"Yes?"

"My name is Kathy. Mrs. Hudson is Ted's mother."

Bridget grinned. Without thinking, she stepped into the hall and wrapped her arms around Kathy Hudson. For a long while the two women stood cheek to cheek, each lost in memories, each looking forward with hope toward a future where affection could be regained. When they parted, neither spoke again. All had been said. Now it was up to time to do the healing.

Bridget closed the door slowly, lingering with one hand on the knob, the other lying over a heart that felt fuller than she ever imagined it could. Ambling over to the low, white sofa, Bridget sat down, listening to the sigh of the leather as she let her eyes roam over the city view.

Transported back in time by her memories, Bridget was once more that young woman from Ireland, her white uniform pressed, her charge resting in the fine house above her. And Bridget, herself, was looking out a window facing a city that was at once frightening and beautiful.

She no longer feared the city of San Francisco, she only thought it beautiful. She was no longer a wide-eyed young lass, but a woman who loved and who was loved in return. Things had changed, just as they had somehow remained the same. Bridget Devlin was tied inexorably to the Hudson family just as Maura Kilburn had wished.

"Sure isn't it just as you wanted, Mrs. Kilburn," Bridget whispered just as the door of the apartment opened.

When she turned to look at Richard, there were tears of joy in her eyes. He came to her, gathering her gently in his arms, sensing that something had changed.

"I love you so, Richard."

He buried his lips in her hair and said back, "I love you, too, Bridget."

Then he smiled, a genuine, heartfelt smile. She sounded like she always had. Once again he

held the Bridget Devlin with the bright emerald
eyes and the fall of curling hair who looked her
best in a blue faille dress with a white collar.
Closing his eyes, Richard hugged her tight,
thinking of his grandmother, hoping one day he
would finally love Bridget without questioning
Maura Kilburn's love for him.

"There she is, Richard. Over there, the
woman with the black hair. That's Jennifer Jen-
sen, she's the artist who did all these pieces.
There, with the curly black hair." Bridget tried
not to point but she was so excited to be at
Jennifer's show she couldn't help herself.

"You mean the one with the black eyes and
the black dress and stockings? The one who
looks a bit like Elvira decked out for Hallow-
een?"

Bridget dug her elbow into Richard's side.
"Hush, now. Sure I think she looks wonderful."

"You look wonderful," Richard said, leaning
close to her ear, kissing her quickly before
standing tall again. "She looks as though she
wouldn't have a face if you took a washcloth to
all that makeup."

"But sure isn't that just the style?" Bridget
furrowed her brow, thinking Richard must be
wrong in his opinion. Everyone in the crowded
room looked quite fashionable to her.

"I wouldn't know. Fashion isn't my forte . . ."

"Finally Richard has realized he's lacking," Michael interrupted, leaning in to kiss Bridget on the cheek she happily presented to him.

"It's not nice to eavesdrop, Payne," Richard retorted, smiling with his lips but not his eyes.

"I didn't need to. You walked Bridget right by me at the door while you were talking."

"Did I?" Richard raised an eyebrow, his arm snaking protectively around Bridget's waist. "Sorry, I guess I just didn't see you."

"Possibly," Michael answered, the one word sounding like a challenge.

Bridget intervened knowing full well the expressions on their faces were sorry excuses for smiles. Though she adored them both, these macho games were getting a bit tiresome, especially when she realized full well it had nothing at all to do with her any longer. Laughing, Bridget put her hands through the arm of each of them.

"Come along, my fine lads. Remember, you both decided a truce was in order. Sure I'm not going to have you break your promise on a night like this. I've never been to a gallery opening before, and I intend to make the most of this one. Now, if you won't enjoy yourselves with me then enjoy yourselves without me or go sulk in a corner, whichever you please."

"You have a point there, Bridget," Michael said, the first to acquiesce. "You look much too beautiful tonight to argue about. Now, how

263

about a drink then hello to Jennifer before w
look around and see what it is you're going t
need for the apartment. I'm sure you'll fin
something here that will be perfect."

"You forget, Michael," Richard broke in
"she's not going to be in that apartment pas
the sublet contract. We'll be moving to m
house soon."

"Perfect. Jennifer has enough canvases to fil
three houses," Michael exclaimed, trying his bes
to get under Richard's skin. Richard, though
would have none of it. Looking around casually
he grasped Bridget's hand, lifted it to his lip
then looked Michael straight in the eye.

"I'm afraid what I've seen so far doesn't strik
me as the kind of thing that might enhance th
home we'll be sharing. I'd prefer the works o
more established artists to hang on my walls."

"And here I thought this was a democrati
country." Michael shot back. "Isn't Bridget go
ing to be living there, too?"

"I said we'd be sharing the house," Richar
answered.

"Then I would hope you'd give her a voice i
how she would like the walls decorated."

"Enough," Bridget cried. "I shall definitel
buy something this evening to help Jennife
along, Michael. But surely I won't hang it any
where you don't want to see it, Richard."

With a dazzling smile she turned to each o
the men as she spoke. Her cheeks were flushe

264

with the excitement of the evening. Glamorous people strolled around them, but none were more glamorous than the three who stood in their tight little circle in the middle of the gallery.

Michael was resplendent in a saffron-colored raw silk jacket with exaggerated shoulders, a shirt of linen that buttoned high up his neck, its standing collar allowing no room for a tie. His slacks were a tad too long and his loafers were the color of cinnamon. Richard looked every inch the man of means, his double-breasted suit cut to European perfection, easing over his narrow hips, buttoning low, emphasizing the sensuous sleekness of his tall body. His shirt was whiter than white and his tie Windsor knotted.

Between them Bridget looked stunning in her short strapless gown, the blistering pink silk a marvelous contrast to her milky skin and red-brown hair. Her face, though seemingly bare, was made up as if by a master. Nude blush and lipstick added a stark vogueness to her look. Only her eyes were widened and deepened with a shadow whose color defied description. In her hand a jeweled Judith Lieber bag winked under the lights, on her feet thongs of silver leather held her pedicured feet to a micro-thin sole, which eased into clear stiletto heels.

Bridget eyed the two men as she cautioned them, far too thrilled with the celebration to worry too much about their fighting. After her talk with Kathy, and given Richard's attentiveness when he heard that fences were on the mend, Bridget was not going to let any thing dampen her spirits.

"You really intend to buy something, Bridget?" Richard reiterated. "Not exactly what I would call a wise investment."

"Sure you don't call many things I want a wise investment, my love," she teased, half meaning to put him in his place as she remembered the one low point of the day. Jerry and his infernal lecturing about how stocks work, Richard nodding in agreement to everything the man said and Bridget trying desperately to get them to understand she didn't have time to wait for her money to work for her. She wanted to make her money work right now. Shaking off the annoying thoughts, Bridget stood on tiptoe and gave Richard a kiss on the cheek.

"Be true now, Richard, you wouldn't mind one of these colorful bits in our new home, would you?" she pleaded nicely.

Richard shook his head, smiling down into her excited face. Despite her lovely hair, her daring dress, when he saw that expectant look in her eye, that marvelously innocent pouting of her lips in her delicate heart-shaped face, he could do nothing less than indulge her. It was, after all, her money. Angry at himself for the last thought, Richard kissed her back lightly.

"Not at all. If you like one of these we'll find a place for a three-eyed harlequin done in the primary colors."

"See, Michael," she cried delightedly, "I told you he was learning to enjoy himself."

"I can see he's having a ball," Michael noted dryly. "Oh, look, Jennifer's free. Let's go say hello."

"I'll be there in a minute, sweetheart." Richard held back, needing to acclimate himself to this place. Monet was as daring as his taste in art took him. Lawyerlike as always, he wanted to gather the facts before making a decision about Bridget's new friends. "I'll pick us up a drink. White wine?"

"Sure that would be lovely. Don't be long," Bridget said gaily, taking Michael's arm just before she was swallowed up by the crowd of very, very fashionable folks.

"She's something, isn't she?"

Richard raised an eyebrow as he glanced over his shoulder to see Michael moving in behind him. He raised his glass, taking a sip of his brandy and soda, before nodding in agreement.

"She is."

"I like her a lot," Michael said, raising a finger toward the bartender. "White wine." Then to Richard. "I don't want to see her hurt."

"I love her," Richard said definitively, turning

to lean his hands on the bar, "and I don't want to see that, either. I especially don't want someone to get the idea that they can take advantage of Bridget's giving nature. Someone who might think she's got money to burn and they've got the match."

"Let's get one thing straight, Richard, I haven't taken a cent from Bridget. I wouldn't dream of doing that. But I also think she needs to really believe that what's happened to her isn't a curse. She'll never have to doubt my friendship for reasons that I might be jealous of her money or want to manipulate it in any way. I realize I have no claim to it. How about you?"

Richard's eyes locked with Michael's as the other man spoke. Michael thought he saw a flicker of conscience deep in Richard's, but then those brown eyes hooded and Michael could read nothing there.

"I have no claim to anything. Bridget or her money." Richard's head swiveled. As he looked over his shoulder he caught sight of Bridget deep in conversation with a man in shorts and heavy black shoes. He seemed like the class nerd grown up.

Bridget was so stunning Richard's breath caught. This was a Bridget he never knew existed: confident, sparkling, sophisticated. He almost wondered if the woman he was looking at was the woman he loved. Then her companion eft, excusing himself to talk to someone else, and Bridget was alone. The old Bridget was back. As he watched, Richard saw her soften, saw a glimmer of shyness replace the studied animation of moments before. In so many ways she was out of her element, and in others she was superior to everyone in the room. But Bridget was changing quickly, banishing the old for the new. Though Richard would care for the new Bridget, he would never love her the way he did the former. He wished she would simply take the best of both worlds.

Reaching into his pocket, Richard withdrew some money and threw it on the bar not bothering to count it.

"Michael, I think you and I know where each other stands. Bridget thinks you're wonderful. Great. You can dance at our wedding. You'll probably help her spend a small fortune on her trousseau. But believe me, you can never give her what I can."

"Love?" Michael asked sarcastically. "I give her that every time I help her enjoy her new life."

Richard shook his head sadly. "What about helping her learn to really live in her new world rather than just enjoy it?"

"But enjoying life is living it," Michael insisted.

"I guess we're just destined to disagree then. Thanks for the invitation. It's been an interesting evening. Bridget will give you a call."

With that Richard was gone. From the ba
Michael watched Bridget's face light up when
Richard held out his hands to her. He saw he
melt into the other man's arms. They spoke. H
could tell they were whispering. She smiled. H
kissed her and she was smiling still. Lookin
over Richard's shoulder, Bridget searched th
crowd, spied Michael and waved. He wave
back, stopping the minute Richard faced him
They looked at each other for an instant befor
Richard put his arm protectively around Bridge
and ushered her away from the noise, the nou
veau riche and Michael Payne. Bridget hadn'
bought a thing, but Richard had convinced he
she was leaving with the best. Michael wondere
how long she would continue to believe it.

Chapter Fifteen

"I still think the cherry wood dining set with the white satin upholstery," Richard called. "Now, the only question is, do we go with the matching sideboard or shall we take a drive to wine country and visit some of those fabulous antique shops that are tucked away up there. Bridget? Come take a look and help me decide."

Bridget switched off the light in the kitchen, picked up the second cup of coffee and joined Richard. Holding out the cup, she knelt beside him. He shook his head.

"Not yet, thanks. Now what do you think of this for the wainscotting if we take the cherry wood table and chairs?"

"It's lovely," Bridget said placing his cup on the coffee table he had shoved aside in order to accommodate his paint chips and fabric samples, his furniture catalogues and design magazines. Idly she picked up a magazine, letting her eyes roam over the exquisitely appointed room pictured on the page.

Every detail was perfect, just like Mrs. Kilburn's home, just like this apartment she was renting, just like the home Richard would furnish on the hill high above the city. Everything was picture perfect these days, Bridget thought as she tossed the magazine onto the pile of lovely samples. Her clothing was perfect, as was her hair and her nails, which had grown long now that she wasn't filling syringes and helping an elderly patient in and out of bed. Richard was perfect, handsome and loving, tender and caring. Yet something wasn't right.

Taking a moment to run her hand down the back of Richard's neck before she put her coffee cup next to his, Bridget unwound her long legs and went to the window. Pressing her hand, opened palm against the pane of glass she looked out onto the black night. For a while Bridget contemplated her new shade of nail polish, wondering why she felt so at odds with everything when the world around her was ... perfect.

"Now the only question is," Richard said, oblivious to her languor, "do we want the white-on-white embroidered satin or just a plain satin? Of course we can always buy black so we won't have to worry about it getting dirty, or we can cover everything in heavy-duty plastic."

"Whatever 'tis you think best," she answered quietly.

"Bridget, I was joking," Richard sighed. "You

know this is getting a little one-sided. You haven't said two words since we sat down to dinner. I thought you were going to help me. I don't want to decide on anything without your input."

"Truly?" Bridget looked over her shoulder, raising an eyebrow lazily.

"Yes, really." Richard laughed uncomfortably. "Do you have a problem with me wanting to know how you feel about furniture for the house we're going to share?"

"Is it positive you are that we're to *share* that house, Richard?"

He shrugged, at a loss. "I assumed we would. I thought we'd reached an agreement."

"Sure and I must have missed the discussion we had about that. You might have even set our wedding date, but my mind must have been elsewhere."

"Bridget Devlin, what on earth is the matter?"

Richard shoved away the paint chips and catalogues, pushed up the sleeves on his oversized coral-colored sweatshirt and, heaving himself off the floor, sat facing her on the low leather sofa.

"Nothing. Just nothing." Bridget waved away his question and turned her face back to the window. She couldn't tell him what was wrong without looking like a fool. Richard was so good with words, she had learned that in no uncertain terms at the office when they met with the banker.

She heard the couch sigh and knew he was coming toward her. In a minute his hands were on her shoulders, pulling her back into him. Involuntarily she resisted. Richard froze. For the first time since they had made a commitment, a touch, a look, a word wasn't enough to bridge a gap between them. Bridget thought her heart would break and wished Richard would simply grab her, kiss her hard and shake her until all the doubts and anger she felt were forced away by his loving. Instead he let his hands trail down her arms, paused to see if she was going to give in and, when she didn't turn into him, went back to his seat and flopped back onto the couch.

"Okay. Why don't we talk about nothing. What did I say? What didn't I say? What did I or didn't I do to deserve this cold shoulder?"

"By the saints, Richard, this is not a cold shoulder I'm giving you. Isn't it just I'm learning to keep my mouth shut when you are talking about making decisions. Sure don't I believe that you prefer to make them all by yourself, so why bother yourself asking my opinion at all?"

"Bridget, that is not true. What on earth ever gave you that idea?" Flabbergasted, Richard stared at her back, wishing she would just turn around and face him, see how surprised he was by her accusations.

" 'Tis true, Richard," she insisted wearily, still looking outside.

"Excuse me," he said evenly, "but haven't we just spent the entire evening going over furniture options for the house? If I didn't want your opinion, if I didn't think you were going to be a permanent resident, do you think I would have bothered to even ask?"

Bridget twirled toward him, her hands clasped behind her back as she leaned into the glass. Framed by the black night, her jet silk dress fading into the background, she looked like an exquisite hologram with her pale skin, her red-brown hair and her emerald eyes. Only the rise and fall of her lovely chest indicated there was a perfect body attached to that beautiful face, those gorgeous bare legs.

"You don't really want to know what 'tis I think. You go ahead and do what you want, anyway. Just like you did at the bank this morning. Just the way you took it upon yourself to cancel the plans for my da's house. Just the way you told me you didn't want to have a painting of Jennifer's. You don't even listen when I try and tell you something."

"Oh," Richard let his head fall back, his eyes closing as the truth dawned on him. "I see. We're not talking about furniture are we? Or our living arrangement? Or how much we care about each other? This is something much more important."

"I think it is. Sure isn't it my money we're talking about now. Seems we're *always* talking

275

about my money." She hadn't meant to blurt it out. In fact, Bridget hadn't been sure until that moment that what was bothering her was Richard's proprietary attitude toward her fortune.

"We're talking about my grandmother's bequest," Richard reminded her.

"My money." Bridget insisted.

"All right. Your money," Richard acquiesced gracefully. "And, if I recall, you asked me to advise you on how to best proceed when it came to *your* money. I don't recall forcing my views on you."

"Naturally you wouldn't. You won't be listening to me about anything. You make me feel a fool in front of these men who control the money," Bridget pleaded, holding out her hands, not wanting to fight, only wanting him to understand.

"I don't make you look like a fool," Richard scoffed, unwilling to even entertain the idea that there was truth in her words. "Of course I listen to you. I listened every time you said you wanted to build a school in Kilmartin, every time you said there was a road you wanted to repave, every time you said you wanted to build a country manor for your father or offer the minister funds for a new church. I did hear it all, Bridget and I didn't ignore you."

"No, you just made it clear I was fairly the idiot," she snapped, unable to remain meek.

"Excuse me," he shot back. "I explained to you why it was better to reinvest the fund that had already been made liquid. We decided that mutual funds for a quarter of that money, futures for a speculative tenth of the funds, and solid, blue-chip stocks for the rest would provide you with a sizable income and enough to make continuing contributions to Kilmartin so that the projects there can be taken care of on a long-term basis."

"Listen to yourself, man!" Bridget wailed, throwing up her arms in frustration. "You talk to me like a child. As though you can offer me a rag doll when I've asked for the one with the porcelain face. Richard, I'm not a child. I know the difference between investing and spending. Your grandmother wanted me to take that money to make life better, not only for myself, but for others in Ireland. Not on a long-term basis, but now."

Bridget walked across the room as she spoke and lowered herself to her knees in front of Richard. He looked so handsome, his brow furrowed with concern. Bridget didn't wonder whether that concern was for her or for himself. His jeans were so old they shone at the knee, feeling more like satin than denim. It made Bridget realize how much they had changed. Now Richard was the one who always seemed so casual, she so pulled together in her new clothes. It took a moment to comprehend that

Richard's fingers were toying with a lock of her hair. She lifted a hand and covered his, smiling sadly, appreciating his attempt to keep the inevitable at bay.

"I love your new haircut," he whispered. "Did I forget to tell you?"

Bridget nodded but reminded him, "We're not talking about my hair."

"I know. We're talking about wealth, and loving you has made me a wealthy man."

"Don't!" She stayed his hand, half pushing it away from her, even as she was drawing it close to her lips so that she could kiss his open palm. She whispered again, "Don't."

Richard stood up so abruptly Bridget fell back onto her heels.

"I don't know what to do, Bridget. You tell me you want my help, but you don't want to accept my best advice. You tell me you want my love, but you don't want me to touch you. What do you want?"

She was on her feet instantly, reaching out for him. Touching him without holding him, trying by sheer force of will to make him not just listen to her but understand her.

"I want all those things. I need you more than you'll ever know. I love you more than anyone ever could or ever will. The thought of not having you near me in the night is enough to make me weep. But, Richard, I will not have you use me. And I feel as if you are doing exactly that. I will not have you jealous of me. And I wonder if that's your feeling. You tell hese men what to do with my money when I want—and your grandmother wanted—it to be used in a much different way, no matter what you think. I will not squander it. I will not reduce myself to a pauper while I build Kilmartin into a village to be proud of. Sure I only want to be able to do what was intended, and I want to do it now. Your mother finally understood that. Why are you making it so difficult for me?"

"Because that is not what an inheritance is meant to do. It's meant to be nurtured so that it can be passed on."

"To our children?" she demanded, knowing that she was laying a trap, unable to help herself.

"Yes," he replied instantly.

"And what if we don't marry?" Bridget challenged him, her heart cold while she waited for the answer, while she remembered Michael's accusations regarding Richard's jealousy.

"But we will," he answered carefully.

"But what if we don't?" she insisted, her cream-colored skin paling to white. "Would you be so concerned if my heirs were not of your blood?"

Richard's face flushed, his hands fisting at his side. Bridget sensed his anger—or was it pain?—just before he was upon her. In an instant she was in his arms, her body crushed against his as he buried his face in her wealth of hair, whispering all the while.

"Our children, Bridget, no one else's. Don't think it, don't speak about it. I love you, and I won't hear you talk like this."

Before she could speak, his hands had grasped her head, pulling her face up so that he could cover her eyes, her cheeks, her lips with hot, insistent kisses. It was as though he would drive a madness from her through his unrelenting loving. Gone now were the Richard and Bridget of months ago. She was no longer a girl from Ireland, he no longer the only favored child, and they both had to deal with who they now were.

Bridget's hands rose between them, pressing against his chest. In her a fever burned, confusing her. Delirious with desire, she wanted him as much as she wanted answers. But could she have those answers without sacrificing her love? Blindly she made her decision.

"No," she murmured fiercely, forcing herself away from his unrelenting affection. "No, Richard. Answer me, damn you, man. Answer me."

With a great push she was away. They were only inches from each other, their labored breathing filling the pristine apartment, ripping through the silence as they stood face-to-face. Quietly, carefully, Bridget posed the question, her voice plunging like a knife into the deepest, most secret part of his heart.

"Richard, do you love me because of your grandmother's inheritance, or despite it?"

Richard, so beautiful, so perfectly attuned to the world, let his shoulders slump as though that world sat upon them. To his credit he met her gaze. His eyes looked deep into hers, their lovely color as warm as a blanket, as clear as a stream.

"I don't know, Bridget. I try not to think about it anymore."

Chapter Sixteen

Bridget walked with her head down, looking at each cobblestone in turn, counting them before they disappeared under the soles of her Italian loafers. Her hands were shoved deep in the pockets of her magenta swing coat, her chin buried in the collar. *Disappointing* was an understatement when describing how her morning had gone, not to mention all the other mornings since she'd arrived in Kilmartin.

After tea and toast with her da, she had set off to do exactly what she'd come home to do: forget Richard and that last horrible night in San Francisco and begin the grand renovation of her home village. Now there was no Richard to tell her what to do with her money, no Michael to urge her toward frivolousness. She would lose her memories and disappointments in hard work. Bridget Devlin had planned to conquer not only this village but her own heart in the process. The only problem was, nothing had gone according to plan.

While the mayor was delighted to see her, having heard of her good fortune "round about from a man whose son often played chess with her father's neighbor," he was quite busy with the milking of his prized cows just when Bridget arrived. He listened politely to Bridget's ideas for improving Kilmartin before shaking her hand heartily and sending her on her way.

After her discouraging meeting with the smiling, busy mayor, her interview with the shopkeeper who doubled as the local realtor "because cottages only sold when someone died, so it was difficult to make a living on real estate," was quite simply disheartening. There were a few properties in the general area that might be suitable for the large manor house Bridget described, but those were far outside the village and was Miss Devlin sure her da, at his age, should be that far from folk who could care for him should he fall ill?

Only her chat with Father Donovan seemed worthwhile—at first. Initially the good father appeared to fully understand Bridget's bright-eyed optimism and had settled her in the rectory with a lovely cup of tea while she told him her story.

"Sure doesn't God work in mysterious ways," he said, beaming at his beautiful visitor. Bridget smiled back hopefully. Wasn't it the parish priest, after all, who carried the weight in village affairs?

"You are a lucky woman, Miss Devlin. Lucky that your parents, and your benefactress instilled in you a desire to do good works. Now after all your years of service to a lady of Irish descent you have been rewarded in this life. How lovely!"

"It is, Father," Bridget agreed, leaning forward, anxious to outline her plans for the town. "Sure wasn't I was hoping you might help me do what Mrs. Kilburn wished. She wanted me to do something in honor of my heritage and hers. What better way than to improve Kilmartin?"

"Well, now, that is grand! Couldn't this town use a bit of sprucing up." Father Donovan laughed, the teacup rattling in its saucer as he did so.

"Exactly." Bridget sighed, thankful that someone finally understood. "But I've been away quite a while, Father, and it appears so much needs to be done . . ."

The old priest nodded sagely, "That it does. That it does."

"And I was hoping you might speak to the mayor for me. I'm afraid I just didn't get very far . . ."

"The church could certainly do with a good painting, I'll grant you that. Of course I'd have to find one of the Carne boys to come and do that now that they aren't working for their father every day. They're the only ones who can paint properly. Have you seen the church, Miss Devlin?"

The old priest fairly popped out of his chair and led the way into the charming sod church. Indeed Bridget could see it needed a whitewash, and she was sure the Carne boys could do an excellent job, but this was not the grand plan that she had envisioned. Promising to write a check to anyone he instructed, Bridget accepted the priest's appreciation and took her leave.

From the church she wandered down the lane that led to town, fighting her odd ennui and wondering why it was that she couldn't make people understand what a wonderful gift she was bringing them. Without hesitation, drawn by the sweet sound of singing, Bridget turned on her heel and headed across the street straight into the pub.

Unbuttoning her coat, oblivious to the hooded glances from some and bold looks from others, Bridget slid into a hard-seated chair and propped her elbows on the table. The woman who was singing slowed her tune a bit, her smile faltering when she looked at Bridget, but she never missed a beat. Bridget smiled her encouragement, recognizing one of Mrs. Slade's girls. Only a colty young thing when Bridget left seven years ago, she was now a black-haired beauty with the fine figure of a woman. The songstress smiled back, earning Bridget's gratitude. She had been recognized as a friend, finally.

Feeling better, Bridget hailed the lady at the

bar who tucked a blanket around her babe before answering Bridget's summons.

"Top of the morning," Bridget said brightly, her spirits returning in full force. "Have you a special today?"

The woman looked at Bridget carefully, full in the face as though in challenge. Bridget's smile faltered, the silence drawing tight between them, pulling the interest of the others in the pub with it. Even the girl who sang let her tune run off her lips as she waited to see what would happen.

"Do I know you?" Bridget asked, wondering what on earth she could possibly have done to offend this lady.

"I should say you do, Miss Bridget," the woman answered, and her voice did have the familiar ring of a friend of old. But Bridget still couldn't put a name to the face, so the woman reminded her. "Didn't we go to school together with the good father before you went off to Dublin and became a nurse? Then it was off to America, wasn't it? Now more American than Irish, I should say, that you don't remember friends."

Bridget looked closer still. It was hard to believe that this woman with her hair pulled so sharply back from her scrubbed face was the same age as she. But yes, there was something in the set of her eyes. If she was twenty pounds lighter. . . .

"My God in heaven!" Bridget breathed, her smile coming back instantly. "Min? Is it really you? Sure 'tis lovely to see you."

"I'm sure 'tis," the woman drawled, still without a smile.

"Of course it is. Sure I'm happy to see a familiar face. I've been gone seven years in the States and four in Dublin. Don't I feel the stranger, as though I don't know anyone anymore."

Min laughed without humor. "Sure 'tis we all feel the same way about you, Bridget Devlin."

"I'm sorry?" Bridget asked, surprised by the harsh words from her school-days friend.

"You might as well be a 'blow-in,' Bridget Devlin, for sure you're not the same girl that left home all those years ago. Your comin' back to Kilmartin all high and mighty in those clothes, drivin' on a street we folk are proud to walk on. Lookin' the way you do was enough to make the tongues wag. Sure weren't we all so excited to see you walk into your da's house lookin' like a queen, carryin' two bags of clothes. Two, by the saints! We couldn't imagine what you had in them. Some of your old friends were going to drop around. But then we hear that you're comin' in here thinking you *are* a queen. Well I'll tell you, we want none of it.

"Sure if you want to come back, Bridget Devlin, we'd be happy to greet you no matter what fancy clothes you put on your back. But don't you think you can throw your money around Kilmartin, pavin' the streets with gold, to make us think kindly of you. Sure 'twas we thought you were coming home to see how we all were."

Min harumphed and looked about the pub to see that heads were nodding in agreement. Fueled by her neighbors unanimity Min crossed her arms and forged ahead.

"Well, if that's not what's brought you home, if you don't even come round to see your friends, if all you want to do is make us feel like little people, put your money where it will do some good, woman. Why not take yourself out to see the factory at the end of town," she challenged with a tart nod of her head. "See if you can't give me husband a job and get us off the dole instead of puttin' new pavement on our streets or a street light not a body will pay attention to. I just wanted to tell you that, Bridget Devlin, to your face." Min gave a curt nod of her head. Her baby was giving a cry and wanted attention. Min's head snapped toward the sound. She muttered the next without looking back at Bridget. "Now, do ya want a pint o' plain or stout?"

Aghast, Bridget sat speechless. How dare this woman tell her what the town thought of her! Bridget looked about, trying to find a man or woman to come to her defense, but none did. They looked away or buried their noses in their cups. Wordlessly Bridget stood up and wrapped her coat around her. Head raised, she looked into the proud eyes of Min Drum.

"Sure and wasn't it lovely seeing you, too, Min," Bridget said, clear as a summer morning.

Moments later Bridget was inside her da's small house. Without thinking, without knocking, she went into his room.

"Da?" she said to his hunched back, the sound of tears already filling her voice.

Slowly he turned to her, his face reflecting the pain she was now feeling.

"I see you've been into town, Bridget," he noted quietly. Bridget's knees felt weak as she realized he knew exactly what had happened. But she had to tell him, anyway. She had to hear him tell her they were all wrong.

"Da, they think I'm lording it over them. They think I want to be the queen of Kilmartin. That's what Min Drum said at the pub," Bridget cried in disbelief, for nothing could be farther from the truth.

"Bridget, darlin'," her father said in his quiet, controlled voice, "sit down, girl."

She did as she was told, waiting for no further instructions. Sitting in her father's sparse bedroom, Bridget talked of everything that had happened since Mrs. Kilburn's death. She spoke of how she had loved Richard and Mrs. Kilburn, of how she had dreamed of Kilmartin and all the wonderful things she could do for the town and how Min Drum had said horrible things to make her feel that those dreams were unfounded. Bridget spoke of her friendship with Kathy and how easily it was almost destroyed because of money. She told of her friendship with Michael and how easily it flourished because of money. Bridget talked and talked and when she was done there was a bit of sobbing left.

When that was done, Bridget looked at her da. He could see precisely what she wanted from him, and he shook his head sadly. He could not give it to her much as his heart wanted to. With a huge sigh, Gil Devlin leaned back in his chair, cradled his chin in his hand, looked her in the eye and said, "Min's right, Bridget. You're not wanted here."

Chapter Seventeen

"Da!" Bridget cried in disbelief. "Sure now you can't mean that. Am I not loved here any longer? Is there no one who wants me?"

Gil Devlin raised his age-spotted hand as if to give her something. Instead he spoke, letting the hand fall to his lap. "But of course you're loved, girl. By me more than anyone. But you've been gone a long time. You've forgotten how it is that life in Kilmartin goes on."

He laughed a little sad laugh, wishing Bridget were younger so he could take her on his knee and stroke her beautiful hair to comfort her. But she wasn't small, and she needed to hear the truth.

"Bridget Devlin, what a fine mess you've made since you've come back here," her father said softly so that she would listen but wouldn't be too hurt. "Sure which of the saints told you that anyone wanted you to change Kilmartin with your American dollars?

"Those of us who have stayed here like our village just as 'tis, thank you. I wouldn't trade this tiny window or this room or the pitch on my roof for a manor outside of Dublin. Nor would any of us want a street painted with white lines for rows of cars. We don't even like to see a car here abouts if it can be helped. And new schools are for places that have children to fill them. In fifty years our schoolhouse hasn't had more than twenty at a time. So just who was it said we were waitin' for you to come save us, lass?"

Taken aback by the question, it was a moment before Bridget could speak. When she did, it was with such conviction her father's heart almost broke. She was so different, so much a part of a world bigger than Kilmartin, he feared she would never understand him.

"But sure it needs changing, Da. When I lived here, that was all I dreamed about—how the town could be so grand if only the streets were wider. And if there was a proper hotel, people would visit and make more business and Kilmartin would be a place to be proud of."

"Bridget Devlin! Stop that prattlin' now." Gil's voice rose, quavering with age but not anger. "I'm proud of Kilmartin as it stands. It doesn't need fine new buildings to make us raise our chins. Nor do we want tourists castin' their eyes about, pokin' their noses in our business."

"But Mrs. Kilburn wanted me to do some good for Ireland with the money she left me.

We'd always talked about Kilmartin and all that could be done. Sure weren't those special times, special dreams that won't come true now. I remember those conversations so well, Da."

"And that was just what it was, lass, conversation. Your lady probably never set foot in this village even when she was a young girl like you, so it wasn't Kilmartin she was thinkin' of changing. And even if she did come back to Ireland, all fancy and rich, from what you told me she wasn't the kind to be tellin' us what to do. Not the woman you wrote about all these years.

"As for your dreams of changing Kilmartin, lass, those were always *your* dreams. Ever since you were a wee one. I knew then, when you sat on my knee, this would never be the place for you to settle, much as I wanted you to. Wouldn't it have been grand if you'd married and had your babes in the cottage next door so I could have watched them grow up. Your mother understood, too, bless her soul. When she died she made me promise not to be selfish and try to keep you with me."

"Da, you never told me," Bridget lamented.

"It wasn't my place to make you feel as though you should be somethin' you were not. I didn't want you to know how much I cared, lass. If I had, you might not have gone on your adventure. You might not have found the place you belong.

"Min Drum said terrible things to you—she always was one with a mouth too big for her. But this time Min spoke true. I know you only had the best of intentions. Sure you would never hurt anyone's feelings on purpose.

"But, Bridget, your dreams aren't ours. Yours are bigger, ours simpler. Your dreams took you beyond Ireland. It was there you found your happiness. It's there you should go if you want to make your final dream come true. Staying here and paving roads and building buildings won't make you content, Bridget me darlin'."

She pushed herself off the bed, unable to look her father in the eye. She was so ashamed. Sure she never meant to force herself or her plans on anyone. And how could her da, who had never been out of Kilmartin, be so wise? The only thing he was wrong about was that happiness lay across the ocean with Richard Hudson.

"Sure I see how wrong I was now, Da. I suppose I'll have to find something else to do. Something that people need and want. Maybe it's a clinic I'll be opening. Wouldn't that be lovely?"

Gil Devlin raised an eyebrow. "And that will make you happy? Working and living without the man you love?"

"I'll stop loving him," Bridget insisted, her voice trembling.

"No you won't. I tell you I still love your mother though she's been dead all these years. Sometimes I still hear her voice calling me from the kitchen. I look up and expect to see her standing in the doorway wiping her hands on that checkered apron she wore. I even talk to her, Bridget. She comforts me when I'm lonely. She guides me to rest when I'm tired. She whispers me to sleep at night. Lass, I remember every word your mother said to me— the harsh ones and the ones of love. Now I wasn't a fancy man like your Richard, but the heart isn't especially smart. Your mother loved me. You love your man the same way. I see it in your eyes. There's no denyin' it, Bridget."

"But, Da, he doesn't love me anymore. Maybe he never did," she told him gently, kneeling down so she could look into his eyes. She lay her hands on his, feeling the fragility of them. "I've got something he thought should be his or his mother's. Giving it back won't help. The damage is done. He says he doesn't know if he loves me because of his grandmother's fortune or despite it."

Gil shook his head sadly, realizing it would take his daughter a bit more time to learn the truth.

"No, me darlin' girl, there's no damage. There's only more love in him than you know. What greater fondness is there than honesty? Sure didn't he love you before all this and tell

295

you that he did? Now he's sayin' he's hurt. He's reachin' out for you, me girl. You're not there because you haven't been honest with yourself. You haven't let yourself believe that Richard might be right about some things. Until you do, there will be no peace for you. When you can truly listen to him and turn your back, then I'll believe you could be happy without him."

Bridget nodded. As her father spoke she felt overwhelmed by what she must do. It was not a simple matter to let go of so much pain, to remember only the good and leave the bad behind.

"Doesn't he still love you, Bridget? And don't you still love him? If you do, then you've found your pot of gold. And if the treasure isn't all you'd hoped for, just remember few even make it to the end of the rainbow, my girl." Gil smiled patiently as his daughter thought about what he said before he continued.

"It's good to have a man who feels deeply enough to question, Bridget. If Richard didn't ache for you, sure you wouldn't mean very much to him. Go on with you now." He waved her away gently, realizing just how much she was in his heart. "Go fix us some tea and cake. And while you're doing it decide which dream means more—the damnable streets, or a man who can love you proper?"

To that question Bridget had no answer, since she felt defeated in all corners at the moment. Her father meant well, of course, but he hadn't heard Richard. He didn't know what the money had done to their love and how it had changed her golden man.

Bridget looked lovingly at her father as he turned back to the book he was reading. Rising, Bridget bent and kissed Gil Devlin's cheek. Quietly she left the room and went to fix him his tea.

When he heard the door click shut the old man sat back in his chair and stared out the window of the home he had lived in for sixty years. "I'll miss you, Bridget Devlin," he whispered to himself. When she'd had enough time to think, his daughter would leave Kilmartin for good. He only hoped she would walk in the right direction.

Richard tossed off the covers and threw his legs over the side of the bed. Leaning his elbows on his knees, he buried his face in his hands with a groan. Sleepless nights were becoming the rule rather than the exception lately, and he was getting damn sick of it.

Pushing off the bed, he threw on a shirt and pulled on his jeans, still finding it difficult to wrap himself in the luxurious robe Bridget had given him.

The tongue-and-groove floor moaned as he made his way down the stairs to the kitchen. Once there Richard realized he was neither hungry nor thirsty. Rather he was lonely. The house he had so coveted was like a morgue. This was not how he had envisioned it: still empty save for his bed, home to only one, cold from lack of companionship.

Halfheartedly Richard opened a cabinet and surveyed the contents. Half a bottle of instant coffee, two tea bags, a can of French onion soup, and three packets of sugar he had found there when he moved in.

The coffee would keep him awake, the soup would lack cheese and croutons so Richard put the kettle on for tea and ignored the sugar packet. Proverbially correct, his pot refused to boil while he stood beside it. In the hopes of hurrying it on he ambled through the house and found himself standing in front of the cathedral windows without really knowing how he got there.

Thumbs hooked over his jeans, his shirt dangling open so that the cold night air pricked his naked skin, Richard felt himself drawn to the leaded panes. Remembering a night so long ago when he watched Bridget take such pleasure in the sight of the city, Richard almost turned away, unable to bear the memory. Instead, as though his body ruled his mind, he pressed his hands against the glass and let his eyes move over the scene below. The bridge undulated with the illumination of headlights even at this hour of the morning. Homes and businesses twinkled with night lights, and he knew most people slept.

For Richard, though, there was no rest. Nor was there any easing of the emptiness he felt not only inside him but in the world around him. Slowly he lowered his head until he could feel the cool glass. He watched the night, wishing intensely that he could once again be filled with wonderment at this sight. His fist clenched and his eyes closed as though he could physically force himself to contentment if not happiness.

But it was useless. The days became longer, melting into nights that brought no relief. Finally, when the kettle began to sing, Richard turned away from the window. Inspiration could not be found in the beautiful view. But Richard had discovered understanding from his memories, and he had reacquainted himself with the boldness he thought had deserted him.

In the kitchen he turned off the fire under the kettle and ignored the tea on the counter. Up the stairs he went, one at a time. There was no need to hurry but he needed to finish what he was about to start as quickly as possible.

In the bedroom he eyed the rumpled sheets, then turned and threw open the doors of the closet. Richard Hudson's world was about to change again. This time he would be the one to change it.

By the time Gil Devlin lay down for his afternoon nap, Bridget was striding toward Connemara's furniture factory two miles outside of town. Gone was the magenta coat, jersey leggings and the kid loafers. Now Bridget walked briskly through the rain with her head held high, her determined steps cushioned by the Wellies she had found in the cupboard. The rubber had stiffened but they fit just fine as did the work pants that had been hanging on a hook way in the back of the dark cubby. Over her sweater Bridget threw her father's slicker.

On the road she passed another pedestrian, his head down as he walked into the wind. Holding tight to his hat, he looked up as they drew alongside each other. He smiled a genuine hello and Bridget shot back a "God bleth ya."

Min Drum's words accompanied Bridget on her long walk. And with each step the memory became less an angry one and more a heartfelt plea for help and understanding. Perhaps her da was right. She had hurt Kilmartin's pride with her grand plans. But wrongs could be righted, and that was what Bridget was set to do.

She saw the huge wooden building a mile before she stepped foot inside. As she approached, Bridget had time to assess the situation, just as Richard had said she should do before making a decision. The paint had faded, even on the large sign a hundred yards from the entrance of the building. To the right stacks of wood lay under a tarp. To the left of the building a huge pile of debris. Two old trucks, one a flatbed, the other enclosed, waited patiently by a loading dock. The place seemed deserted, but Bridget forged ahead. She had come this far, she wasn't about to go back now.

"Hello," she called, once inside, "anybody here?"

Her Wellies made squishing sounds over the wooden floor. Curious, Bridget strolled through passages made by the long work tables by the door. Her fingers ran appreciatively over a half-finished rocker. It was wondrous to feel as well as see how fine the workmanship was. Not just in the building of the chair, of course, but in the carving. Such a chair should grace her new home — Bridget stopped herself immediately, remembering she would never live in the house on the hill with Richard.

"Can I be helpin' you?"

Startled, Bridget turned toward the sound of the voice. Far back in the cavernous building she saw movement, then a shadow and finally the figure of a large man. He came toward her slowly, wiping his hands on a rag that seemed no cleaner than whatever dirt he had gotten himself into.

"Sure I hope you can. I'm lookin' for the owner. I'm Bridget Devlin," she said, stepping forward and holding out her hand. He ignored it.

"Sean Doyle. I'm the owner," he answered with a nod, "and I don't think I'll be needin' to meet with you about anything, especially your money. Good day to you, Miss Devlin."

"Sure did I say I've come to throw it at your feet, Mr. Doyle?" Bridget called to his back.

Her reputation had preceded her, and she was losing him before they had begun. But this was the place where she could make a difference. Bridget could feel it, and she wasn't going to let the opportunity get away.

"And if you're so stubborn as not to want to even speak to me, I'll find another man who will. Someone will want me to give them my money if it means putting a factory back to work, if it means real jobs and real profits."

Sean Doyle stopped but did not turn around. She bit her lower lip, every fiber of her being praying he would face her with interest.

"I don't want a fancy woman telling me what to do in my own business," Sean Doyle growled, confronting her at last.

"What exactly is it you want to do in your factory, Mr. Doyle?" Bridget asked, not daring to step closer to him for fear she would break the spell.

Slowly the man removed his cap and looked around his building. Sean Doyle saw a barnful of men working hard, their muscles rippling as they whittled the designs and screwed the legs and sanded the tabletops with pride. He saw a place that at one time had been a proud workshop. Now, after years of being Kilmartin's only hope, it was fading like the rest of the village.

"I want my factory to take care of itself, Miss Devlin. Sure I have the men, I have the designs, but I canna get my goods to a market that wants them. I haven't the knowledge to do that or the money. I don't know where to go in a world that moves so fast it makes my head spin. Me and my lads are craftsmen. Can you buy me knowledge, Miss Devlin? Can you make it so when you leave and your money goes with you, we won't fall right back to this?"

Stunned by the man's honesty, touched by his simple desire to be self-supporting, Bridget remained silent for a long while. Finally, her hands stuffed in her pockets, she spoke, remembering what Richard had told her, realizing that he had been right all along.

"I can make my money work for me, Mr. Doyle, by putting it to work for you. That was what my benefactress wanted. Giving you money to paint a building or get your trucks running would be meaningless. It's exporting that will make this factory solvent. Let me help you. I have a friend in San Francisco. A very smart man by the name of Brandon Madison. He'll know how we start. Put your lads to work building fine furniture and I'll make sure there's money for wages and wood and new equipment. Sure if I've learned anything since I've come into my good fortune, it's that people in the United States will pay top dollar for goods that are well made. And don't they just love anything that's crafted across the sea! Sure now tell me, have you heard about limited partnerships, Mr. Doyle . . . ?"

Bridget moved beside the huge man and they fell into step as they wandered out into the rain and high grass while they talked. From the depths of her memory Bridget pulled every piece of information she had gathered from the bankers and stock brokers, every piece of business and legal wisdom she had heard Richard or Brandon or the brokers and bankers utter.

And when Sean Doyle bid her goodbye, when she stood alone halfway on the road between the factory and Kilmartin, Bridget took a moment to make peace with herself. Sure Richard had been right in so many ways. By investing in Mr. Doyle's factory, Bridget would gain, as would Kilmartin. Her money would be working for all of them.

But she was right, too. Only she could have found the way to do what Mrs. Kilburn had asked. If Kathy or Richard had come here, they would have been outsiders, blow-in's as Min so kindly pointed out. No one would have spoken to them the way Min Drum had spoken to her. The Hudsons would have left Ireland without accomplishing a thing. Bridget Devlin had done what was asked of her in a way Richard never could. Hopefully, someday he would understand that his feelings of inadequacy were ill founded. Only if Maura Kilburn had entrusted him with this task would he have been allowed to feel the failure.

"Richard, my love," she murmured for no reason other than to hear herself commit to him. Slowly Bridget Devlin headed back to her father's house knowing now it wasn't truly home.

"It looks fine, Father. Truly fine," Bridget said, stepping back and shading her eyes from the glare of the weak sun. The whitewash on the church had made an amazing difference. The little place looked brand new. Even the statue of the Virgin, its paint peeling and the babe in her arms a bit dusty, seemed brighter.

"That it does, Bridget. But sure doesn't it make the pews seem a bit old and worn, lass?" the priest lamented, his heavy brows pulled

305

together in all seriousness.

Bridget took her time surveying the pews, the wood shining from hands clasped in prayer, knees bent in homage. She'd been in Kilmartin long enough now to know exactly how the priest played his game. No sense in spoiling his fun by simply writing a check.

"I don't know, Father," Bridget answered. "Sure don't they give the church a nice rustic look?"

"Rustic? Is that what we want when we have visitors coming here to see the new factory and such?"

"Perhaps you're right, Father. I should talk to Mr. Doyle about possibly having him craft new pews for the church. I'm sure we can see our way to give you a good price, Father."

"Now, Bridget, is that what Our Lady would be wanting? Just a good price?"

"Right, again. Perhaps a donation, then. If we had each lad at the factory carve his own pew we could be putting his name on a little brass plaque. What would you say to that? And I would donate the wood."

"Now that does sound like a plan. Sure aren't you the businesswoman."

"I try, Father," Bridget said, seemingly with great timidity. "But if I don't try a bit harder, Mr. Doyle will have my head. We're going over the new designs for a limited edition of that willow rocker."

"Isn't that fine, Bridget. Just fine. Time to go about our business, then. I must stop to see Mrs. Fahey, poor thing. Still down with the flu she is."

"Give her my best, Father. I'll let you know what the lads say about the pews."

"Goodbye, then, Bridget."

And she was waved off with complete confidence that the pews would be made and delivered before the next season. Bridget headed down the road, her mind on a million things. Brandon had put her in touch with a wholesaler who was making a bid to carry their line. But an independent representative from England had also been to see them. Then there was the problem of securing the proper woods at a better price. It was no wonder the little factory had been floundering. Crystal, tapestries or wool clothing would have been a better choice of product. But furniture she had bargained for and furniture she would make.

Lifting her head higher, she heard herself hailed heartily as she came in sight of the factory. And as she called back to the men, Bridget Devlin felt more whole than she had in months. If only the gratitude and enthusiasm of the villagers could fill that void she felt when she lay alone in her bed at night. Shaking her head, she plunged into work, grateful that she at least had this.

* * *

Exhausted at the end of the day, tired of the paperwork she'd been reviewing since three, Bridget sat back in her office chair and picked up her tea. It was cold. She was tired, and Mr. Doyle was the only one left in the factory.

Slowly, knowing she would sleep well tonight, Bridget rose and slipped into her coat, not caring a fig what it looked like over her worn dockers. All she wanted was a warm meal, a pint and a fire. Da would certainly have all that waiting for her. It seemed her venture had breathed a bit of life into him, as well. He was proud as a peacock as he walked about the village now. Talked a bit more in the bargain, too. With a chuckle Bridget headed out the door.

"Night, Mr. Doyle. Don't be too late."

In response he raised his hand but not his head. The piece he was working on was exquisite and would fetch a pretty penny. They had just begun a program to manufacture one-of-a-kind pieces, and Bridget was sure they would find an immediate market. She only wished Brandon would hurry up with his report on warehousing possibilities.

Outside Bridget raised her head. Twilight was hovering on the horizon, but there was still plenty of early-evening light. Forcing herself to a quick pace, Bridget tried to push the cobwebs from her mind. Paperwork was not her favorite thing. There were times when she wished she could work alongside the men, carving and fitting and sanding. Her hands would be so busy there wouldn't be time to think about that heartache she couldn't shake. She might even banish the vision of Richard's face that insisted on haunting her.

She was walking quickly down the road, her hands stuffed into her pockets. Bridget thought of nothing but the funny reflections that run through a body's mind when a road has been trod a thousand times. And in this state she saw the figure coming toward her and thought only how odd it was that a man from the village should be dressed so lovely on a Friday night. Bridget slowed her pace, realizing she had seen that fine coat before and recognized the stance of the man. His determined, confident step was as familiar to her as the rising of the sun, though it had been a long time since she had seen it.

He was drawing closer now, and Bridget stopped to watch. He was becoming recognizable as the distance closed, but the twilight was coming on fast and Bridget cautioned her heart that this might be a trick of the light. Standing her ground, she faced the man in the camel coat. He stopped, too. Far enough away that she could not feel the warmth of his skin or smell that clean scent he wore. Far enough that she couldn't reach out and take the lock of brown hair and smooth it back from his fine forehead. But he was close enough that she could see a shining hope in his eyes and a surge of life in his expression. He faced her, tall and strong, his lips set, his eyes watchful.

"Sure and it's you, Richard," Bridget murmured, trying to keep the tremor from her voice and the weakness from her knees.

"Bridget," was all he said.

The depth of his voice, the resonance of emotion, pulled her toward him, but she refused to give in. She would not move. Hadn't there been too much hurt to start again? "You've come a long way."

"Farther than you can imagine," he responded, his eyes drinking in the simplicity of her wind-tossed hair.

He smiled gently, seeing that her nails were no longer long and polished but short and buffed as when she had worked with her hands. Here, certainly, was the lovely Bridget he had longed for in his dreams. Unadorned, natural as the first time he loved her. But in her eyes there was now a light of wisdom, the look of a woman who had come to know herself and her heart.

"Is that so?" Bridget asked, breaking into his reflection. "And what's made your journey so tedious?"

"I didn't say it was tedious," he corrected, allowing his smile to widen a bit. How like Bridget to confront him. "Actually it was a wonderful journey, filled with twists and turns. Quite an adventure that brought me right back to where I started."

"I don't think you're talking about your trip, Richard. I think you're talking nonsense."

"For the first time in a long while I'm speaking about the truth," he said, holding out his hand as though afraid she might move, somehow disappear into the lush greenery around them. "It was a trip through my heart and soul, Bridget. And it was a tough one."

"Make sense, man," Bridget responded sternly. The only defense against her desire was poorly feigned anger.

"When you left, I thought it was for the best. I patted myself on the back for my honesty. I told you that I wasn't sure if I loved you despite Grandmother's legacy or because of it." Richard lowered his head and stuffed his hands in his pockets. He looked about him and breathed out into the clean air, creating little trails of condensation. He smiled that glorious smile of his. "It's damn cold here, Bridget."

She laughed despite herself.

"Anyway, I was sitting there in San Francisco patting myself on the back for my honesty, my forthrightness. Oh, I was such a sophisticated sop, telling myself that you deserved such integrity. Well, you didn't deserve it.

"After all my poetic waxing about how my mother should forgive my grandmother and

311

welcome you back into the fold, about how you had to understand that what we were feeling was natural and right. Oh, Bridget, what a sap I was," Richard chuckled sadly as though hope still lingered somewhere in his heart but it was as elusive as a puff of smoke. "Still calling the shots, creating my own little world. It's amazing you could ever love me."

There was a beat of silence as a small breeze teased Richard's hair. It was then Bridget realized he hadn't actually been looking at her. In that moment he turned his eyes toward her and locked his gaze on hers, losing himself in the depth of her emerald ones.

"I did love you," she said quietly. Tears welled as she felt the evening cold push its icy fingers through her heavy coat. She longed for his warmth, the comfort of his arms. But he was here in front of her as though beaten, and she didn't know what she could offer to heal his wounds.

"When I loved you," she said, "I saw that you had command of everything you touched. You picked what made you happy, banished what made you sad. You created a world so inviting I stepped into it without a thought for anything but loving you. Then I realized it wasn't enough for you to create, you needed to control it, too. Ah, Richard, that was painful. Sure didn't that mean we could never be partners?"

Richard nodded but said not a word.

"And aren't I to blame, as well? Acting like a silly child wanting her own way. I was certainly put in my place when I came here, I can tell you. I expected Kilmartin to reaffirm my righteousness. They showed me that I had been wrong in so many ways." Bridget lowered her gaze, kicked at a stone and watched it skip off the road. "Weren't we the sad ones to throw away what we had."

"Bridget?" Richard asked, taking a step forward, one hand sneaking out of his pocket to reach out to her. "Do you think it's gone? Can't you love me a bit so we can start to build again. I've come so far because I couldn't bear to be without you. I couldn't go forward. And I couldn't go back to the way I was. I woke to an empty bed and wanted to cry. I saw other women on the street and compared them to you. I hadn't realized that your voice colored every waking moment of my day and your love grounded me so that I knew what direction I had to go.

"I've moved into that house I wanted to share with you. By myself it will never be a home. Bridget, I've come to *ask* you, not beg you, to come back with me. Or, if you want, I'll stay here. I'll help you pave the whole damn island of Ireland if you like. I'll roof your father's manor house. I'll raise sheep. Bridget Devlin, I need you. I love you. Come back to me. Please. Or let me follow you. Please, Bridget, come back into my life."

Now both hands were held out to her, and in an instant his arms were wrapped about her. They clung together on that narrow, worn road to Kilmartin until the sun had set and the cold forced them away.

There was a fire waiting when they reached Gil Devlin's house, and soup in the kitchen. But Gil had gone to the pub knowing his ears were not for the conversation his daughter would be having that night.

"Hurry, Bridget. Sure wouldn't you think you had all day!"

"I'm coming as fast as I can, Min. I just can't seem to get this right. I've never done this before, you know," Bridget called back.

Min crossed herself and raised her eyes heavenward. "And sure you'll only do this once, if any of us have anything to say about it."

"I feel the same way, Min. Only once," Bridget murmured as she turned her back and allowed Min to lace her satin gown.

"Now, aren't you the picture," Min said, satisfied that only she could have made Bridget look perfect.

"I suppose. Oh, Min, I'm so nervous. I just don't know how it came to this."

"Sure I don't, either. From what you've told me I'd say 'twas a miracle. Now no more thinking this way and that. I'll be getting your da."

"Thank you."

Left alone Bridget turned once more toward the mirror. Not so much to admire herself, but to reaffirm that it was indeed she standing there. Could it possibly be she, this beautiful woman in white, a cloud of veil pinned into her tumble of curls, a bouquet of fern and daisies in her hand.

She closed her eyes to keep her tears of joy from falling. She closed her eyes and remembered Richard and the road and the moment they were once again in each other's embrace. Sure he didn't have to ask twice. Her heart, once so carefully put away, had burst from its protective confines and filled with a love both pure and wise. No hurt could overshadow what she felt for Richard. Neither time nor distance could keep her memory from him. They were meant to love each other and so they would. But first . . . first. . . .

"Are you ready, darlin'?"

Bridget turned and smiled at her father.

"Yes, Da. I'm ready."

"Then we'll be off." He took her arm and patted it protectively as he led her out of the cottage and into the street.

Together they walked over the cobblestones until they came in sight of the newly whitewashed church. The little building seemed to sparkle on this clear and perfect day. The rain had fallen softly in the wee hours of the morning, then given way to clear, blue skies and the odd, high, white cloud. All around her the streets were clean and the countryside sweet smelling.

Lifting her skirts a bit higher, Bridget stepped over a puddle and her da handed her into the church. There the organist began the wedding march. The people of Kilmartin and the Hudsons of San Francisco rose to watch the heiress marry her handsome man. But most had forgotten about Bridget's good fortune. Most simply thought of her as Gil Devlin's lass soon to be wed to a gentleman.

Proudly, confidently, Bridget walked down the aisle toward Richard. He stood straight and tall, with eyes that looked only into hers. When they were close enough, he stretched out both his hands and drew her to him.

"I promise you it will be wonderful," he whispered.

And Bridget smiled at him knowing there was a lifetime of happiness in that vow. Gently he pulled her close and, in front of Father Donovan and the congregation, kissed her sweetly on the lips. And when Bridget opened her eyes, there through the tall, plain windows of the church, she saw a rainbow sitting pretty as you please in the sky. Sure and didn't it end right there at the church, streaming through the window, melting into a splash of color at their feet.

Confidently they turned toward the priest. As he began to read their troth, Bridget knew that she was finally, truly wealthy. Sure and at the rainbow's end wasn't there always something to be treasured?

OFFICIAL ENTRY FORM
Please enter me in the

Lucky in Love

SWEEPSTAKES

Grand Prize choice:_____

Name:_____

Address:_____

City:_____ State _____ Zip _____

Store name:_____

Address:_____

City:_____ State _____ Zip _____

MAIL TO: LUCKY IN LOVE
P.O. Box 1022A
Grand Rapids, MN 55730-1022A

Sweepstakes ends: 2/26/93

OFFICIAL RULES
"LUCKY IN LOVE" SWEEPSTAKES